Hannah forced her gaze away from the touching sight of father and child.

She wanted the earl to persist at the tasks of fatherhood even when they did not come naturally. She wanted him to see that he could improve with practice and not take temporary setbacks as a sign of failure.

Baby Alice seemed willing to teach her father those vital lessons, for she gradually quieted. Finally the earl announced with a muted ring of pride, "I believe she is asleep now. Give her a little more time, then you may take her."

Hoping to take advantage of his good humor, she ventured to ask, "May I still bring the babies to visit you, sir?"

He considered for a moment. "Of course, if you would be so kind."

"I should be happy to, sir."

Happy she would still see him for a while each day? She had no business feeling anything remotely like that for the earl, Hannah's sense of propriety warned her. Was it seeing him interact with the babies that called forth the softer emotions she tried to conceal behind a mask of cool resourcefulness?

Books by Deborah Hale

Love Inspired Historical

The Wedding Season
  "Much Ado About Nuptials"
*The Captain's Christmas Family
*The Baron's Governess Bride
*The Earl's Honorable Intentions

*Glass Slipper Brides

DEBORAH HALE

After a decade of tracing her ancestors to their roots in Georgian-era Britain, Golden Heart winner Deborah Hale turned to historical romance writing as a way to blend her love of the past with her desire to spin a good love story. Deborah lives in Nova Scotia, Canada, between the historic British garrison town of Halifax and the romantic Annapolis Valley of Longfellow's *Evangeline*. With four children (including twins), Deborah calls writing her "sanity retention mechanism." On good days, she likes to think it's working.

Deborah invites you to visit her personal website, www.deborahhale.com, or find out more about her at www.Harlequin.com.

The Earl's Honorable Intentions

DEBORAH HALE

Ⓗ **HARLEQUIN**® LOVE INSPIRED® HISTORICAL

Recycling programs
for this product may
not exist in your area.

 ™ LOVE INSPIRED BOOKS

ISBN-13: 978-0-373-82969-9

THE EARL'S HONORABLE INTENTIONS

www.LoveInspiredBooks.com

Printed in U.S.A.

My flesh and my heart may fail, but God is the
strength of my heart and my portion forever.
—*Psalms* 73:26

To my aunts:
Ada, Audrey, Carol, Doris, Dolly, Eileen, Evelyn, Georgina, Joan, Kathleen and in memory of Maymie. What a blessing it has been for me to have such smart, capable women as role models!

Chapter One

Kent, England
June 1815

What kind of man would not do everything in his power to attend his wife's funeral?

From her place several pews back, Hannah Fletcher stared at the cluster of family members mourning the late Countess of Hawkehurst. It was a pitifully small group led by her ladyship's detested half brother. Not one of them had cared for the countess as much as Hannah, her young son's governess. The man who should have cared most of all was not even there to pay his final respects.

Hannah usually made an effort to think charitably of others, as the scriptures bid, but that was not easy when it came to Gavin Romney, Earl of Hawkehurst. It was one thing to turn the other cheek to someone who had wronged her personally. Hannah had always found it much harder to forgive those who hurt the people she cared about.

Besides, if she let go of her righteous anger to-

ward his lordship, she feared her exhaustion and grief
for Lady Hawkehurst would get the better of her and
she would disgrace herself with an outburst of weeping. Such a lack of restraint would violate the com-
mandments of the Pendergast School, which had been
drummed into Hannah and her friends far more vigorously than the creed of Christian charity.

The Bishop of Kent had come to conduct her ladyship's funeral. Though Hannah followed the funeral
service in her prayer book, listening attentively to the
readings and making all the proper responses, part of
her mind remained preoccupied with the earl's absence.

For the past several weeks, he had been in north-
ern France with the Duke of Wellington's army, preparing to battle Bonaparte's forces once again. At the
pleadings of her ladyship, Hannah had written to Lord
Hawkehurst begging for his return, but he had failed
to heed her urgent summons. Hannah felt certain his
timely appearance at his wife's sickbed, and a show of
concern for her welfare, might have given her ladyship
the will to fight for her life. At the very least, it would
have brought comfort to her final hours.

Hannah's hand still ached from where the countess
had clung to it, hour after hour, the grip growing gradually feebler. Her ears still rang with the poor lady's
repeated pleas for her absent husband and demands to
know when he would come.

"Soon, ma'am, soon," Hannah had crooned the comforting lie until she almost believed it. Then she'd made
excuses for him. "It is a long way from France with the
Channel to cross. And there is a war on, remember?"

Hard as she strove to sound convincing, Hannah

could not persuade herself. This was not November or March, after all, when the Channel crossing might be delayed by rough seas. And His Majesty's army had been marshaled on the French borders for weeks now, gathering strength and coordinating with Britain's allies for an attack that would oust Bonaparte from power once and for all.

There had been reports in the newspapers of some noble ladies setting up house in Brussels to be near the action and keep the officers entertained. To Hannah that sounded more like an enormous house party than a war. Surely one man would not be missed, even if he did command a regiment of cavalry. If the earl had begged leave to attend his dying wife, Hannah was certain his superiors would have granted it at once.

But clearly Lord Hawkehurst had made no such request. Bad enough he had ignored her summons to his wife's deathbed. Surely he could have made an effort to attend the funeral and *pretend* to mourn her passing.

So deeply absorbed was Hannah in her indignant brooding that she scarcely noticed the mournful hush of the congregation fall quieter still, as if everyone present were holding their breath. It was a hesitation in the bishop's eulogy that roused her attention. Only then did she hear the ponderous tread of footsteps making their way up the aisle and see the heads of those around her turn toward the sound.

She followed their gazes just in time to see a man walk past her wearing the scarlet coat of the Royal Dragoons.

His lordship had arrived at last.

He might have done better to stay away, Hannah

reflected bitterly, than to disrupt his wife's funeral by turning up late and in such a state. As he walked past her aisle seat, she noted with disapproval his disheveled appearance. His coat was dirty, and he stank of horses. Granted, the earl must have traveled in haste, but surely he could have taken the opportunity of the Channel crossing to make himself presentable.

Instead he looked as if he had not bothered to wash, shave or comb his hair in days. Besides the pungent reek of horse, Hannah also detected the sharp odor of spirits. How dare the earl show so little respect for his wife's memory by coming to her funeral in a state of intoxication?

His lordship's labored, unsteady gait further persuaded Hannah that that was precisely what he had done. The harsh lessons of her girlhood and her regard for the late countess were all that prevented her from surging to her feet and denouncing Lord Hawkehurst in front of his family and neighbors.

To the bishop's credit, he did not let the earl's tardy arrival interrupt his fine eulogy. Hannah doubted many of those assembled heeded a word of it as Lord Hawkehurst reached the family pew and his brother-in-law budged over to make room for him. When the earl dropped heavily into the pew, the breathless silence of the congregation shattered into a buzz of muted whispers.

Jane, the head housemaid at Edgecombe, nudged Hannah, but she ignored the sharp dig in her ribs, keeping an indignant glare directed at the back of the earl's head. She only wished he were aware of it. But in his disgraceful state, she doubted he would notice even if she were staring him in the face.

The final prayer was uttered, the final hymn sung and the soul of Clarissa Romney, Countess of Hawke-hurst, was committed to the care of her Lord and Savior. Hannah took comfort in knowing her ladyship would find the peace and love in Heaven that had been denied her in this world.

The congregation stood while the family of the deceased made their way back down the aisle led by the earl. He was visibly staggering at this point, Hannah noted with barely suppressed outrage as he lurched toward her.

His dark eyes appeared glazed and absent at first. Then he met her glare, which seemed to penetrate his befuddlement.

He stumbled to a halt in front of her. "I got your message, Miss Fletcher."

Though Hannah could smell the spirits quite distinctly now, they did not seem to be on his breath. How could that be?

"Thank you for sending for me," his lordship continued in a heavy, slurred voice. "I came as soon as I could."

How could he make such a disgraceful spectacle at a ceremony that was meant to be solemn and dignified? The thought of such an insult to her ladyship's memory brought a sting of tears to Hannah's eyes. The rest of the mourners faded from her awareness as she focused with baleful intensity on the dark, rugged man before her. She forgot that he was a powerful peer of the realm and her employer.

"I sent that letter *days* ago," she replied in a fierce whisper through gritted teeth. "Could you not have shown her ladyship a little more respect in death than in—"

Before she could say anything more that she would surely regret, the earl's dark eyes suddenly rolled up and his rangy frame pitched toward her. Fortunately others nearby had the presence of mind to swoop forward and break his lordship's fall. The brunt of his weight still fell on Hannah, who instinctively opened her arms to catch him.

She heard sharp gasps and a louder buzz of whispers as the earl's dead weight pressed down on her, his head resting on her shoulder and his black hair grazing her cheek. Then, as swiftly as he had collapsed, other hands pulled him away from her and lowered him into the aisle.

His late wife's physician rushed forward, tugging loose the earl's neck linen and wrenching open the buttons of his coat. Though many people crowded around, Hannah had a clear view of it all from her place at the end of the pew.

A gasp burst from her lips when she saw that the right side of the earl's shirt was drenched in dark blood.

From nearby she heard someone murmur, "He must have ridden here straight from the battlefield."

Those words smote Hannah's conscience a heavy blow. While she had been entertaining the worst possible thoughts about him, Lord Hawkehurst had been shedding blood for his country traveling all the way from France wounded. Though she still could not excuse the unhappiness he had caused his wife, it seemed that in this instance she had misjudged the man.

As the doctor strove to revive his lordship, Hannah overheard a doleful whisper from one of the other on-lookers. "Those poor children. I pray they will not lose *both* their parents within the fortnight."

The children! Hannah jerked a hand to her lips to stifle a cry. Five-year-old Peter had taken his mother's death very hard. What would become of him if he lost his father so soon after? And the precious newborn twins—she could not bear to think of them being or-phaned before they were a month old. Their mother had entrusted all three children to her care with practically her dying breath. If their father lived, he might respect his late wife's wishes. Otherwise guardians would take charge of the Romney children. Those guardians might have their own ideas about how they ought to be raised and educated—ideas that would not include a humble governess making decisions about their upbringing.

For the sake of those dear children and the promise she had made to their dying mother, Hannah knew she must do everything in her power to make certain Lord Hawkehurst survived.

Every time the hooves of his charging horse hit the ground, it jolted Gavin and drove a red-hot poker of pain through his side below his ribs. But he dared not slow his mount's headlong gallop. Indeed, he must urge it to greater speed. A narrow gap in the French lines was closing fast. If he could not squeeze through, that would be the end of him and poor Molesworth.

Gritting his teeth against the stabs of pain, Gavin

tightened his knees around his horse's straining barrel. Then he bent low in an effort to secure his wounded comrade, who hung over the beast's withers. Gavin had no idea where he'd found the surge of strength to hoist Molesworth up in front of him. Perhaps it had come from the same source his horse now called on to fuel its final dash.

As it galloped through the gap in the lines, Gavin caught a confused glimpse of scarlet coats. Some of his Royal Dragoons must have braved the murderous French fire to wedge open a route of escape for him.

The fools! A groan of dismay rumbled through Gavin's chest and rose to his parched lips. Somehow it wrenched him away from the battlefield into a place of dark, eerie silence.

"There now." A quiet voice penetrated the stillness to reach him. "Don't fret yourself."

Not fret? How could he? He must find out what had become of Molesworth and the men who had risked their lives to give him a chance. There was someone else, too—someone who needed him as urgently as his fallen comrades.

"Rest and try to recover your strength." It was a woman's voice. Her words were accompanied by a swipe of something cool across his brow.

His strength? Now that she brought it to his attention, Gavin realized he did feel weak. Though the pain in his side had eased to a dull throb, it cost him enormous effort to move his leaden, aching limbs. But he could not just lie there, wherever *there* might be.

He had a vital mission to carry out, and there was

no time to lose. If only he could remember what he was meant to do and muster the strength to do it.

"You must not give up!" another woman insisted. Her tone was emphatic and determined, in sharp contrast to the other's gentle murmur. "You are a soldier and a very brave one. You must fight now for your life!"

Her peremptory order roused his resentment. He had spent years in His Majesty's service, driving Bonaparte's forces out of Portugal and Spain. He did not need anyone telling him to fight!

That flash of anger roused his consciousness, forcing the darkness to loosen its grip on his mind. He must open his eyes to discover the identity of these women who hovered about, by turns soothing and inflaming him. He had a nagging conviction that he should recognize their voices, but his memory refused to cooperate.

When he struggled to raise his eyelids, he found them every bit as obstinate. His thoughts seemed mired in thick black mud, sucking him into the depths of oblivion, where neither entreaties nor commands could reach him.

For a time he surrendered to it. Part of him felt ashamed for not fighting harder, but another part welcomed the opportunity to forget.

A while later—he could not tell whether it had been an instant or many long hours—one of the voices again invaded his tranquil darkness and strove to lure him out of it. "You *are* going to live. You must, for the sake of your children. They need you, and I refuse to let you abandon them."

His children! Gavin could not ignore the challenge and the plea in the woman's words. Was that the mission he'd sensed deep in his bones but could not remember? He must return to his children and protect them.

He wanted to tell the woman he would never think of abandoning his family. But his tongue felt parched and swollen. When he tried to speak, it would not budge. The best he could do, with enormous effort, was turn his head away from the voice in denial of her accusation.

"You *can* hear me." The other woman spoke—the gentle one. She sounded exhausted but encouraged. "I feel certain you can. It was the mention of your children that roused you, wasn't it? You cannot bear for them to be left all alone without a parent's love and protection."

Gavin knew more about parental judgment and censure. He was far from certain he had it in him to be a better kind of father. But what choice did he have?

An arm slipped behind his shoulders, raising his head. The pain in his chest sharpened again, and a wave of dizziness washed over him. Unpleasant as those sensations were, they pushed him closer to full consciousness.

He felt the rim of a cup press against his lips. When a trickle of cool liquid ran into his mouth, he was able to swallow it gratefully.

"I cannot bear that thought either," the voice whispered, from so nearby it seemed almost to come from his own thoughts. "I know how it feels to grow up that way, and I would not wish it on any child, least of all your dear little ones."

The wistful sorrow of her entreaty penetrated deep and sank a hook into Gavin's heart.

"Have a little more water," she urged him. "Then I

will give you some broth. You must be starved, and you will need your strength to get well."

Though the darkness tried to tug him back into its peaceful depths, Gavin found he could not give in so easily this time. Something in the voice made him want to keep listening, even when he must exert himself to maintain a glimmer of awareness.

He swallowed several more sips of water, then received the promised broth. He savored the hearty flavor on his tongue, and his empty belly welcomed the warm nourishment. He was completely at the mercy of the woman who tended him.

Never in his life could he recall being so tenderly cared for.

Would the earl recover?

An anxious shadow in the physician's eyes chilled Hannah. Yet it made her more determined than ever not to give up the fight for his lordship's life. For as long as she could recall that had been her natural reaction to any challenge or hardship—to work harder. It had not always yielded the result she desired, but the effort helped to keep her fear at bay.

"You should get some rest yourself, Miss Fletcher." The doctor shook his head gravely as he rose from examining Lord Hawkehurst. "First the birth of the twins, then her ladyship's illness and now this. You must be exhausted."

He did not mention that it was most irregular for a governess to tend the master and mistress of the house in this manner. Everyone at Edgecombe had become accustomed to the dependence Lady Hawkehurst had on Hannah Fletcher. Her position in the household had become more like that of a trusted relative than a mere hireling. Because she did not take advantage of her authority or impose on the servants, they had long since accepted the situation. Now, with her ladyship in her grave and his lordship's life hanging by a thread, everyone looked to her for leadership.

"I appreciate your concern." Hannah struggled to suppress a yawn that would betray her fatigue. "But I have been accustomed since childhood to do without a great deal of sleep."

Her answer did not appear to satisfy the doctor. "Be that as it may, you must not allow yourself to become run-down and prey to illness. How would they manage at Edgecombe if you were incapacitated?"

His suggestion that she was indispensible to the family acted like a tonic on Hannah, infusing her with new energy—though she doubted it would last long. "I promise I will not neglect my own health, Doctor. But until his lordship is out of danger I feel I owe it to his wife's memory and to their children to do all I can for him."

"I understand," Dr. Hodge conceded, perhaps because he'd witnessed the promise Lady Hawkehurst had exacted from Hannah in her final hours. "When there is an outbreak of sickness, I am often obliged to tax my strength for the good of my patients. But do try to let some of your other duties slide a bit in the meantime."

"I have," she admitted, relieved to receive the doctor's support. "Young Lord Edgecombe is still too upset by his mother's passing to concentrate on his lessons. I thought it better for the poor child to have as much diversion out of doors as possible. The servants have been very kind to assist me. They take him to dig in the garden and visit some of the tenant farms to see the animals. He enjoys going for rides in the pony cart with the coachman."

"Excellent." The doctor began to pack away his instruments. "The more fresh air and activity the child gets the better he will eat and sleep—all of which will help him recover his spirits."

Hannah tried to spend as much time with her young pupil as she could, so as not to disrupt his life any worse than it had been already.

"Have you been to check on the babies lately?" she asked. "From what I can tell, they seem to be thriving."

She made an effort to visit them as often as possible, taking Peter along in the hopes of fostering a bond between the three children that might compensate a little for the loss of their mother. Hannah knew from experience how important that could be.

The physician nodded. "They are indeed. Growing nicely and both good-tempered from what their wet nurses report. I congratulate you, Miss Fletcher, on getting them so well settled in the midst of such a difficult time."

"Thank you, sir." Hannah appreciated his recognition of her efforts.

She did not expect any such praise from the earl, if and when he recovered. During his brief time at home during the fleeting months of peace, Lord Hawkehurst had seemed to resent her special position in his household and her closeness to his wife. Hannah reminded herself she could accept his ill will if only he would live.

"What about his lordship?" She glanced toward the

master, his rugged features so unwontedly still and his skin strangely pale beneath his soldier's tan. It made a stark contrast to the bristling black stubble over the lower part of his face. "Will he live to see his new son and daughter? I cannot abide the thought of them losing both parents with no memory of either."

An anxious look gripped the physician's craggy features. "I still cannot say for certain. The bleeding has been staunched, and the wound is healing. Both of those are in his favor. But he lost a great quantity of blood when his wound reopened during the strenuous journey from France. He should have waited to travel until it had healed better. But I suppose, under the circumstances…"

A sharp barb of guilt worked its way beneath Hannah's defenses. It was her letter that had summoned the earl home, fresh from the battlefield. Since then, news of the near-run allied victory at Waterloo had spread through the country. It made Hannah repent many of the harsh things she'd thought about Lord Hawkehurst during those anxious last days of the countess's life.

If only God would grant her an opportunity to make it up to him.

Too often, in the past, her failings had cost others dearly. Always those she cared about most. Each time she had vowed to do better in the future. Would it ever be enough? Perhaps the answer was to keep herself from caring too deeply.

"Why will he not wake?" Hannah fought a rising tide of helplessness that threatened to sink her spirits. She would work harder to bring about the earl's recovery if only she knew what to do. "Now and then I feel as if he can hear me. But other times he seems scarcely to be alive."

"It is worrying." Dr. Hodge sighed. "Though I hope it may only be his body's way of allowing itself time and rest to heal. I have known Lord Hawkehurst since he was a boy, and he has never been one to keep still for long. Provided this state of unconsciousness does not persist too long, it may ultimately benefit his recovery."

Hannah tried to draw encouragement from the doctor's words as she bid him good-night. She would have found it easier if his tone and gaze had not betrayed quite so much doubt.

All the while Dr. Hodge poked and prodded, Lord Hawkehurst had seemed altogether insensible. Once the physician left, however, the earl grew suddenly restless. His eyes moved beneath their closed lids with a darting glance. His powerful hands began to twitch over the bedclothes. Low, incomprehensible sounds escaped his lips.

Hannah kept an anxious vigil over him. Perhaps the doctor was right about his lordship's earlier deep sleep giving his body an opportunity to recover. She feared this agitation might have the opposite effect. What if his movements grew more violent? Might the earl tear open his wound again? According to the doctor, he could not afford to lose more blood.

"Hush, now." She spoke in a gentle murmur she might have crooned to young Peter when he woke from a nightmare. "You must not upset yourself. There is nothing you need fret about. You are tucked up safe at home now, and no more harm will come to you if I can help it."

Was this her fault? Had her exhortations to fight for his life somehow roused his soldier's spirit before his wounded body was ready?

"Lie still now." She clasped the earl's nearest hand in both of hers, hoping her touch might reach and quiet him if her words could not. "Rest and be easy. You are safe here, I promise."

All her efforts seemed to have the opposite effect from what she desired. The earl began to thrash his head from side to side. Now and then he winced, as if aware of the pain from his wound. His utterances grew more forceful and more distinct.

"*Please,* your lordship!" Hannah begged, tightening her grip on his hand.

Then suddenly his eyelids flew open. The earl clasped her hand with greater strength than she had thought he possessed in his present state. He gazed deep into her eyes, his rugged features furrowed in an expression of intense concern.

Hannah could never recall him looking at her with anything warmer than barely concealed disdain. A breathless feeling of relief that the earl was finally awake collided with another emotion she could not readily identify. She had no time to sort it out, for no sooner did Lord Hawkehurst open his eyes than he began to speak.

"Hang on, Molesworth!" he rasped, clearly addressing his words to Hannah.

Had she misheard him?

The earl's next words did nothing to dispel her confusion. "Come on, man. I didn't pluck you out of Boney's grasp only to have you desert me now. The surgeons will patch us both up good as new. Then we'll make certain that warmonger gets his just deserts. No Mediterranean holiday to rest up for his next conquest."

Though some of the earl's words puzzled her, Hannah understood what he meant about Bonaparte. After years of war that had brought much of Europe under his domination, the French emperor finally had been defeated the previous year. The summer of 1814 had been crowded with jubilant celebrations of victory and peace at long last.

But the man whose towering ambition cost so many lives had never been made to answer for his actions. Instead, he had been permitted to retire to a small island off the coast of Tuscany to plot his return to power. Scarcely more than ten months after his defeat, Bonaparte had returned to France in triumph, plunging Europe into war once again—a war that need never have been fought. Small wonder Lord Hawkehurst was anxious to put an end to the emperor's career of conquest once and for all.

The earl's silence stirred Hannah from her reflection. He seemed to expect some answer from her. What could she say that might reassure him?

"I shan't go anywhere, sir. I promise." She wondered if there had ever been such a person as Molesworth, or if he was only a figment of the earl's troubled dreams. If the fellow did exist, what had become of him? "But you must lie still. So…er…the surgeons can patch you up. Will you do that for me?"

Would her answer help…or only make matters worse? Hannah wished she had not taken pity on the yawning footman and ordered him to bed once he'd seen

Dr. Hodge out. She could have used a man's help to subdue Lord Hawkehurst, if that should prove necessary.

She prayed it would not.

Fortunately her wordless supplication was answered
for the earl's anxious tension deserted him as quickly
as it had come on.

"You have a bargain," he replied in a thick, drowsy
murmur. His grip slackened, and his eyelids drooped.
"We will let the surgeons do their work so we're fit to
go after Boney. He won't be leading any more armies
after we're done with him."

No sooner had those words left the earl's lips than his
eyes slid shut and his breath settled into a deep, rhythmic drone. For a time Hannah continued to clasp his
hand, for fear he might stir again if she let go. The sensation reminded her of how the poor countess had clung
to her through the painful hours of labor and later how
her grip had eased with her waning strength.

Blinking back tears she could not afford to let fall,
Hannah released the earl's hand. Then she raised hers
to brush the hair back from his brow with a gentle touch
that was almost a caress. His life still hung in the balance, but now it was not entirely for the children's sake
that she wanted him to live.

Chapter Two

How long had he been like this?

Gavin felt as if he were immersed in a deep pond. Often he sank to the still, dark bottom, knowing nothing and caring even less. But at intervals he would float closer to the surface, near enough to hear and feel—or was he only dreaming? All the while, that flimsy barrier between sleep and consciousness remained strangely impenetrable. Certain sensations could pass through it to reach him. But for him to break through required a greater effort than he could muster.

Among his few connections with the waking world, were those voices—one softly pleading, the other fiercely challenging. They seemed to wage a tug-of-war over him. At times he longed to flee them both in search of peace, though he sensed they would follow and continue to plague him until one or the other prevailed.

Besides, he had heard one other voice—that of his fallen comrade. It reminded him of urgent unfinished business.

That reminder gave Gavin the strength to pry open

his eyes and look around him. He found he was not lying in a pool of warm water after all, but tucked up in his own bedchamber back at Edgecombe. It must be very late at night for the room was wrapped in deep shadows with only the fitful flicker of a single candle to relieve the darkness.

How had he come to Edgecombe? Gavin plundered his memory for the answer to that question. The last thing he recalled with any clarity was the cavalry charge at Waterloo.

In the stillness of the darkened room, he fancied he could hear echoes from the battlefield—the rolling thunder of horses' hooves punctuated by the crash of artillery, the crack of rifle fire and the cries of wounded soldiers. The whiff of gunpowder, sweating horses and blood seemed only a breath away.

While those sensations hovered, just out of reach, the tumultuous emotions of that day seized hold of his heart once again. First came the grim satisfaction of being on the move and able to strike a blow at last after frustrating hours of waiting. Then he relived the fierce rush of triumph as their charge turned the tide of battle, bringing hope to the beleaguered infantry. Beneath both of those roiled a sickening sense of futility that his men should be fighting and dying once again, scarcely a year after their last hard-won "victory."

A spasm of alarm caught him by the throat when he realized some of the hussars had ridden too far and risked being cut off from retreat. Among those were his commander, General Beresford, and his dearest friend, Anthony Molesworth.

A faint sound and a flicker of movement from nearby

wrenched Gavin away from the battlefield and thrust him back into the shadowed tranquility of his bedchamber. His gaze flew toward a slender figure slouched in an armchair beside his bed.

It took him a moment to recognize Hannah Fletcher. Even then, part of him had trouble believing it could be her. Amid his hazy memories of recent days, he had one vivid recollection of Miss Fletcher's face. Her fierce blue glare had accused him of all manner of shortcomings that he could not deny.

Was that why she had chosen to sit a vigil by his bedside—so she could be on hand the moment he woke to take him to task for all his failings? She need not have put herself to the trouble. His own conscience was capable of reproaching him with greater severity than even his son's formidable governess.

Not that she looked very formidable at the moment, Gavin had to admit. Seeing her features softened and relaxed in sleep, he judged them a good deal more attractive than he ever had before. Strands of honey-colored hair had fallen loose from the severe braided knot in which she usually wore it, gently framing her face. She looked far younger than her years and rather vulnerable. Her pallor and the dark smudges of exhaustion beneath her eyes heightened that impression and roused Gavin's protective instincts in spite of himself.

He wondered how long Miss Fletcher had been sitting by his bedside. Ever since he'd reached Edgecombe? And how long ago had that been? Days? Weeks?

Could one of the voices that had pierced his darkness and ordered him to live have belonged to his son's brisk, disapproving governess? That would not have surprised him. But what about the other voice—the gentle, coaxing one? Could that have belonged to his wife? A returning memory struck Gavin a stinging blow and warned him it could not have been Clarissa he'd heard.

He tried to stifle a groan, but it escaped his lips before he could clamp them shut.

Faint though it was, the sound brought Miss Fletcher bolt upright in her chair, her eyes wide with alarm and her features tensed in a look of urgent concern.

Could that worried expression be on *his* account? Gavin wondered. Surely not. In all his life, no one had ever looked so anxious about his well-being.

"Sorry I woke you." It cost him considerable effort to produce that softly rasped apology.

To his astonishment, he was rewarded by a complete transformation of Miss Fletcher's face. The corners of her mouth flew upward in a smile of almost blinding radiance, while her eyes glittered like the dew on bluebell petals at the break of dawn.

"You're awake!" She surged up from the chair to clasp his hand with a degree of fervor Gavin would never have expected from her. "You're alive!"

Her first exclamation of relief muted to a sigh of prayerful thanksgiving. "What a mercy."

Gavin scarcely knew what to make of the lady's reaction. If Miss Fletcher cared in the least whether he lived or died, he had assumed she would favor the latter. He never imagined a simple thing like his return to consciousness would provoke such a joyful outburst from her. Yet the tone of her voice, husky with unaccustomed emotion, betrayed the fact that *she* was also the woman who had hovered nearby, tending him and pleading with him to live.

The clasp of her hands around his was a strangely familiar sensation and a surprisingly welcome one. The gesture made no demands on him, nor did it judge him. It only seemed to celebrate his continued existence.

But no sooner had he begun to savor the feeling than Miss Fletcher abruptly let go. "I beg your pardon, sir! I did not mean to take such a liberty. I was only half-awake and not in full possession of my wits."

What was she making such a fuss about? Gavin wondered. He was not offended by her unexpected gesture. On the contrary, it seemed to infuse him with fresh life.

"I was so pleased to see you awake at last," Miss Fletcher rattled on, more flustered than he had ever seen her. "I forgot my place. I assure you nothing of the sort will happen again."

Her place? The woman had never seemed concerned about that before. From what he could recall, she had been almost as much mistress of Edgecombe as his wife. The thought of Clarissa raised questions that demanded answers while he was still sufficiently awake to ask. "How long…have I been…like this?"

"Three days, sir." Miss Fletcher stepped away from the bed as she spoke, her gaze avoiding his. Her face, so pale just a moment ago, suddenly looked flushed. "Or was it four? Ever since you collapsed at her ladyship's…funeral."

The instant that final word left her lips, she grimaced, as if wishing she could take it back.

So he *had* arrived in time for Clarissa's funeral. A brief flicker of satisfaction was quenched by a surge of guilt that he had not been in time to prevent his wife's death.

Gavin turned his mind from that troubling thought to a subject that promised welcome diversion from his regrets. "The battle…was it a victory?"

He must find out before the darkness overcame him again. Perhaps Bonaparte had been killed on the field and he could rest a little easier.

Miss Fletcher nodded. "Waterloo was a great victory for the Alliance. Word arrived yesterday, and the church bells rang for so long I am surprised they did not wake you. The French army is in retreat with the Duke of Wellington and Prince Blücher chasing them to Paris. I hope it will put an end to this wretched war once and for all!"

Relieved as Gavin was by news of the victory, Miss Fletcher's final pronouncement sent a qualm of misgiving rippling through him. Waterloo was a good beginning, but there could be many more lives lost before peace was secured. As the French army retreated, Bonaparte would be able to consolidate his forces while the Alliance would need to stretch theirs thin in order to secure the country through which they advanced toward Paris.

Lasting peace would never be possible while Bonaparte remained at liberty. Gavin knew he had a vow to keep. And he *must* keep it, no matter the cost.

It was all very well the army had been victorious, Hannah reflected. But why must the earl have inquired about military matters before asking about his children?

Hard as she tried, she could not quench a spark of her

old antagonism toward him. She told herself not to be so foolish. His lordship was awake at last, with wit and energy enough to speak. Was that not what she had prayed for during these past anxious days and nights? Surely his thoughts would turn to his children soon enough.

A strenuous examination of her conscience forced Hannah to admit she was partly vexed that the earl had opened his eyes just when she'd closed hers. She had only meant to rest them for a moment, but fatigue had gotten the better of her.

Now she berated herself for the lapse. What had been the point of sitting up with her patient night after night if she could not remain alert to keep watch over him and respond if he needed her? Worse yet, his lordship had caught her napping. She had compounded her disgrace by seizing hold of his hand and crying out her relief at seeing him awake. What must he think of her for behaving in so forward a manner?

In response to her report of the battle, Lord Hawkehurst nodded. "Lasting peace is my wish, too, Miss Fletcher. And of many others, I am certain."

His words came as a relief to Hannah. When the earl had returned to Edgecombe the previous year, he'd seemed distracted and restless, as if he could not fully embrace a life of peace. Perhaps his latest taste of warfare had made him ready to settle down to quiet family life at last.

The earl seemed to rally his strength to continue. "I fear any hope of lasting peace will be in vain as long as Bonaparte remains free to plot his next conquest. The man must be stopped!"

His right hand clenched into a fist, which he pounded

on the bed with some force. The instant he did, his features twisted in a grimace of pain.

Hannah chided herself for getting him started on a subject that provoked such strong feelings. The man needed to stay quiet to give his wound a chance to heal. "I am certain he will be, sir. The Duke of Wellington will see to it."

Hoping her assurance would calm the earl, she sought to divert his mind to quieter channels. "Now that you are awake, you must be hungry and thirsty. Dr. Hodge recommended beef tea to help you regain your strength. Let me heat some for you."

For the next little while, Hannah busied herself pouring a quantity of broth into a long-handled copper saucepan then warming it over the glowing coals in the hearth. She hoped by the time it was ready, Lord Hawkehurst would have calmed down.

Perhaps his outburst had tired the earl, for he lay still and silent while she prepared his beef tea. Was he also beginning to wonder what she was doing here? The Edgecombe servants, and even the doctor, might not question her tending the earl. But now that he was aware of her presence, Lord Hawkehurst might have a very different opinion on the subject.

After several minutes, Hannah tested the beef tea with her finger to make certain it was warm enough to be appetizing but not so hot that it might burn his lordship's mouth. Then she decanted it into a spouted cup, which she bore back to his bed.

As she brought it toward him, the earl scowled. "I am not an infant, Miss Fletcher. Now that I am conscious, I am perfectly capable of feeding myself."

Hannah bit back a sharp retort. It had been a good deal easier to feel caring and protective toward Lord Hawkehurst while he lay unconscious. Now he turned his dark gaze on her and spoke in a gruff parade-ground tone, as if he expected his every order to be obeyed without question. On top of her exhaustion and grief, his imperious manner stirred turbulent feelings within her that she was hard-pressed to subdue.

"As you wish," she replied through gritted teeth. "If you believe you are equal to the effort."

She drew back and watched his lordship struggle to sit up. From the way he moved, she could tell he was weaker than he'd realized, and perhaps light-headed, as well.

"Don't just stand there." He seemed vexed at being forced to ask for help. "A little assistance, if you please."

"Of course, sir." His request brought Hannah a flicker of satisfaction, but she took care to conceal it. Instead, she set the cup on a nearby table, then slipped her arm beneath his for support.

Several times during the past days, she had lifted the earl's head to give him a drink and thought nothing of it. Now that he was aware of the contact between them, she found herself intensely conscious of it, as well. With an awkward effort, she adjusted his pillows, then helped him lean back on them.

When she offered him the spouted invalid cup, his lip curled. "I would prefer to eat by spoon from a proper bowl."

Keeping *her* mouth firmly shut, Hannah poured the broth into a bowl and fetched his lordship a spoon. Then she stood back and watched him try to feed himself. As he raised the spoon to his lips, his hand trembled. Some of the beef tea spilled onto the breast of his nightshirt.

He muttered something under his breath.

"Would you like my help, sir?" she inquired.

"I can manage."

He persisted, though Hannah wondered whether he was getting more beef tea on his nightshirt than into his stomach. Exasperated as she was with his stubborn independence, she could not help but admire it, just a little.

She did not want to admire *anything* about the Earl of Hawkehurst, Hannah reminded herself. She had cared for him well, perhaps even tenderly, while his survival was in doubt, forgetting the veiled tension that had existed between them and all the complaints her poor mistress had voiced about him. Now that he was awake, gruff and obstinate as ever, she could no longer forget.

"Now that you have inquired about the military situation, perhaps you would care to know how your children are faring." She sank back down onto the chair beside his lordship's bed, her spine stiff as a poker.

"My *children*." The earl lingered over that word as if it referred to something strange and possibly frightening. "Your letter arrived just as my regiment was summoned from Nivelle. We were obliged to ride through the night to Waterloo. I did not have an opportunity to read your message until before the battle. By then it was too late to…"

His voice trailed off, and for the next few moments he concentrated on spooning the broth into his mouth as if his life depended on it.

Did he expect some response from her? Hannah sat

stubbornly mute. Clearly she had been wrong to assume Lord Hawkehurst had ignored her summons to his wife's deathbed. Still she could not bring herself to say anything to assuage his conscience. It was up to God to forgive him, not her.

Finally his lordship broke the brittle silence that had descended between them. "I tucked your letter into my sabretache before the charge. It must still be there."

Must he bring *everything* back to military subjects? Hannah pressed her lips tightly together to keep from saying something she might regret. No matter what her opinion of the man, she must try not to aggravate the friction between them or he might decide to engage a more congenial governess for his children.

"Twins." The spoon in his hand trembled again. Had he overtaxed his strength already? "A boy and a girl, I believe you wrote."

"That is correct, sir. Her ladyship asked to have them christened Alice and Arthur. In honor of her late mother and His Grace the Duke of Wellington." A lump rose in Hannah's throat as she recalled the vicar performing the sacrament at the bedside of the children's dying mother.

When she managed to get her voice under control, she added, "Her ladyship asked me to stand as their godmother."

Though she was able to keep her voice from quavering, Hannah could not prevent a note of defiance from creeping into her tone. Being a godparent conferred certain obligations and rights regarding the child's upbringing, especially if one or both parents were deceased. It was an honor usually bestowed on a relative or close friend of the family. Among the nobility, it was common to ask someone of higher rank. Certainly not a mere governess.

"Did she, indeed?" There could be no mistaking the earl's disapproval as he scowled down at his beef tea. "I suppose there was no one more suitable at hand. How *have* the little ones been faring? Are they well?"

Hannah gave a stiff nod. "As well as can be expected, I believe. I placed them with wet nurses. They seem to be thriving."

"Very good. And Lord Edgecombe?"

"Your son is well enough in body, sir, but very much affected by the loss of his dear mother, as you may imagine."

The earl would have to *imagine* his young son's feelings, for Hannah was under no illusion that he shared them. From the moment he regained consciousness, Lord Hawkehurst had shown far more interest in whether Bonaparte lived than the fact that his wife had died.

"Indeed." His lordship's voice sounded suddenly weary. His hand sank onto the bedcovers, the spoon lightly grasped between his fingers. "I have had enough of this beef tea. Kindly take it away."

Hannah doubted he'd managed to feed himself as much as he might have been able to eat if he'd accepted her help.

"Is there anything else I can fetch or do for you, sir?" she asked as she retrieved the bowl and spoon. "A clean nightshirt?"

The instant she asked the question, Hannah wished she could take it back. She had not been able to resist the urge to remind Lord Hawkehurst that if he'd accepted her help, he might not have ended up with a damp, stained garment. As a consequence, she had left herself open to a most awkward possibility. If his lordship agreed to her suggestion, she would either have to go wake the footman or assist the earl herself.

"That will not be necessary," he replied, to her vast relief. "It can wait until morning. Then I will want a footman to help me wash and shave."

"I will make the arrangements, sir." Hannah returned to the bed to help him lie down again, but he warned her away with a stern look.

With obvious effort, he inched down in the bed until he lay nearly flat again. By the time he was settled, his eyelids were beginning to droop.

When Hannah resumed her accustomed place beside his bed, he cast her an exasperated glance. "I have no intention of dying, Miss Fletcher, so there is no need for you to watch over me. Go to your own bed and get a proper sleep. You look as if you could use it."

By the time the earl finished speaking, his eyes were closed.

"I will, sir." Hannah did not budge from the chair. "If you insist."

As she expected, no such insistence came. The earl's fierce features gradually relaxed and his breath soon came in slow, deep waves.

An answering sigh escaped Hannah's lips. In part it expressed her relief and gratitude that Lord Hawkehurst seemed likely to live. But it also contained a note of frustration. Now that he was conscious, she feared the earl's stubborn independence might be the greatest obstacle to his recovery.

* * *

Gavin could not remember closing his eyes. But when he opened them again the room was bathed in muted red-gold light. This waking did not disorient him as the last one had. He recalled his late-night conversation with his son's governess and his pitiful effort to feed himself.

"Good morning, sir." Hannah Fletcher's greeting made him start, and that provoked a sharp twinge in his wounded side.

Had she deliberately tried to startle him in retaliation for catching her sleeping last night? "What are you still doing here, Miss Fletcher? I thought I ordered you to bed."

"You did mention it, sir." She tried to smother a yawn but failed. "I asked if you insisted, but you did not."

Gavin scowled. As colonel of a regiment, he was accustomed to being readily obeyed. "I am not in the habit of giving orders I do not insist upon. I expect you know that. So why did you choose to ignore me?"

"As I said, sir—"

He did not need to hear her excuse again. "From now on, you may take my insistence for granted. Is that understood?"

"Perfectly, sir." Her answer sounded meek enough, but a mutinous tilt of her chin suggested otherwise.

If he was not careful, Miss Hannah Fletcher might soon be running his household and him along with it, just the way she had with his wife. An unexpected pang of sympathy for Clarissa stung his heart. Poor creature, overborne by two strong-willed people with very different ideas.

"Good." Gavin wished he could stand. It was difficult to exert the proper authority while he lay flat on his back and had to look up at Miss Fletcher. Not to mention that the woman had recently seen him at his most helpless. It rankled his pride and inflamed his temper.

As this point in a conversation with him, any of his junior officers would have had the good sense to hold their tongues and make themselves scarce at the earliest opportunity. It seemed his son's governess had less discretion than they…or perhaps more courage.

"I can assure your lordship it was never my intention to disregard your orders. When you went to sleep so quickly, I was afraid you might have fallen unconscious again. I felt it would be unwise to leave you alone in case you took a turn for the worse."

So she had disobeyed him for his own good? It made Gavin feel rather a fool for speaking so sharply to her. So did the vague memory of having been tenderly cared for while he was incapacitated.

"What *other* time?" He did not recall any waking before last night.

"The night before last. Or was it two?" Clearly exhaustion had muddled Miss Fletcher's memory. Gavin had seen the effect often during the grueling Peninsular campaign. "You began speaking quite clearly, as if you were awake. But you did not appear to know where you were. You addressed someone named…Molsely? Molesby?"

"Molesworth." The name burst from Gavin's lips before he could contain it.

"That's right." Miss Fetcher rubbed her eyes. It made Gavin weary just to look at her. "You kept telling him not to go. You said the two of you must put a stop to Bonaparte."

Her words revived a wrenching memory. If she had struck him hard on his injured side, Gavin doubted it could have hurt worse. But it was worth the pain to be reminded of his vow and his mission. Valuable time had already been lost while he'd lain there useless.

"If I might ask, sir," she continued, "who is Mr. Molesworth?"

"You may *not* ask!" Gavin snapped. "And he is… *was* Major Molesworth."

Before the impertinent creature had the audacity to quiz him further, he seized command of the situation. "Enough of this. I am in full possession of my faculties now and I want you to summon a footman to help me make myself presentable."

He wished his aide-de-camp had been able to accompany him back from Waterloo. Then he would never have been placed in the awkward position of being tended to by Miss Fletcher. But the lad had sustained wounds of his own, so Gavin had insisted he stay behind to recover.

In case Miss Fletcher should be in any doubt about whether he meant to be obeyed, he added, "I insist upon it."

"Yes, sir." The governess shot to her feet, her spine stiff and straight as a ramrod. Gavin half expected her to snap a mocking salute. "Will there be anything else, sir?"

"As a matter of fact, there will. I want breakfast ordered. Not gruel or broth or jelly, but a substantial meal that will put some strength back in me—eggs and bread and meat."

Miss Fletcher's lips, which had looked so soft and innocent while she slept, were now tightened in a frown of disapproval. "Are you certain that will be wise, sir?"

"It is not for you to question the wisdom of my instructions, Miss Fletcher, only to carry them out at once. I also want the newspapers fetched so I can find out how the situation in Europe stands."

She did not agree with that, either. Though she managed to hold her tongue, Miss Fletcher's countenance expressed her opinion most eloquently.

"Very well, sir." She started for the door.

"One more thing," he called after her.

She came to an abrupt halt.

"And what might that be, your lordship?" she inquired through clenched teeth.

"After you have carried out my other instructions, get to bed and do not stir from it for at least eight hours. Or better yet, ten. I reckon you look worse for this whole ordeal than I do."

She stalked away without another word—at least none he was meant to hear.

But as she withdrew from the room, Gavin thought he overheard her mutter, "That's because you have not looked in a mirror yet."

For reasons he could not fathom, her insult made him break into a foolish grin.

Chapter Three

That man!

The moment Hannah woke, she began to fume again. The arrogance of him, ordering her off to bed in that domineering manner! As the earl's employee, she was paid to do his bidding in her position as governess. That did not give him control over every aspect of her life. How much she slept or ate was her own business, not his.

She also chafed at his rudeness in pointing out how haggard she looked. Would it have pained him to spare her a word of thanks for watching over him night after night?

Thoughts like those had run through her head before she lay down to snatch a brief nap, making her fear they would prevent her from sleeping a wink. Badly as she needed the rest, part of her wanted to defy Lord Hawkehurst by remaining awake. But the moment her head touched the pillow, she had fallen into a deep, exhausted sleep from which she did not stir for…

Hannah glanced at her clock. *Eight* hours!

She sprang from her bed as if slumber were a crime.

She could not recall sleeping so long in years. Perhaps the earl had been right after all, much as it pained her to admit it. Even after eight long hours, she still felt tired, though not so bone-weary. If his lordship had not commanded her to sleep so long, she would have felt unbearably self-indulgent. Instead she was able to place the responsibility squarely on his broad shoulders.

The thought of being beholden to him for *anything* irritated her.

Might he feel the same way about being tended to by her during the past few nights? Hannah resented the possibility that they might have something in common.

Now that she was awake, she must attend to the duties she had neglected for the past eight hours. As she donned fresh clothes, then plaited and pinned her hair in its usual plain, trouble-free style, Hannah chided herself for her preoccupation with the earl.

She tried not to dwell on her reflection in the looking glass, but she could not ignore her pasty complexion, hollow cheeks and the dark shadows under her eyes. Unchivalrous as his remark might have been, the earl had not exaggerated when he had claimed she looked worse than he did. It was vastly unfair that a man with a gaunt face, disheveled hair and a bristle of dark whiskers on his jaw could still appear ruggedly handsome, while a few late nights had left her looking a perfect wreck.

Once she had made herself presentable, Hannah considered going to check on his lordship. Who knew how badly he might have set back his recovery by overeating or fretting himself about the war news? She did not relish the prospect of another confrontation with the earl, but she had made his dying wife a promise and she intended to keep it.

She was about to head toward the sick room when a plaintive wail rose from the nursery, which adjoined her bed chamber. "Why can I not see Miss Hannah? Has she gone away like Mama? If she has, I want to go, too!"

As the nursery maid tried to quiet little Lord Edgecombe, Hannah flew in the direction of the ruckus. The earl was old enough to manage for himself, and her first responsibility was to the children. His lordship's well-being only concerned her so far as it affected them.

"Here I am." She stooped to catch the child, who had pelted toward her the instant she appeared. "You mustn't fret anymore. Everything will be all right."

Peter hurled himself into her embrace and buried his face against her shoulder, where he proceeded to weep his small heart out. It was all Hannah could do to keep from joining him. For days she had held back her grief, afraid it would prevent her from carrying out her duties. Now it threatened to engulf her.

"I am not going anywhere." She stroked the child's dark hair, which she suddenly realized was the very color of his father's. "You couldn't get rid of me if you tried."

Peter would never try any such thing, but what about his father? It occurred to Hannah that she should make an effort not to antagonize the earl. She would not put it past him to dismiss her if she disobliged him once too often. How would it affect the children if she were forced out of their lives—especially sensitive little Peter?

"I th-thought you went away!" the boy sobbed. "I d-didn't see you all day."

Holding him tight, Hannah backed toward the nearest chair and sank down on it. "I had some matters to see to, and I thought you would have such jolly times with Maisie and Matthew and Mr. Jennings that you wouldn't miss me at all."

Speaking in a soft, soothing voice, she rubbed Peter's back and pressed her cheek against his hair. She found it difficult to show affection, except with children.

The child's weeping eased to sniffles. "Couldn't Papa look after those things now that he is home from the war? I heard Jane tell Edgar he was back."

Hannah stifled an exasperated sigh. How often must she remind the maids and footmen that little pitchers had big ears? Lord Edgecombe was a clever child for his age; he took in more than people realized. What could she tell him about the earl? She did not want to make him worry that his father might soon join his mother in Heaven.

At the same time, she did not want her young pupil to wonder why his father had failed to look in on him and assume it was because the earl did not care. Hannah was far from certain if that might be true, though she prayed it was not.

"Your papa is very tired out from the war, and he must rest a good long while." No doubt her excuse would sound ridiculous to anyone over the age of five, but her young pupil did not question Hannah. "Until then, I must take care of some matters for him the way I used to for your mama."

She hoped her mention of the countess would not

upset the boy just when he had grown calm. Clearly they could both use a diversion. "Would you like to go visit the babies and see if they have gotten any bigger since last time?"

A glance and a tilt of her head signaled the nursemaid to fetch a handkerchief. When the girl brought it, Hannah thanked her and set about wiping Peter's eyes.

"Visit them now?" The child gave a doubtful frown. "But it is nearly time for tea."

"We won't stay long." Hannah held the handkerchief for him to blow his nose. "And the fresh air may give us an appetite."

Peter seemed prepared to accept the change in routine. "When will the babies get big enough to play with me?"

"Not for a while." Hannah helped him on with his little blue jacket and cap. "But it will not be long until they begin to smile at you."

She fetched her bonnet, then they headed off to a nearby tenant farm where little Alice had been sent to nurse. All the while Hannah told her young pupil of the changes he could expect to see in his brother and sister, how they would learn to hold up their heads, roll over, sit, crawl, stand and walk. By the time they neared the cottage, Peter was skipping along at her side, asking all sorts of questions.

"Good afternoon, Mrs. Miller," Hannah called to the farmer's wife, who was removing washing from her clothesline. "I hope we are not disturbing you. We wanted to look in on the baby, if we may."

"It's no trouble," the woman replied. "Go right on in. Our Bessie is rocking the wee one in her cradle. She does love to be rocked. A sweet-tempered lamb she is and growing prettier by the day."

They went inside the clean, snug cottage, where a fair-haired girl only a little older than Peter was rocking the cradle and singing to the baby.

"That's a nice song." Peter gave the girl a shy smile. "What is your name?"

"Bessie, my lord." The child scrambled up and bobbed a hasty curtsy. "That is…my name's Elizabeth, but Ma only calls me that when I vex her."

Peter laughed at that, causing poor Bessie to look even more flustered. Hannah could not help thinking what a pity it was that her young pupil was cut off from the local children by his rank. No wonder he was anxious for his baby brother and sister to grow up quickly into playmates for him.

"Would you like to hold Alice and say hello to her?" Hannah asked Peter as she scooped up the baby, who was beginning to fuss. "There, there, little one. Your big brother has come to visit you."

She lifted the precious little creature to her shoulder for a moment and rubbed her back, inhaling her sweet, milky scent. Holding a contented baby must surely be one of the most satisfying pleasures in the world! A tide of tenderness rose in Hannah's heart as she caressed the child's downy cheek with her forefinger.

Wee Alice and her brothers were the closest thing she would ever have to children of her own, Hannah mused. Though her friend Marian Murray had recently wed and Rebecca Beaton was engaged, Hannah held no such hopes for herself. She had always been guarded in her dealings with other people, men especially. Even if she could have found one who would be interested in a penniless governess, she had let down too many people she cared about and lost them as a consequence. She dared not risk her heart on marriage. But she did regret missing the opportunity to become a mother.

"Miss Hannah." Peter gave her skirt a tug. "I thought you said *I* could hold the baby."

"Of course." Hannah stirred from her maternal brooding. "I only wanted to get her settled first. Climb up in that chair and I will give her to you."

Peter did as he was bid, then Hannah did as she had promised, though it cost her a pang to surrender the small, precious bundle to other arms. Even then, she hovered close, making certain Alice's small head was supported and that she was in no danger of falling from her brother's arms.

"You're very pretty, Alice," Peter informed his tiny sister with grave courtesy. "Your eyes are the same color as Mama's. I wonder if you will look like her when you grow up."

"She will be a fortunate girl if she does." Hannah's heart overflowed with love for both twins and their brother. She was relieved Peter had been able to speak about his mother without becoming upset. "You know, Alice and Arthur are too young to have any memories of your dear mama. When they get older, it will be up to you and me to tell them all about her."

"Don't forget Papa," replied the boy. "He can tell them, too."

"So he can." Hannah strove to keep her tone from betraying any doubt. "How silly of me not to think of him."

The earl's children would need their father for so many things in the years to come, Hannah reminded herself. She must do everything in her power to make certain they did not lose him, too. Even if it meant standing up to him in a way no one else in his household was willing to do.

Alice seemed very content in the arms of her big brother. She didn't fuss at all and soon drifted off to sleep.

"Shall we go visit Arthur, then head home for tea?" Hannah whispered, so as not to wake the baby.

Peter gave a solemn nod and let Hannah gently place his sister back in her cradle.

On the way to the Wilkeses' cottage, Hannah found herself wondering if Lord Hawkehurst had spent the day resting quietly as he should. Their confrontation that morning made her fear he might not. What if he tried to get out of bed too soon and risked compounding his injury? If he did, it was no use hoping any of the other servants would try to stop him. None of them would dare to gainsay the earl's commands, even if his stubborn independence might cost him his life. What it might cost her young charges, Hannah could not bear to think.

If only she could persuade him not to rush his recovery. But she was the last person he would listen to. Unlike his dear wife, he clearly considered her opinion of no value because she was only a woman and a governess.

"Are you feeling ill, Miss Hannah?" Peter's question jolted her out of her thoughts.

"Ill?" She glanced down at the child. "Not at all. Only a little tired. What makes you ask?"

"The look on your face." He twisted his own features in an imitation of hers—mouth tight and brow furrowed. "Are you sure you're not ill? Perhaps you should see the doctor."

The doctor! Hannah felt the tension in her face ease. She smiled to reassure her anxious young pupil. "That is an excellent idea. I feel quite well but I reckon I should consult him to be certain."

It was not for herself that she intended to consult Dr. Hodge. She was certain the physician would agree with her about Lord Hawkehurst. And his lordship might conceivably heed the doctor.

Gavin had not thought *anything* could make him pleased to see Miss Fletcher. But when she appeared that evening with Dr. Hodge, the earl was forced to admit he'd been wrong. Not that he had the slightest intention of telling her so.

Since their exasperating, yet strangely invigorating, exchange that morning, he had spent the rest of the day surrounded by obliging servants who deferred to him in every particular. They never presumed to disagree with anything he said. They readily carried out his orders to the letter. He could not recall when he had last spent such a tiresome day.

It did not help that the news from France was so uncertain. Waterloo had been hailed as a great triumph, yet Gavin knew the cost of that victory in human terms had been appalling…on both sides. What a terrible waste it had been—a terrible *needless* waste! If only the man responsible had been dealt with properly a year ago, all those men, including his friend, might still be alive and healthy now.

It was no good casting stones at others, Gavin admitted to himself. He was as much to blame as anyone. He was a peer of the realm, after all. He should have gone up to London and demanded Bonaparte be put somewhere he could be properly watched and prevented from returning to power.

Gavin could not let the same thing happen this time.

To be certain it would not, he needed reliable information. Since that appeared to be in short supply, the void was filled with rumors instead. He must find out what was going on, but he could not do that by lying in bed and reading newspapers that printed more fiction than fact!

The arrival of Dr. Hodge and Miss Fletcher provided a surprisingly welcome diversion from his anxious brooding.

"I was most relieved to hear that your lordship had regained consciousness." The doctor laid down his satchel and reached for Gavin's wrist.

"No more pleased than I am," Gavin replied. "How soon can I expect to be on my feet again?"

The doctor exchanged a look with Miss Fletcher before he answered. "I shall need to make a more thorough examination before I can hazard an opinion, sir. But I must stress it is important not to hurry the process. The body heals from injury in its own time as the Lord has ordained. Any attempt to speed it may have the opposite result. In your case it might even place your life in danger."

Gavin scowled as the doctor continued his examination. That was not the response he had wanted to hear. The prospect of a long succession of days like this one appealed to him as much as a plague of boils! Being confined to his bed while Bonaparte slipped through the Allies' fingers again would be some of the worst torture he could imagine.

He resented the smug look on Miss Fletcher's face as she stood by the mantel waiting for the doctor to complete his examination. No doubt she had fetched Hodge here to lecture him about not trying to rush his recovery.

Had he given her any choice, his conscience inquired, after making it clear he had no intention of heeding her advice? What puzzled him was why she was not eager to see him up and speeded on his way. All the time he'd been home last year, Miss Fletcher had made little secret of her disapproval of him. She should be happy to see him gone again.

That was it! Gavin flinched and sucked in his breath as Dr. Hodge removed the dressing from his wound. Miss Fletcher did not know that he meant to leave Edgecombe once he was fit to ride again. She must assume he intended to settle down and take over running the estate, perhaps interfere with her management of the children. Nothing could be further from his plans—for the time being at least.

Perhaps if he explained why he could not afford to linger in bed for days on end, Miss Fletcher would seize the opportunity to be rid of him.

The doctor shook his head and clucked his tongue as he examined the wound. "It appears to have opened again just when it was beginning to knit. What happened, sir?"

Gavin's scowl deepened. He felt as if he were eight years old again and being brought before his father to answer for some mischief he'd gotten up to. "I retched up my breakfast, if you must know. The…heaving was rather violent."

His words brought a furrow of worry to the doctor's brow. "What did you have to eat that disagreed with your digestion? I gave instructions for—"

"An invalid diet," Miss Fletcher piped up. "Water gruel, beef tea, calves' foot jelly. When his lordship woke this morning he had an appetite for…heartier fare."

"Ham and eggs," Gavin growled. "Kippers, hot rolls and coffee."

The doctor looked aghast. "Not much wonder you cast up your accounts, eating like that after a long fast. I cannot stress strongly enough that you must rest in order to heal. The longer that wound takes to knit, the greater risk you run of an infection. After the quantity of blood you lost, your constitution might be too weak to fight it."

Gavin was still not convinced his injuries could be that serious. Civilian doctors were such alarmists. Army surgeons would stitch a soldier up and send him straight back into action.

"But I feel quite well. Apart from the odd twinge of pain…and being weaker than I'd like…perhaps a trifle light-headed." He jammed his mouth shut before he admitted to anything worse. If he added much more, he feared the doctor might declare him a permanent invalid.

Once again Miss Fletcher spoke up. "Dr. Hodge, could you perhaps advise his lordship how long it will be before he may resume his normal activities?"

Gavin shot her a baleful look. Had he truly been pleased to see her a few moments ago? He must have been off his head.

The doctor considered for a moment. "I should say you must not stir out of bed for at least a fortnight, sir, and eat only those foods that will be easy on your digestion. After that you might slowly begin to resume your accustomed activities. Provided you do not cause yourself a setback by trying to hurry the process, I believe you should be quite well recovered in a month's time."

"A month?" By then Bonaparte could have slipped out of France on a ship bound for the Caribbean or America to wait for his next opportunity to seize power. How many more would die then? Far more than Gavin cared to contemplate.

"A fortnight?" he cried. "That is ridiculous! I cannot lie about for days on end while my country is at war."

"The war will soon be over thanks to men like you." The doctor dismissed Gavin's protest. "Now I must apply a fresh dressing. Miss Fletcher, would you be so kind as to help his lordship sit upright while I bind his wound?"

The look on Hannah Fletcher's face told Gavin how little she cared to approach that close to him. Had he only dreamed of the devoted care she'd given him while he had lain unconscious? She did not permit her aversion to interfere with doing what she considered her duty, however. Gavin could respect that. The governess gave a curt nod of agreement, squared her shoulders and strode toward the bed.

"I am perfectly capable of sitting up on my own," Gavin insisted. But when he tried, a hot stab of pain made him inhale sharply.

"Very capable, indeed," Miss Fletcher muttered.

Before he could stop her, she swooped down, wedged her shoulder beneath his right arm and eased him to a sitting position. Once there, she continued to support him. Gavin wanted to dismiss her gruffly, but the room was beginning to tilt this way and that, making him fear he might humiliate himself further by falling over if she let go. So he gritted his teeth and prepared to endure what he could not avoid.

As Dr. Hodge wound a length of loose-woven cotton around his midriff, Gavin found himself grateful for Miss Fletcher's capable strength. Her hair grazed his cheek, and the clean, tangy scent of lemon filled his nostrils.

"I commend your devotion to king and country," the doctor continued as he went about his work. "But you must not forget the duty you owe to your children, especially since they have lost their poor mother."

Something in the man's tone suggested he was only parroting the opinion of another person. Gavin had no trouble guessing who that meddlesome someone might be.

"What have my children got to do with any of this?" he demanded, addressing Hannah Fletcher as much as her puppet, the doctor.

True, he had not originally intended to become a father, and he had very little experience with children. That did not mean he would ever neglect his duty to his offspring. He resented having anyone question that.

The doctor tucked in the end of the bandaging that held the dressing in place. "Your children have a great deal to do with it and a great deal to lose if you jeopardize your health by not taking proper care of yourself."

Hodge might have spoken those words, yet they sounded as if they had come straight from Miss Fletcher. No doubt she had lectured the poor man half-deaf on the subject all the way here. Much as it exasperated Gavin, he could not deny her devotion to his eldest son, which now clearly extended to the little ones, as well.

"I have no intention of neglecting my duty to my children," he repeated, sensing Miss Fletcher might not believe him. "If you say I must rest for a fortnight in order for my wound to heal properly then…I suppose…I must."

That final admission came out almost painfully, like a rotten tooth being extracted. He did not know how he would withstand the tedium and uncertainty for that length of time. Somehow he must, for the sake of his young family and the mission he had sworn to carry out. Neither would benefit from his death.

"I was certain your lordship would see reason," the doctor replied.

If Miss Fletcher had not been so near, Gavin might have missed her faint sniff of doubt.

The doctor nodded to her. "I am finished. You may lower the earl now."

Her muscles tensed, preparing to bear his weight. "Just relax and let me do the work, sir."

Gavin tried, but it was not easy to surrender control to another person. His sinews instinctively tightened to keep from falling back too quickly. A sharp pain in his side warned him that he had likely torn a bit of flesh that was trying to knit itself back together. By a great effort of will, he managed to relax as Miss Fletcher had bidden him and let her ease him down the rest of the way.

As she slid her arm out from beneath his shoulder, her face hovered near his. Gavin found himself suddenly intrigued by the shape of her lips, which suggested both fierce determination and profound generosity.

His conscience denounced him fiercely for entertaining such a thought. He had no business noticing any woman's lips when the mother of his children was barely in her grave. Poor Clarissa! He had married her for all the wrong reasons, believing she would be content as the wife of a soldier seldom home from war. He had let her down in so many ways, but at least he had never looked at another woman.

And he was not about to start. He would have quite enough to occupy him with his mission. Once it was accomplished, he would be busy raising his three motherless children. Any connection with a woman would be a needless complication in his life.

If he *had* been inclined to think of a woman in that way, his son's strong-willed governess was the last one he would ever consider. The two of them were like oil and water. Though he had discovered more admirable qualities in her of late, it was clear Hannah Fletcher still found him as odious as ever. The speed with which she backed away once she'd carried out the doctor's orders left no doubt of that.

It galled him that she had managed to compel his agreement to a fortnight's tedious convalescence through the underhanded use of Dr. Hodge. A soldier never liked to accept the necessity of surrender. He must show Miss Fletcher there could be unpleasant consequences to meddling in his life. Otherwise she might continue to call the tune around Edgecombe until his children were grown.

The doctor packed his satchel and promised to call again in two days' time unless he was summoned sooner.

When the governess offered to see him out, Gavin spoke up. "I would like a word with you after that, please, Miss Fletcher."

Dr. Hodge waved her back. "In that case I can see myself out. No need for you to go all the way down to the entry only to return. Good evening, Lord Hawkehurst. I wish you a pleasant rest."

Pleasant rest. Gavin barely suppressed a sniff of derision. There was no such thing as far as he was concerned. He was a man of action and had been for as long as he could recall. He had already exhausted his tolerance for lying about doing nothing. The coming fortnight stretched ahead of him like an endless wasteland. If he must endure such tedium he had no intention of enduring it alone.

The doctor closed the door behind him.

Miss Fletcher turned toward Gavin, but she made no move to approach him. "What did you wish to say to me, sir?"

"Pleased with yourself, are you?" he asked.

"I beg your pardon, sir? Pleased on what account?"

Gavin shook his head. "Come now, Miss Fletcher. It will not do. We both know you put the doctor up to that, so let us not insult one another by pretending otherwise."

For a moment the lady looked as if she intended to continue protesting her innocence, but then her chin tilted upward and she met his challenging gaze with one of her own. "Very well. I did speak to the doctor. But only because you refused to heed a word *I* said. I thought you might take more notice if the advice came from a man and someone outside your household."

Well, well. It appeared Miss Fletcher was capable of giving as good as she got. Her frankness put Gavin in mind of the Duke of Wellington, the commander he revered. Her words hit home, for he knew all too well the frustrations of having his sound advice ignored by his superiors.

"Neither of those changed my mind," he insisted.

Miss Fletcher's brows rose. "Then pray what accounted for the alteration?"

He was enjoying this. The unlikely feeling crept up on Gavin just as it had the previous morning when he and Miss Fletcher had sparred verbally. Somehow the sluggish minutes passed more swiftly when he was diverted in this manner. He asked himself why and decided perhaps it was the nearest thing to combat he could experience while confined to his sickbed.

Yes, of course, that must be the reason.

"What changed my mind?" He readied his next salvo. "Why, experience, of course. You tried to warn me that a hearty breakfast might not be the best idea, but I thought otherwise and learned a hard lesson."

Miss Fletcher blinked rapidly and took a step closer to him. "You did?"

A faint glow of satisfaction provided some relief for Gavin's chagrin. He never liked admitting he'd been wrong. But it might be worth the minor humiliation to keep his adversary off balance.

He nodded. "Hard but valuable—as most worthwhile lessons are. I realized that any attempt to hurry the natural rate of my recovery would only delay it. Therefore, the quickest way to get on my feet again would be to remain on my back for as long as I must."

Miss Fletcher seemed to sense something amiss. "Then why did you argue with the doctor if you already knew what he was trying to tell you?"

"I was not entirely prepared to admit defeat. I would rather fight a division of the French Imperial Guard than spend a fortnight doing absolutely nothing."

"I can understand that," Miss Fletcher replied in a tone of sincere sympathy.

"You can?" Who had been caught off balance this time?

Miss Fletcher gave a rueful nod. "I might not prefer to face down the Imperial Guard, but I do like to keep busy and feel useful. The prospect of a fortnight with nothing to do would hold no appeal for me."

Who would have thought they might have something in common? Certainly not Gavin. "Then you *can* see why I would not want to agree to it except as a last resort."

"But you did agree for the sake of the children." She sounded as surprised as he felt. "That was well done."

Would wonders never cease? There was something

about him of which Miss Fletcher approved. "May I assume you would not object to helping make my ordeal more bearable?"

She went for the bait without a moment's hesitation. "I should be happy to assist you in any way I can, sir. Pray, what can I do?"

"You can keep company with me." The instant he spoke, Gavin realized he had phrased his request quite the wrong way. A man and woman were said to *keep company* when they were courting. "I mean…you can keep me company. Help me pass the time so I do not go mad from boredom."

He prepared for her to argue and make excuses, but he would counter them all until he won his way at last, as she had won hers to keep him bedridden. If he must suffer such imprisonment, so must she. That was only fair, surely.

The last thing he expected was for Miss Fletcher to reply, "Very well, sir. If that is what you wish, I shall be happy to oblige you."

Gavin's well-honed military instincts warned him that he had just blundered into an ambush.

Chapter Four

Why had the earl asked her to keep him company while he recuperated? Hannah pondered that question from the moment he ordered her away to get a decent night's sleep until the morning when he summoned her back to attend him.

It was not because he enjoyed her company. She had no illusions about that.

Perhaps Lord Hawkehurst considered it some sort of punishment she deserved because he held her responsible for the dreary confinement he faced. Could he not understand that was *his* fault? If he had not tried to rush his recovery, he might only have had to endure one week or less.

Whatever his reasons, Hannah was not altogether displeased with the result. True, it might be rather disagreeable to spend so much time in the company of a man who seemed to go out of his way to antagonize her—a man she found it difficult to forgive for making his late wife so unhappy. It would also keep her busier than ever trying to accommodate the children's needs and his lordship's. Besides that, there was a disturbing undercurrent of tension between her and the earl that she could not comprehend. Did it spring from her aversion to the man…or feelings that were quite the opposite?

Hannah dismissed that ridiculous notion before it was fully formed in her mind. Instead she turned her thoughts back to the children. It was on *their* account she welcomed the opportunity to supervise their father's recovery.

Just because his lordship had assured the doctor that he would stay quiet and not overtax his strength did not mean he would be able to keep his promise—especially if the hours dragged by too slowly or he received upsetting news from the Continent. If he took it into his head to disobey his doctor's orders, none of the servants would have the nerve to intervene. But she would, in order to preserve his health for the children's sake.

She had another aim in mind, as well. No matter how difficult it might be, she intended to win the earl's trust so he would never consider replacing her as his children's governess.

Fearing that might be a task beyond her ability Hannah knelt by her window for a moment, clasped her hands and gazed up into the serene blue of the summer morning sky. "Please, Lord, help me to get on well with the earl and make his healing time pass as quickly as possible."

It wasn't often she pestered God with pleas on her own account. Past experience had taught her to be self-reliant and do for others. But surely it was no great failing to ask for a little help now and then. She hoped her

Heavenly Father would appreciate that this was a request of particular urgency and grant it.

The very act of phrasing her prayer gave Hannah a boost of energy and optimism. With divine assistance nothing was impossible, though she feared that keeping Lord Hawkehurst amused for a fortnight might come close.

Firmly dismissing that thought, she practiced smiling in front of the looking glass. The expression she managed to produce looked more bilious than cheerful.

"For the children," she reminded herself. Closing her eyes, she pictured young Peter, Alice and Arthur.

When she opened her eyes to peer in the glass again, Hannah was relieved to find her features relaxed in a doting smile.

"Thank You, Lord," she breathed. "Now I suppose I'd better not delay any longer. It won't improve his lordship's temper if I keep him waiting."

She discovered just how truly she'd spoken when she entered the earl's bedchamber a short while later.

"What kept you?" he demanded. "You claimed to be so eager to be of service and yet you have left me lying here with nothing to occupy me. I am only hours into this wretched convalescence, yet it already feels like a week."

All Hannah's good intentions evaporated in a flare of annoyance. "At least you are alive and have all your limbs and senses about you. Rather than bemoaning two weeks' rest, you ought to be thankful your wound will heal that quickly!"

Though she meant every word of it, inwardly Hannah cringed at her shrill, priggish tone. What was it about this man that brought out the worst in her? She spun toward the window and yanked open the curtains so the earl would not witness her grimace of regret. Not that it mattered. He would likely order her out of his presence after such an insolent outburst. She would be fortunate if he did not dismiss her from his service on the spot.

She heard him inhale sharply at her rebuke and braced for the counterblast she knew would come. One she deserved, no doubt.

"You are right, Miss Fletcher." Those were the last words she expected to hear from Lord Hawkehurst. Could her ears be playing tricks on her?

"I...I am?" She turned back toward the bed, fighting to rally her composure.

"Of course you are." There could be no mistaking the earl's tone of chagrin. "You need not have been so brutally blunt about it, but that does not make you wrong. When the surgeons were patching up this pinprick of mine, I heard men screaming in agony as their shattered arms and legs were sawed off. Others had bandages wrapped around their eyes, never to see again. I am an ungrateful wretch to complain of a situation which will soon pass."

The earl's frank acknowledgment made Hannah feel worse than any reproach. Was this how a soft answer could turn away wrath? Perhaps she ought to learn a lesson from it. "I beg your pardon, sir. It was not my place to speak to you that way."

Lord Hawkehurst raised his shoulders in a rueful shrug. "Even if you were right?"

"Even then." Hannah sank onto the chair beside his bed. "It is not always easy to remember our blessings."

She recalled the relief and grateful elation she'd felt when his lordship had finally regained consciousness. How quickly she had taken that blessing for granted to focus on some new dissatisfaction. She had no right to take him to task for a failing they shared.

"It is no blessing being forced to spend time with a person you detest," the earl muttered. "Is that why you were so quick to lose your temper with me?"

A reflexive denial rose to Hannah's lips. "I do not detest—"

The earl's dubious stare stopped her in midsentence. "If we are to spend the next fortnight together, I reckon we ought to clear the air, don't you?"

Before she could answer, he continued, "I know you disapprove of me and my profession. I suppose you think it sinful of me to have fought for my country and its allies."

His accusation caught Hannah off guard, uncertain how to respond. She could not pretend she had approved his decision to return to war the last time. But what would become of the world if every soldier and sailor put domestic concerns ahead of military duty?

"It is not for me to judge whether anyone else has done wrong. Scripture says *all* have sinned in some way and have fallen short of the glory of God." She hoped her words would appease him. Instead his dark gaze grew stormy and his features clenched in a fearful scowl that compelled her to ask, "Do you not believe in God?"

"Of course I do!" The earl sounded surprised and offended by her question. "Though I sometimes wonder about the contradictory demands the Almighty places upon humanity. It seems no matter what we do, or how hard we try, we can never measure up. We are always wrong, always judged and found wanting."

The bitterness in his voice took Hannah aback. It made her wonder what had given him such a harsh impression of the Lord. Discretion urged her to drop the subject, but something else made her persist. "I do not believe that passage of scripture was meant as blame, only to warn us against self-righteousness. Perhaps I should have paid it more heed."

Hannah could not recall the last time she had spoken so openly with anyone about her faith. Lord Hawkehurst was a most unlikely confidante. Yet it felt strangely natural to talk this way with him. Could it be because they had both confronted death so recently?

"I do not condemn your military service," she continued, "quite the contrary. I know there will always be people who seek to oppress anyone weaker than they."

She recalled how the biggest girls at school had always crowded around the fire, preventing the younger ones from receiving any of its meager warmth. "Fortunately, there are others willing to defend the weak, even at risk of harm to themselves. Anyone with a sense of right and wrong must admire them."

"But…?" the earl prompted her. "I sense one coming. Out with it. I would rather have an open disagreement than silent hostility seething beneath a polite surface."

Was that how he viewed her attitude toward him? Hannah wished she could deny it, but her conscience would not let her. "Very well, then. I cannot pretend I agreed with your decision to return to your regiment the last time troops were called up. Your wife and son needed you."

The earl looked as if he regretted urging her to speak freely. "You needn't remind me that I was a poor excuse for a husband and father, Miss Fletcher. No one knows it better than I. But I had a duty I felt obliged to see through."

Then, more to himself than to her, he added, "And I am not finished yet."

What on earth had made him think it would be a good idea to have Miss Fletcher as a companion while he was forcibly bedridden? Gavin asked himself that question as they played a game of backgammon. The rattle of the dice sounded like a mocking chuckle at his folly.

He had been so busy anticipating her discomfort and wanting to punish her…for what? For caring more about his well-being than he did? For thinking ill of him when he knew she was perfectly justified? For being right and seeing him proven wrong?

His resentment of the lady was unfair and his wish to penalize her quite unworthy. Now he was getting his just deserts.

The black-and-white marble disks made a sound like a clicking tongue as they struck one another while being moved across the board. Well, they should reproach him.

If he'd thought that sparring with Miss Fletcher and needling her would make the time pass quicker, he'd been wrong. For the lady had not hesitated to tell him a few unpalatable truths about himself. He hesitated to provoke her again for fear she would unleash more on him. Tiresome as it might be to lie in bed for days on end with only his painful conscience for company, it was even worse to pass the time with a person whose presence was a continual unspoken reproach.

Miss Fletcher counted up her final moves under her breath, bringing the last of her counters to their destination.

"Gammon," she announced. The softly spoken word betrayed a faint ring of triumph. She had beaten him quite handily. Only backgammon would have been a more humiliating defeat.

"Congratulations," Gavin replied in a flat, hollow tone. "You win more than you might have guessed, Miss Fletcher."

Her head snapped up. "I beg your pardon? What have I won?"

Her blue-gray eyes glittered with suspicion at his riddle. Gavin could not deny she had good reason to mistrust him.

"Your freedom." He swept the backgammon disks back into the hinged box that served as a playing board. "This imprisonment is tiresome enough for a man like me to bear. Forcing you to suffer with me does not make it easier. Go about your usual duties and leave me to my own miserable devices. It is no worse than I deserve."

He expected the lady to greet his announcement with relief. Instead her eyes widened in a look of distress. "Give me another chance. Please, sir. I know I have not been good company for you today, but I promise I will do better."

Gavin shook his head. "You mistake me. I am offering you a reward, not a penalty. It takes two to make good company. When I am one of those two, I fear it is a lost cause from the beginning."

She pondered his words for a moment, then one corner of her lips inched upward. "That sounds like a challenge."

Why did she not simply accept his offer and make her escape? "If you relish attempting the impossible."

"Does a good soldier accept defeat before the battle has been properly joined?" *That* certainly sounded like a challenge—one he was hard-pressed to resist.

"I would rather fight a battle every day for the next fortnight than this." Gavin barely stifled a sigh. "There I go falling into self-pity again. You were right to chide me for it. It is as contemptible as it is tiresome."

Though she must surely agree, Miss Fletcher refrained from saying so. "You could not have fought a battle *every* day of that long war. How did you occupy yourself between times?"

"There was never any difficulty to pass the time." Gavin thought back to his recent weeks in Nivelle and his years in Portugal and Spain. "There were scarcely enough hours in the day between drilling my regiment and meeting with the senior officers to discuss strategy. Dispatches to write and scouting patrols to assign. Making certain my men were properly fed and supplied, our horses well cared for. Breaking camp, riding to the next one and making camp again."

As he recited the litany of his duties, Miss Fletcher began to nod her head slowly. "No wonder you could find little time for writing to your wife."

Gavin winced, though his wound was giving him little pain at the moment. "You need not remind me of my deficiencies as a husband, Miss Fletcher. My difficulty was not a matter of finding *time* to write as of finding anything to say that might have interested Clarissa. She had no patience for military news. It was almost as if she were…"

He searched for the word, not certain what he was trying to say.

"Jealous?" Miss Fletcher suggested. "I believe she may have been."

"Jealous?" Gavin dismissed the possibility with a wave of his hand. "Of what? The army? The war?"

"Of something that took you away from her." The governess sought to explain what perhaps only another woman could understand. "Something she thought you cared about more than her. Something with which she could not compete."

"Must we talk about this?" Gavin squirmed. Suddenly his position on the bed did not feel so comfortable. "There is nothing to be done about it now."

"I suppose not." A shadow of sorrow darkened Hannah Fletcher's eyes. Almost as if *she* had been to blame for his wife's unhappiness rather than he. "Forgive me for raising the subject, after I promised to be a more agreeable companion. I believe I may have thought of a way to make the coming days pass more quickly, if you would care to hear it."

Gavin doubted anything could accomplish that, but he strove not to concede defeat too soon. "By all means, speak. If anyone can devise a solution, it might be the incomparable Miss Fletcher."

"Must you mock me, sir?" She lowered her gaze.

"You may not think well of me, but I have endeavored to do my best for your family since I came to Edgecombe."

He had never expected to hear such an injured tone in the voice of his son's cool, capable governess. She tensed, as if preparing to spring up and hurry away. If she did, Gavin feared she might never come back.

His hand shot out to clasp hers. "I did not mean to mock you, Miss Fletcher. In the past, I may not have valued your service as highly as you deserved, but I am beginning to see my error."

Another thought occurred to him. Though discretion urged him to keep it to himself, he felt compelled to offer Miss Fletcher a token of atonement. "Perhaps I was a trifle jealous of…you."

"Of me?" She still looked dubious of his sincerity.

"Of your pivotal place in my household." Suddenly conscious of the impropriety of holding her hand, he released it. "Of how well you succeeded in a role where I never could."

"I am certain you could have succeeded if you had tried harder."

Could he? The possibility skewered Gavin's conscience as surely as that shot had pierced his side. He hastened to change the subject. "Tell me about this idea of yours to pass the time. I would welcome any hope, however slight."

"As you wish." Miss Fletcher inhaled deeply, whether to compose herself or to master her annoyance with him, Gavin could not be certain. "I thought the time might not stretch so long ahead of you if it were divided into shorter units."

She looked so deadly serious, Gavin could not resist

rallying her a little. "I believe it already is. Those divisions are called hours and minutes. When I am obliged to lie about doing nothing, each minute seems as long as an hour and an hour as long as a day."

"That is not what I meant," Miss Fletcher replied tartly, though Gavin glimpsed a faint twinkle in her eyes. "I propose dividing the day into units of activity, none of more than an hour's duration. Frequent changes of activity might make the time pass more quickly for you."

"Like a schedule?" The notion intrigued him. "That does sound promising. What sort of activities do you propose to fill my time?"

"Necessary ones to begin with. Your meals. Time in the morning for grooming. Then…" Her eager words trailed off.

No doubt she had grasped the flaw in her fine plan. There would still be many blanks to fill in this schedule she proposed and very few activities suitable for a bedridden patient.

Just as Miss Fletcher's hesitation stretched into an awkward pause, she was rescued by the sudden appearance of Edgecombe's elderly butler. "The newspapers, my lord."

News! Gavin's spirits bounded. No one at Edgecombe could tell him more than that the Allies had been victorious at Waterloo and Wellington was pursuing Bonaparte toward Paris.

Miss Fletcher sprang from her chair. "I will take those, Mr. Owens, and read them to his lordship if he wishes."

"Very good, miss." The butler handed the papers

over with an air of deference, as if she were Gavin's sister or...

"Thank you, Owens," Gavin said. "I am most anxious for news from the Continent."

"I trust the reports will be to your liking, my lord." The butler bowed and withdrew.

Miss Fletcher resumed her seat. "Are you sure you want to hear all this? I am afraid the news may only upset you and hinder your recovery."

"Of course I want to hear." In fact, he could hardly wait. "Are there any reports from the French or Flemish papers?"

It occurred to him that perhaps he could put the coming fortnight to productive use after all, gathering information, laying plans and making preparations for his mission once he was fit to undertake it.

"After we are finished with these—" he gestured toward the newspapers "—I have thought of a number of activities with which we might fill that schedule of yours."

The following day, Hannah once again scanned the newspapers for reports from the Continent. She was not certain how she felt about this activity. Reading the newspapers to his lordship certainly helped to pass the time. No other activity seemed to occupy his attention quite so well. Once they'd finished reading all of yesterday's news, the earl had ordered her to fetch writing materials and compose a letter to the Foreign Office. Then he had asked her to fetch a map of the Continent and mount it on a board for him to examine.

Though she welcomed any diversion that would occupy him, his obsession with the war troubled her. She hoped he did not plan on returning to active duty as soon as the doctor let him leave his bed.

But how could she stop him if he was determined to go?

"Here it is." She focused on one particular news item. "A report from the French Chamber of Representatives when it sat six days ago."

"Six days?" The earl plowed his fingers through his thick black hair. "Do you know how much the situation could have changed in that time? Is there nothing more current?"

"I will check, sir, if you will calm yourself. It does no good to fret about any of this. There is nothing you can do about it."

The earl muttered something under his breath that sounded like "not yet."

"Here is the latest news from London," Hannah began to read. "There was a report current upon the Exchange yesterday morning that Bonaparte had surrendered himself into the hands of the Duke of Wellington at Compiègne. But no authentic advice of any such event was received by Ministers, though the fact is mentioned in the Brussels papers."

As she read, Hannah lifted a silent prayer of thanks. "That is excellent news! If Bonaparte has surrendered, the war must be over for good."

"*If* he has surrendered." Lord Hawkehurst gave that first word the most doubtful emphasis. "I would not credit a rumor from the Exchange that assured me the sky is blue."

"But the Brussels papers…" Hannah protested,

wanting the report to be true quite as much as the earl seemed to wish it proven false.

"Even if the report is correct—" the earl drummed his fingers on the bedclothes "—that is no guarantee Bonaparte will not be sent into comfortable exile once again, long enough to lay plans for his next return to power. I cannot allow that to happen!"

His fingers ceased their drumming and clenched into a tight fist. "Week-old news and unsubstantiated rumors—I must have more accurate information! Has there been any reply from my letter to the Foreign Ministry?"

"Not yet." Hannah spoke in a soothing tone she might have used with young Peter when he was upset. "But it has only been one day, and I daresay the Ministry has plenty of business to occupy it at the moment."

Her words seemed to ease the worst of his agitation. The earl's fingers unclenched, and he exhaled a deep, slow breath. "You are right, of course. Perhaps we will receive an answer on Monday. In the meantime, put a pin in the map at Compiègne."

Hannah laid down the newspapers and did as he'd bidden her.

"Are you only following the doctor's orders so you can recover enough health to return to your regiment?" Hard as she tried to keep her tone neutral, notes of challenge and accusation crept in.

The earl must have heard them, for he responded accordingly. "What if I am? I owe a duty to my country."

"You have a duty to your *children*." Hannah wanted to throw up her hands in exasperation. "Or do you care nothing for them?"

Discretion warned her it was not her place to question her employer's feelings toward his family. But beneath that insistent warning, a quiet insight dawned on her. How *could* his children mean more to him than his military career? He had lived with it night and day for years. But he had spent very little time with Peter, and he had never even *seen* the babies.

If she hoped to make the earl's obligation to his children something more than an abstract concept, he would need to get to know them. What better time to do that than this fortnight while he recovered?

"Of course I care for them!" The earl bridled. Clearly her question made him defensive. "They are my children, after all. Besides, I know what it is like to grow up without a mother."

He did? Hannah's gaze flitted toward the portrait above the mantel, which showed a dark-haired young woman dressed in an elaborate brocade gown of the past century. She had never thought to inquire how long ago the previous countess had died. History seemed to be repeating itself at Edgecombe.

"I am relieved to hear that you appreciate your paternal responsibilities, sir. For the children's sake, I urge you to give up any idea of returning to your regiment. It is clear General Wellington will vanquish Bonaparte. And surely the Allies will have learned their lesson about the folly of leaving such a man at liberty. Let others deal with him. *He* is not your responsibility, but your children are. You cannot risk your life while they need you."

Lord Hawkehurst flinched at her words as if each one had dealt him a blow. "I appreciate your concern for my children, Miss Fletcher, but you must understand that I cannot rest until I am *certain* there is no possible way Napoleon Bonaparte will ever return to power. I made a vow to a dying comrade, and I must honor it."

A dying vow? Hannah folded the newspaper with trembling fingers. How could she ask his lordship to abandon such a sacred promise when she had made a vow of her own—one that ran contrary to his?

Chapter Five

Had he managed to get through to Miss Fletcher at last?

Gavin marked the change that came over her face when he'd mentioned his vow to Molesworth. The resolute thrust of her chin faltered, and the challenging flash of silver in her blue-gray eyes muted. Had she assumed his determination to return to duty was only a headstrong whim? A love of war? Perhaps a selfish effort to avoid his parental responsibilities?

Much as he resented her doubts, Gavin could not entirely suppress his own. And they sickened him.

While he had been fretting about having nothing to do, he could have been getting to know his young son at last. Perhaps even comforting the boy after the death of his mother. Not that he had any idea where to begin. Miss Fletcher would be better suited to *that* task, yet he had robbed the poor little fellow of his governess just when he needed her most.

Gavin wished he could blame his thoughtlessness on the tremendous upheaval in his life. He had been wounded in a great battle, lost his wife and closest friend and became a father to two more children all in a matter of days. It was no excuse for thinking so little about his children.

"Major Molesworth," Miss Fletcher murmured. "Was he the comrade to whom you made your vow?"

Gavin's first impulse was to wonder how she knew. Then he remembered her saying he had called out for his friend.

"I take it you were close comrades." Miss Fletcher seemed to forget he had refused to answer her earlier question about his friend.

Somehow he could not refuse her this time. "The closest. We met at school when we were only little shavers. He was deadly homesick at first."

"But you were not?" Miss Fletcher's question pursued Gavin as he sank into his memories.

He shook his head. "I got on much better at school than at home. I was not terribly studious, but I did well at games and got on well enough with the masters and the other boys. I looked out for Molesworth until he settled in, fought some bigger lads who tried to bully him. Over time he became more like my brother than… When I purchased my commission in the cavalry, he followed my lead and we rose through the ranks together."

"It must have been very hard for you to lose him." The sympathy in Miss Fletcher's voice surprised Gavin. "It would grieve me to the heart to lose any of my dear friends from school, even though we have not set eyes on each other for years."

The woman had friends and a past life of which he knew nothing. Somehow that came as a revelation to Gavin.

"I am not certain I have taken it all in yet. Part of me wants to believe it was a terrible mistake. I know he is gone. I watched him die. Every time I think of him, I am reminded that it should never have happened. We came through that long, blood-drenched slog up the Peninsula without a scratch, and we beat Boney once." Without realizing it, his voice rose as he spoke until his final words rolled like thunder. Hot anger was easier for him to accept than the chill void of loss. "That should have been an end to it!"

Gavin expected Miss Fletcher to shrink from his outburst as Clarissa would have. Instead, when he shot her a guilty glance, he found himself caught in a gaze of understanding and compassion.

Surely when he explained it all, she would understand why this meant so much to him and why even his paternal responsibilities would have to wait until he had seen his mission through. "If only Bonaparte had been dealt with as he deserved, a year ago, there would never have been this bloody postscript. Molesworth would have lived to a ripe old age, surrounded by his children and grandchildren."

"Did he have a family?" Miss Fletcher sounded almost as if she mourned his fallen friend.

"No." The word gusted out of him like a sigh. "There was one young lady who caught his fancy during the peace celebrations. But he did not want to propose to her until he was certain the war was over for good. Now he will never get that opportunity."

"That is a tragic misfortune," the governess mused. "But even if Bonaparte is made to pay for his actions, it will not bring back your friend."

"I know that," Gavin insisted, though a small, irrational part of him wanted to believe otherwise. "But it will prevent others like him from losing *their* lives in another repetition of this wretched war. And perhaps the soul of my friend will truly rest in peace. Can you not understand the importance of such a vow, Miss Fletcher, and why I cannot rest until I have done everything in my power to fulfill it?"

"I understand better than you may imagine, sir." The lady looked so deep into his eyes, Gavin had the uncomfortable feeling she could see straight into his heart. "You see, I made a vow much like that to your wife not long before she died. I promised her I would watch over your children and do everything in my power to protect them."

Somehow, Miss Fletcher's mention of her promise to his wife brought home to him the reality that Clarissa was truly gone. In the six years of their marriage he had spent far less time in her company than he had away on some distant battlefield. He'd grown accustomed to her absence, which made it difficult to believe that she was not still going about her life elsewhere. Now he grasped the truth that her life was over, just like his friend's, far too soon.

Her brief span of years had not been as happy as they might have been. That was his fault. He had hoped to make it up to her once the war was over. But would he have been able to? Or would it have been another dismal failure?

"I beg your pardon, sir." Miss Fletcher's words pierced Gavin's bemusement. "Did you hear what I said?"

"You mentioned a vow you made to watch out for the children." He was tempted to resent Clarissa entrusting their children's welfare to a paid governess when they had him. It showed whose capability and caring she trusted more. But how could he blame her? He was the first to admit his lack of experience with children, while Miss Fletcher had amply demonstrated her concern for them.

"Is that why you sat up with me while I was unconscious?" he asked. "And why you agreed to keep me company while I am bedridden? For the children's sake?"

"Of course, sir," she answered with only the briefest hesitation. "Why else?"

Why else, indeed? Gavin was not certain why her answer came as something of a disappointment. Surely he knew better than to think the lady cared about *his* well-being for his own sake. But she took her vow to Clarissa seriously. If she believed her worst enemy was essential to the welfare of his children, she would do everything in her power to safeguard that person. Gavin supposed he must admire that depth of dedication.

"I do not want your children to grow up without a mother *or* a father," Miss Fletcher continued with a vague air of unease, as if the seat of her chair had grown too warm for comfort. "That is why I wish you would give up any thought of placing yourself in danger by returning to the Continent."

What she proposed made sense. Gavin could not deny it entirely.

And yet…the sting of knowing she only tolerated his company for the children's sake stirred his instinct to oppose her. "Would you have me abandon *my* solemn promise to my friend without a second thought or even an attempt to fulfill it?"

"I am certain if Major Molesworth was as true a friend as you say—"

"He was my friend without a doubt," Gavin interrupted her sharply. "If I had asked the same of him, he would not have hesitated."

Miss Fletcher refused to back down. "That is because he had no family to consider. I feel certain he would not want to place this vow, worthy as it is, above the well-being of your children. Especially when there are others who can accomplish the task with greater ease and less risk."

"What would *you* say if I told you to forget your promise to my wife?" Gavin sensed a weakness in her position and sought to exploit it. "After all, I am the children's father, and I am home now. I can take responsibility for them."

Miss Fletcher sprang from her chair. "That is different!"

"Is it?" Gavin demanded.

"Entirely."

"Why?" he asked. "Because you do not trust me to care for my children as well as you can?"

"No," Miss Fletcher responded too readily, without giving herself time to consider.

But the moment the word left her mouth, it was clear she did not believe it any more than he did.

Oh, that vexing man! No one had ever ruffled Hannah's composure as much as the Earl of Hawkehurst.

That thought dogged her footsteps the next afternoon as she hurried down to the Millers' cottage while his lordship took a scheduled nap, to which he strenuously objected.

A short while later she returned to Edgecombe, bearing a warm, sweet-smelling little bundle.

"I must admit," she murmured to the sleeping baby. "Over the past few days, my opinion of your father has improved a great deal. He has a number of qualities one must admire—courage, determination, protectiveness, honor. He is willing to admit his mistakes, sometimes too quickly I think. He can even laugh at himself, which I never expected. When you are my age, you will realize it is an underappreciated virtue."

Baby Alice stirred in her sleep and gave a soft coo that imbedded itself deep in Hannah's heart.

"But why can he not see what a terrible mistake he is planning to commit?" She shook her head, torn between perplexity and exasperation. "I can understand wanting to keep his promise to his friend. Who would not want the man responsible for so much bloodshed to be prevented from waging war ever again? But that is a task for other hands, and I am certain they will accomplish it."

The baby continued to sleep, her peace undisturbed by the knowledge of her father's plans. She was still too young to realize she *had* a father, but Hannah hoped to lay the foundation for that precious knowledge today.

"If your papa puts duty to his dead comrade ahead of his living children, I may be the only one who can raise you and your brothers the way your dear mama would wish. Do you suppose he trusts me with your upbringing as much as I trust the Duke of Wellington to bring General Bonaparte to justice?"

The possibility kindled a warm glow in Hannah's heart.

"Or am I fooling myself?" she muttered. "More likely it is his faith in his own invincibility that blinds him to the possible consequences of his plans. That is why I need your help, little one. I believe the better your papa comes to know you and your brothers, the less inclined he will be to risk your future by chasing off after Napoleon Bonaparte."

Was she taking a risk now, Hannah wondered, with the welfare of her precious little goddaughter? Surely not! Lord Hawkehurst might not have been the most attentive family man, but he would never allow any harm to come to a helpless child.

"I hope you will do your part," she whispered to baby Alice as they approached the earl's bedchamber. "Just stay asleep and look sweet and endearing. Within half an hour, you will steal his heart entirely."

She brushed a soft kiss on the baby's tiny nose by way of reassurance, then pushed open the door and slipped into the earl's room.

"Thank heaven you are back," he greeted her with a mixture of relief and annoyance. "You must omit this cursed rest time from my schedule. I am not tired in the least, only bored witless. It would be better to keep me well occupied through the day so I may be able to sleep at night."

The words came out in a rush as though he had been rehearsing them for some time and could not wait another moment to speak. Once he'd had his say, the earl took notice of her at last.

"What's that you're carrying?" A note of unease in his voice suggested he already guessed.

"This is your daughter." Hannah approached his bedside. "I'm sure you have wanted to meet her, and you seem well enough to tolerate a little visit."

She took her accustomed seat and held the child up so her father could get a good look. "Your lordship, may I present Alice Clarissa Beatrice Romney. Is she not the most exquisite little lady?"

The earl gazed at his tiny daughter with an air of gentle yearning tempered with baffling wariness.

"She is so tiny," he breathed as if terrified the sound of his voice might wake the child. "Peter was nearly weaned when I first saw him, yet I was still afraid he might break if I held him the wrong way."

Hannah's lips relaxed into a tolerant smile. There was something strangely endearing about such a powerful man being frightened by a small, defenseless child. "But your son did not break, did he?"

She meant to reassure him, but instead the earl grimaced. "Perhaps not, but he did wail fit to burst my eardrums. Hard to believe such a tiny creature could be capable of producing such deafening noise."

He peered toward his infant daughter, clearly expecting her to explode into violent bawling at any moment. "I appreciate the thought, Miss Fletcher, but do you reckon it is wise to keep the child away from her wet nurse at such a young age? She might wake up hungry."

Did he think that had not occurred to her? Hannah suppressed a flare of irritation with Lord Hawkehurst.

There was too much at stake for her to indulge such feelings.

"I made certain Alice fed fully just before I brought her here. I doubt she will stir at all for quite some time, let alone wake hungry. Babies sleep a great deal at this age, you know."

Perhaps the earl did not know about the habits of infants. By the sound of it, he'd had no younger brothers or sisters. If he had gone straight from school to war, he might never have seen a very young child up close before his elder son. Hannah could picture his reaction to Peter's loud crying. Had that incident sown the seeds of awkwardness between father and son that persisted to this day? Hannah resolved to tackle that problem once she had properly introduced the babies.

Her assurance that little Alice was likely to sleep peacefully seemed to ease his lordship's mind. He regarded the child with greater interest and less worry.

"What a dainty little creature she is." A glimmer of paternal pride lit his dark eyes. "Doesn't take after me in the least. For her sake, I hope she will grow up to resemble her mother."

A faint sigh escaped the earl's lips, the first indication Hannah had heard of grief for his late wife.

"Alice's hair is dark like yours," she told him, anxious to establish a connection between father and daughter. "Shall I take off her cap to show you?"

His lordship blanched as if from a mortal threat. "That will not be necessary. I am quite prepared to take your word for it. I would not want to disturb her while she is sleeping."

"I see a resemblance to *your* mother, as well." Hannah nodded toward the portrait above the mantel. "Her wide-set eyes and the shape of her mouth."

The earl's hand twitched over the bedclothes as if he wanted to reach toward his daughter but something prevented him. Much as Hannah would have loved to cradle the sleeping baby in her arms all day, she reminded herself of the reason she had brought the child to visit her father.

"I really must go look in on Peter." She rose from her chair. "He doesn't understand why I am gone so much. I have been reluctant to tell him about your wound. He is very worried that other people he cares about will go away and leave him, like his mother."

"Poor little chap," Lord Hawkehurst murmured. "Perhaps it was a blessing I lost my mother before I was old enough to miss her."

"No loss like that can ever be a blessing." Hannah thought of the twins and how it might affect them to grow up with no memory of their mother. "But sometimes, even in the worst of circumstances, we can find small mercies for which to be grateful."

She must quit stalling, Hannah chided herself, and get on with what she had come here to do. "While I go check on your son, I shall leave you to get better acquainted with your daughter."

Before his lordship could do more than sputter vague sounds of protest, she leaned forward and deposited the sleeping baby in his arms.

"That is not necessary." He tried to hand the child back, but Hannah had already moved out of reach. "Do not leave her here. You should take her with you!"

"I will not be long." Hannah gave an airy wave as

she headed for the door, though the edge of panic in the earl's voice gave her second thoughts about her plan. "I'm sure she will not be any trouble."

"Miss Fletcher." His voice pursued her. "I must insist you return and take the child back at once! What are you thinking to leave her here? I am in no shape to take care of an infant. I am not even capable of caring for myself!"

Hannah stopped just outside the door. Every feminine instinct urged her to go back at once and retrieve the baby, but she strove to resist.

Lord Hawkehurst was not going to form a bond with his daughter by watching her from an impersonal distance. He needed to see up close the plump curve of baby Alice's cheek and the gossamer fringe of lashes on her closed eyes. He needed to hear the steady whisper of her breathing and the tiny coos and gurgles she sometimes made in her sleep. He needed to feel her warm weight in his arms and smell her milky-sweet scent. Only then might she begin to make a place for herself in his heart.

Keep your voice down or you might wake her up! Hannah longed to warn the earl. That was clearly the last thing his lordship wanted.

But it was too late.

The baby had slept serenely while Hannah carried her from her nurse's cottage and then talked for some time with her father. But the transfer to his tense, unwelcoming arms and the ragged edge of panic in his voice must have jarred little Alice from her tranquil repose.

The child gave a fussy little bleat, which prompted

her father to cry out even louder. "Miss Fletcher, come back here at once!"

It was everything Hannah could do to resist his desperate plea and her womanly instinct to soothe a crying infant. But she dared not rush to his rescue too soon. She must give the earl an opportunity to discover that tending a baby was not as frightening and fraught with failure as he appeared to believe. If she swooped in the moment things went a little wrong, she would only confirm his belief that the task was beyond his ability.

So she stood and listened as the baby's cries grew louder and shriller, each one slicing into her like a blade. Silently she implored the earl to find a way to quiet his tiny daughter.

What was Hannah Fletcher trying to do—terrify his tiny daughter and drive him gibbering mad?

As the baby's face grew red and her wails became louder, Gavin would rather have been anywhere than lying there so helpless and ill equipped to comfort her. A litany of unkind words ran through his mind, all directed toward the heartless woman his late wife had trusted to watch over his children. Was this an example of how she meant to safeguard their well-being?

"Hush, now," he begged the crying infant. "Please, please, hush. I know you must be frightened that Miss Fletcher dumped you upon me. I am no happier about it than you are, but I swear I will not let any harm come to you."

In spite of how it might set back his recovery and thus his mission, Gavin considered rising from his bed and marching off to the nursery with the baby. There he would hand her over to someone other than Miss Fletcher and order little Alice returned to her nurse at once.

But he dared not take the chance that he might become light-headed and fall with his tiny daughter in his arms. He could not even reach the bellpull to summon assistance without loosening his hold on her and leaning over dangerously far. The safest action he could take was the one that came hardest to him—do nothing and wait. Miss Fletcher would have to return eventually.

The baby's cries seemed to demand he do more than that. Perhaps she was not frightened of him after all, but angry at being woken so abruptly.

"I sympathize with you." He knew the child could not understand a word he was saying any more than his horse might.

The pitch of her cries reminded him of the shrill whinny of a spooked horse. It was a sound that did not stop at his ears but penetrated his chest, making his heart gallop and his breath race. It set all his nerves jangling and made him want to do anything that might make it stop.

Then he recalled how his roan gelding, Severn, responded to the sound of his voice, especially when nervous. His touch had calmed the beast, as well. Was it possible this small creature might respond in the same way?

"There is no sense bellowing." Fighting every instinct to the contrary, he pitched his voice soft and low, barely audible above his daughter's screams. "Believe me, I tried. It will not bring Miss Fletcher back a moment sooner. Until she decides to return, I'm afraid you are stuck with me."

As he spoke, he held the baby securely, passing one hand over her tense little body, the way he would have caressed Severn's neck or flank before a charge. He wasn't certain it was doing the child any good, but at least it made *him* feel calmer and more in control.

"I'm sorry to be such a dunce about all this, but it is rather uncharted territory for me." Was it his imagination or were the cries becoming less shrill? "I wish you could tell me what is wrong and how I can help, but I suppose that would be too much to expect from someone of your age."

Horses could not speak either, to explain their troubles, yet over the years he had learned to interpret the different sounds they made and the physical signs that indicated their moods and their needs. Did women learn to do the same with babies?

His daughter was definitely growing quieter. That certainty brought Gavin a rush of relief, charged with a flicker of triumph that he'd seldom felt, except after winning a battle. Could little Alice be responding to his easing tension?

"That's better." He wiped away a tiny tear with the tip of his forefinger. He could not resist grazing it over the baby's cheek. He had never felt anything so soft. Not the finest kid leather. Not even the petal of a flower. Something this small and soft called forth all his strength and courage to protect it.

"Shh, shh. Everything will be well. You'll see. I will hold you safe until Miss Fletcher returns." Gavin kept talking about anything and nothing, for the words would have no meaning for the child, only the tone of his voice.

At last, after a series of little grunts and sniffles, Alice's crying subsided. Had she gone back to sleep? Gavin angled his head and titled her slightly to check.

No. His daughter was wide awake. She fixed him with a solemn stare, as if she was committing every feature of his face to memory. He could not help smiling. All thought of his earlier unease faded, eclipsed by feelings that were entirely new to him.

"Isn't that better?" Without conscious effort, his voice took on a tone unlike any he'd ever used before. "Shall we just lie here and enjoy one another's company? I must confess I find the prospect of raising a daughter rather daunting. I hope you will not hold it against me if I make some mistakes over the next twenty years or so."

He could not resist grazing his knuckle over the delicate roundness of her cheek. To his surprise, she raised one tiny hand and grabbed on to his finger with surprising strength.

"Looking to shake hands, are you?" Gavin's smile stretched wider as he bobbed his finger up and down. "Good day to you, Lady Alice. Allow me to present my compliments."

He drew her hand toward his lips and pressed a soft kiss on it.

A chuckle bubbled up in his throat only to find it strangely constricted. What in blazes had come over him?

He was still trying to sort out his feelings when Miss

Fletcher breezed back into the room. "There, I said I would not be long and the baby would be no trouble."

Gavin managed to wrench his gaze away from his daughter to direct it at her godmother. "Why did you thrust her upon me and run off like that? It woke her. She began to cry. You must have heard. I thought you promised to safeguard her welfare."

"I did," Hannah Fletcher protested. "I was! Your children's well-being will always be my first concern."

Gavin detected a quaver of guilt lurking beneath her words. It suggested she was not as confident of her motives as she pretended to be.

When he continued to stare at her without another word, Miss Fletcher's conscience got the better of her.

"Perhaps it was not my best idea." She heaved a contrite sigh as she dropped heavily onto her chair. "But I knew no harm would come to your daughter, and I was right. You managed to soothe her, which can take some doing. I suspect you have far more skill with little ones than you realize."

"With *big* ones, actually." His gaze strayed back to his daughter's small face as if drawn by a powerful magnetic force.

When she stared back at him with rapt interest, the corners of his lips arched upward quite against his will. How was he supposed to impress on Miss Fletcher the gravity of her error when he was grinning like a fool?

"Big ones, sir?"

"Horses." Gavin raised his forefinger again and watched with wonder and amusement as baby Alice reached out and clenched her diminutive fingers around it. What a strong grip she had for her size! That would be a great asset to her when she grew older and learned to ride. "I have never been good at understanding people—what they want from me and what makes them behave the way they do. I understand horses, though, and it occurred to me that babies might not be so very different."

He cast a quick glance at Miss Fletcher to find one of her eyebrows raised in a look of doubtful puzzlement. "Indeed? How so?"

"The way they respond to a certain tone of voice and touch." Gavin wondered what compelled him to make her understand.

"I believe you may be on to something," she replied. "In my experience babies also like to be rocked and bounced about gently. I'm not sure how you would manage that with a horse."

She concluded with a sputter of laughter, the first time Gavin had heard any such sound from her. Until that moment, he would have sworn Miss Fletcher did not know how to laugh. It was a very pleasant, infectious sound that coaxed an answering chuckle from him.

Then he remembered his wife and his best friend had been dead for a very short time. Everything that had happened since then and the endless hours he'd been confined to bed made it feel much longer. But in the eyes of the world both bereavements were still fresh. He had no business laughing and feeling happy when he should be mourning Molesworth and Clarissa.

With ruthless force, Gavin forced his mouth into a severe line.

Miss Fletcher stifled her chuckle just as quickly, making Gavin wonder if he had only imagined it.

"However you managed to settle your daughter, I knew you would rise to the occasion. I felt it would do her far less harm to fuss a bit than to grow any older at a distance from her father. Alice needs you, sir. They all do. And this seemed the perfect opportunity to bring the two of you together."

Gavin wondered if Miss Fletcher might be right. Could this be his chance to become a better father than he'd been a husband? An opportunity to put the horrors of war behind him and become a man of peace?

With his infant daughter cradled in his arms, he wanted to believe it was possible. But experience had taught him that a single victorious skirmish did not ensure a successful campaign. He could not hope to achieve that goal on his own any more than Britain could have defeated Bonaparte without the assistance of its allies. Was it possible he might find an ally in his former adversary, Hannah Fletcher?

Chapter Six

"Is it quite necessary that you desert me to go off to church?" Lord Hawkehurst asked Hannah the next morning as he ate his breakfast. "There are no newspapers for me to read today. How am I to pass the time until you return?"

A few days ago such complaints might have irritated Hannah, but closer acquaintance with the earl had made her more tolerant. Considering how hard he found it to stomach inactivity, he seemed to be trying his best. He had not given in to the temptation to rise from his sickbed without the doctor's permission, not even when Hannah had left baby Alice in his care.

Listening to the gentle way he spoke to his infant daughter and watching the way he held her, Hannah had found herself strangely drawn to him. No doubt that was due to their mutual bond with the child. Whatever the reason, she was relieved her attitude toward him had begun to soften. It would be far more difficult to keep her promise to his late wife if she must constantly battle her aversion to the children's father.

"As to your first question," she replied, "yes, it is

quite necessary for me to go to church. With all that has happened of late, I need to seek comfort in the words of scripture and pray for strength and guidance. It is vital that I take your son with me. After losing his mother, he needs the consolation only faith and love can provide."

"I suppose that is all true." The earl finished his last spoonful of buttered eggs. "I beg your pardon, Miss Fletcher. I did not mean to be so beastly selfish. Being confined to a sickbed for days on end does not bring out the best in me. I reckon you need all the divine assistance you can get to put up with it me."

Hannah did not disagree, though in truth she found him much easier to tolerate when he recognized his own faults. "To answer your second question, you might pass the time and observe the Sabbath by reading from your Bible. It may not be as current as the *Times* or the *Morning Chronicle,* but it contains words of wisdom that could well apply to the present situation. Or you could pray about matters on the Continent."

The earl did not greet her suggestions with much enthusiasm. "I am accustomed to taking more direct action. But since I am unable to do that…"

"You might be surprised at the power of prayer." Hannah removed his breakfast tray to the butler's table beside the door. "If nothing else, it might help you decide upon a course of action to pursue once you are well again."

She hoped the spirit would move him to remain at Edgecombe with his children and leave the fate of Napoleon Bonaparte to a higher power.

"Perhaps." The earl did not sound hopeful.

Hannah wished she had taken Sunday into account

when she'd made up his lordship's schedule of activities. It was meant to be a day of rest, but he clearly needed as much activity as possible.

"Before you go," said Lord Hawkehurst, "I wish to speak to you about my daughter's visit yesterday."

"Very well, sir." Hannah braced for a reprimand she'd been expecting ever since.

Perhaps she deserved it. Had she taken too great a risk by leaving the baby alone with a father who had little experience with infants and even less liking for them? Just because her gamble had paid off did not mean it had been wise.

"Apart from a little crying, her visit did not appear to do the child any harm." The earl sounded oddly defensive, as if he expected Hannah to disagree.

His remark was so different from what she had expected that it took Hannah a moment to recover from her surprise and produce a reply. "On the contrary, sir. I believe an opportunity to meet her father could do your daughter nothing but good."

Though he tried not to show it, the earl seemed pleased with her answer. "In that case, I would not object if you were to bring her for another visit sometime soon. Tomorrow, perhaps, if the weather permits."

This was so much better than she'd dared to hope. Hannah made no effort to conceal her happiness. She did have one reservation, however. "I can bring Alice again if you wish, sir. But what about little Arthur? You have not met your younger son yet, and I am certain you would not wish to favor one of your children over the others."

"No, indeed." His lordship's brow furrowed and his

features settled into a pensive frown. "I would never want that."

The matter was clearly of great significance to him. Hannah could not help wondering why.

"I never expected to have a family, you know," the earl mused as if in answer to her unspoken question. "I never *intended* to have one. I was devoted to my military career, and I did not feel it would be compatible with family life."

"What changed your mind?" Was it impertinent to ask such a personal question of her employer? Hannah feared it might be. Yet she could not resist the inclination to know his lordship better. Perhaps if she learned more about his past and came to understand his motives, it might help her persuade him to do the right thing for his children.

If the earl resented her question, he gave no sign of it. "My elder brother fell ill and died. Did Clarissa never tell you?"

"No, sir." Why should she?

Her face must have betrayed her puzzlement, for his lordship offered an explanation. "As the new heir, I was expected to perform the duty for which I had been bred—step in to ensure the succession of the family title. My father insisted upon it. Clarissa had been engaged to my brother. After a suitable period of mourning, she seemed agreeable to accept me in his place."

So he had wed his late wife out of duty, not love. That explained a great deal about their marriage. Hannah wished she had known sooner. While there were some who might not approve of the earl's actions, she had always set a high value on duty. If his lordship did too, it seemed all the more likely she might help him recognize the duty he owed to his children.

But what about their mother? Why did the earl suppose she had married him? To secure the title of countess, perhaps, or a fine home and fortune?

"Why are you telling me this?" She was not comfortable with any knowledge that cast his marriage in a different light from the one she had seen.

"I'm not certain, to be honest." The earl sounded almost as puzzled by this unexpected confidence as she. "Perhaps I do not want you to think I care nothing for my children. I *want* to be a proper father to them, but I have no idea where to begin or whether I have it in me."

Would he rather not try at all than try and fail? Hannah found that attitude difficult to fathom. Her instinct in the face of possible failure had always been to try harder, do better, give more. "You have already made a good beginning with Alice, sir. You clearly demonstrated that you have it in you to be a fine father, if you are willing to try."

"Of course I will *try*. But if I am to have any hope of succeeding, I shall need…help." The earl sounded almost ashamed to admit it. "*Your* help, Miss Fletcher. You have done a fine job helping me to endure my recovery. That schedule of yours has made the time pass more quickly. I can see now why her ladyship placed such great reliance upon you."

"Thank you, sir." Hannah's face blazed. Past experience had made her much more accustomed to accepting slights and criticism than praise. For some reason, she found herself particularly uncomfortable receiving a compliment from Lord Hawkehurst.

She told herself not to be so foolish. The more his lordship came to depend on her, the better chance she would have of dissuading him from returning to his regiment once he recovered. "I shall be happy to do everything in my power to assist you."

"Good." The earl sounded relieved, as if he had expected her to refuse. "I hope that means when you fetch my son to visit you will not simply dump him upon me, then disappear, but rather stay and offer some advice on how to handle him."

"I did not *dump...*" Hannah began to protest. The words faded on her lips when she realized he had spoken the truth. "Er...that is...of course, your lordship."

She glanced at the clock on the mantel. "Dear me, I must be going, or Peter and I will be late for church. Since you have less than usual to occupy you today, perhaps I could call at the Wilkeses' cottage on my way back and bring Arthur for a visit this afternoon."

Hannah wondered if she might be pressing her luck with that suggestion. But she wanted the earl to spend as much time as possible with his children while he was confined to bed with few other matters to claim his attention.

His lordship hesitated for a moment, then replied, "That is an excellent idea. I look forward to it."

After what seemed like a very long time, but what the mantel clock insisted had only been two and a half hours, Miss Fletcher returned to Edgecombe. It struck Gavin that she looked rather attractive in spite of her black mourning dress and bonnet. Her cheeks had a dapple of healthy color, and there was a becoming softness about her features that might have something to do with the baby she held in her arms. Or perhaps he was so desperate for company that even the old butler would have looked attractive in his eyes.

"Lord Hawkehurst." She perched on the edge of his bed and held up the baby for his inspection. "May I present your younger son, Arthur Gavin Horatio Romney."

The child was dressed in identical garments to his twin sister, a white gown and cap with a blanket wrapped around him. Yet Gavin thought he could detect subtle differences in their looks. Little Arthur had darker brows than his sister and a tiny dimple in his chin. Unlike Alice, he was wide-awake and seemed less placid. His small fists flailed and his gaze swept the room, gradually focusing on his father's face.

"Well," said Gavin. "That is an impressive name for such a little fellow to live up to. I suppose you will have no choice but to pursue a military career. Which do you fancy—the army or the navy?"

Both were popular choices for younger sons of the nobility who would not inherit the family lands and fortune…unless some harm came to their elder brothers. Most peers liked to have at least one extra son—a spare who could inherit if anything happened to the heir.

"Would you like to hold him?" Miss Fletcher asked with a warm flicker of encouragement in her eyes. "I will not run off, I promise. I shall stay right here, prepared to take him back if you need me to."

Gavin's face must have betrayed his misgivings.

"There is no danger of breaking him." Miss Fletcher bounced the child gently in her arms. "He is sturdier than he looks. Remember how well you managed with little Alice yesterday."

"Very well, then." Gavin held out his arms, not wanting to appear a coward. "I suppose I cannot do much worse than yesterday. I will keep try to keep my voice down to begin with."

"That would be a good start." Hannah Fletcher leaned closer to transfer the child into Gavin's waiting arms. Somehow, she seemed more awkward about it than the previous day when she'd foisted his infant daughter on him without ceremony.

Today she proceeded with much greater care. "There we go. Make certain you support his head. He is a bit too young to hold it upright on his own yet. But he will be soon, won't you, Arthur? You're strong for your size. I reckon you will grow up to be a big, strapping man like your papa one day."

Her remark ambushed Gavin. Was that truly how Hannah Fletcher saw him? Even the way he was now, unable to rise from his bed and as dependent on her care as any little child? His chest seemed to expand even as he fumbled to get a proper hold on his small son.

Yesterday, with Alice, he'd been too much taken by surprise to notice the brush of Miss Fletcher's arms against his or the whisper of her breath in his hair. Now he was acutely conscious of the whole procedure. Part of him wished the governess would draw back as soon as possible, but another part wanted her to linger near him.

Meanwhile the baby wriggled his small body and batted his arms about, making all sorts of gurgling noises that his father found strangely endearing.

"He doesn't seem to like keeping still any more than

you do." Miss Fletcher gave a breathless chuckle as she abruptly surrendered the child to him and pulled away. "You appear to have a good hold on him now."

With her hands free, she tugged the strings of her bonnet loose and pulled it off. Several strands of her honey-brown hair came free and fell about her face in winsome disarray.

Gavin had little opportunity to notice for the baby began to fuss. Perhaps young Arthur did not like being parted from his godmother. Or perhaps, like a spirited horse, he sensed uncertainty in the person now handling him. The movement of his arms grew more agitated. His small face reddened, and his features screwed up. A lusty wail erupted from his tiny mouth.

Hard as Gavin tried to remain calm, he could not help but grimace. "Perhaps you ought to take him back. I don't think he likes me."

It dismayed him how much that thought stung.

"Nonsense." Miss Fletcher set her bonnet down on the foot of his bed and proceeded to smooth back the wayward wisps of hair that framed her face. "Babies cry about anything and nothing. You must not take it personally. I'm certain he will soon settle down just like Alice did."

In the past Gavin had not appreciated the governess's brisk, capable manner, but today he was grateful for it. She radiated greater confidence in him than he felt in himself.

"I'm afraid this young lad may not be as coopera-tive as his sister." In spite of his resolve not to raise his voice, Gavin was forced to in order to make himself heard over the child's piercing howls.

"He is certainly rambunctious," Miss Fletcher agreed. "Just as you may have been at his age. He might be more content if he had something to occupy his attention. Try bouncing him a little and talking to him."

The tension building inside Gavin began to ease. Surely if they put their heads together he and Miss Fletcher could get his noisy young son to settle. The bouncing seemed to help. As for talking, he wasn't certain. With Alice, he'd just been thinking aloud. But with an audience, he wasn't certain that would be a wise idea. "What should I say to him?"

"Anything that comes into your head." Miss Fletcher flashed him an encouraging smile. Or was she amused to watch him struggle with the crying baby? "As you discovered yesterday, it is the sound of your voice that matters, not the words. Tell him about some battle you fought or interesting facts about horses. Try exaggerating your expression, as if it is the most exciting thing you can imagine. That might divert him."

Gavin racked his brains for an engaging topic, one he could talk about at length with some animation. And then it came to him.

"What do you suppose General Bonaparte is up to, Arthur?" He followed Miss Fletcher's suggestion, posing the question as if it were of vital importance, which he believed it was.

His son responded with a little gasp, his eyes widening in a startled look that made Gavin want to laugh. Best of all, the crying ceased entirely.

"I thought a future soldier might be curious about that," he continued. "The newspapers reported that the three Bonaparte brothers set sail to England from Le Havre, but I do not believe a word of it. Do you?"

Young Arthur stared at him with the most intent look, almost as if he did understand. Then he made a rude wet sound, appropriately derisive.

Gavin broke into a broad grin. "I agree. It is all nonsense. Bonaparte is likely planning to make a stand in Paris or retreat further south. If he does try to escape, it will be to the Americas or some French possession in the East Indies."

The baby wriggled and seemed to shake his fist at the idea of Bonaparte making a successful escape.

As he continued to talk, Gavin found himself thinking about Napoleon Bonaparte's young son, who must be halfway in age between Arthur and Peter. After last year's defeat, the child had been taken to Austria by his mother. As far as Gavin knew, the family had not been reunited after Bonaparte returned from Elba. Tempting as it was to condemn the French emperor for neglecting his son, Gavin realized he was in no position to cast stones.

One thing he knew for certain. He would never make little Arthur feel like a barely necessary *spare*.

What intelligence would the newspapers and the post bring today? Hannah wondered on Thursday morning when the butler delivered them with great ceremony. The past few days had left Lord Hawkehurst in a fever of suspense. No reports from Paris had reached the English newspapers since the previous week, and no one knew why. Uncertainty had spawned conflicting rumors and speculation that changed from day to day.

"What do you suppose we shall hear today, Miss Fletcher?" the earl inquired as Hannah opened the *Morning Chronicle* and scanned the columns of print for news from France. "Another report of Bonaparte applying for asylum in Britain? If it is true, what gall the fellow has! Surely the government would have more sense than to permit such an outrage. It would be a mortal insult to every soldier and sailor who died fighting against him!"

Hannah gave a sympathetic nod. They had been through this on Monday in response to a report in the papers. The earl had become so outraged she had feared he might do himself an injury. She suspected part of his anger stemmed from a sense of helplessness that there was nothing he could do to influence events.

"I'm certain your letter to the Foreign Secretary would make them think twice about any such action, sir. If the report was true in the first place."

"It was a good idea, getting me to dictate that letter." The earl gave a nod that seemed to signify approval and thanks. "It made me feel as if I was doing something, however little. You would make an excellent aide-de-camp, Miss Fletcher…if you were a man, of course."

His lordship's words of praise had kindled a blaze of happiness inside Hannah that frightened her with its intensity. For some reason his afterthought quenched that happiness entirely. But why? Surely it was a great compliment that the earl considered her capable of doing a man's job. And it was only proper that he should value her as he would a male comrade.

Then why did she feel slighted by a remark the earl had obviously meant as sincere praise? Hannah refused to consider that question too deeply. She would do better to focus on her duty to the Romney children.

"I trust Lord Castlereagh will take your advice into consideration, sir. He should, considering you are a peer of the realm *and* an officer who has seen action in His Majesty's cavalry."

Hannah's reply came out stiff and prim, in contrast to the easy camaraderie that had grown between them in recent days. Surely such informality was a natural consequence of spending so much time together. But she must remember the earl's convalescence was already half over. In a week's time he would be allowed to leave his bed and resume many of his normal activities. He would no longer be dependent on her to occupy his time. She would return to the nursery, and they might hardly ever see one another. The prospect sank her spirits to a degree she would not have thought possible a few days ago.

"There cannot be any news of significance," his lordship prompted her in a jesting tone. "Or it would not take you so long to locate."

"I fear you are correct." Hannah put aside any thoughts of the future to concentrate on the time at hand. "I can find nothing but complaints about the continued interruption of mail from Paris. There is not even a confirmation or denial of yesterday's report from the *Brighton Herald*."

That item claimed the Allies had surrounded Paris and charged the provisional government not to let Bonaparte escape or *their* lives might be forfeit. If they'd been certain the report could be trusted it would have cheered both Hannah and his lordship. Instead they were both wary of getting their hopes up.

Last night she had prayed for it to be true. If the French would surrender and hand over their former emperor to the Duke of Wellington, Lord Hawkehurst could rest easy, his battlefield vow fulfilled at no further risk to him. He could retire from active military service and devote himself to his family.

Every day that week, except Tuesday when it rained, she had brought one or the other of the babies to visit their father. It delighted her to see how much more skilled and confident the earl had become at handling infants in such a short time. Even more encouraging were the signs of his growing attachment to them. When the weather prevented Alice's visit on Tuesday, her father had been positively downcast. Though Hannah tried to cheer him up by losing a chess match, she could barely contain her pleasure that her plan appeared to be working.

"What else do the papers say besides bemoaning a lack of mail from Paris?" The earl's warm, rustling voice broke in on Hannah's thoughts. "Has the Exchange recovered? What is all the latest society tattle? If I do not soon get on my feet, I fear I shall become preoccupied with such trivialities."

Hannah read to him from the newspaper, though she knew he was capable of doing it for himself. The earl interrupted now and then with some observation or question. Sometimes their discussion grew so lively that the news was forgotten for as much as half an hour at a time.

"There," she announced at last, folding up the newspaper and setting it aside. "You are now quite current with all that is going on in the world."

"What about the post?" asked his lordship. "Is there any reply from the Foreign Secretary yet?"

Hannah glanced at the first letter and shook her head. "This one does not look official. It is addressed in a woman's hand."

She passed it to him and heard him break the seal as she turned her attention to the second letter.

"From Molesworth's mother, poor lady." Lord Hawkehurst sighed. "He was her only son. I wonder how many homes around the country are grieving after Waterloo. What is that other letter?"

"It is for me." Hannah held it to her bosom. "From an old friend who recently married. I should like to have attended the wedding, but with her ladyship's confinement approaching, it was not a convenient time for me to be absent from Edgecombe."

That was probably more than the earl cared to know about the personal life of an employee. Hannah slipped Rebecca's letter into her apron pocket. It was kind of her friend to take the time to write her. Hannah had feared the bride of a viscount might not care to maintain her friendship with a mere governess. But clearly Rebecca was as kind in that regard as Lady Hawkehurst had been. Hannah felt blessed to have had such good friends.

With a pang she recalled that the earl had lost his closest friend under tragic circumstances. Was it any wonder he was so fiercely determined to bring the man he considered responsible to justice? Would she not want to do the same if anyone harmed one of her friends?

"It was admirable of you to place your duty above personal inclinations." The earl stared at Mrs. Molesworth's letter as he turned it over and over. "I am glad Clarissa had you with her when I could not be. I know you must have been a great support and comfort to her. Far more than I would have been, no doubt."

His words brought those wretched days back for Hannah all too vividly. Yet the memory of them troubled her less than the realization of how recent they'd been. She told herself she had been too busy caring for his lordship and overseeing the children's care to grieve properly for Lady Hawkehurst. But those excuses did nothing to ease the guilt that gnawed at her heart.

"I did my best." She hung her head. "But it was you she wanted. All I could do was tell her you were on your way and beg her to hang on."

Silence stretched between them, cold and brittle.

Lord Hawkehurst was the one to break it, of course. He could bear anything but inactivity. "What does your friend write, if you do not mind my asking? An account of the wedding perhaps? I could use a bit of happy news at the moment if you would be willing to share it."

There was a pleading note in his voice that Hannah could not resist. Besides, she was curious to read Rebecca's news. The earl was right. After a week of anxious uncertainty, a helping of glad tidings would be most welcome.

"Very well, sir." She fished the letter out of her apron pocket, broke the seal and unfolded it. "Rebecca begins by saying how sorry she was that none of her school friends could attend the wedding, but she understands that it is a great distance to travel and we all have responsibilities to our employers."

"Old school friends are the best kind," the earl mused. "Properly tended over the years, such an acquaintance can ripen into a very special attachment. I take it there were others in your circle?"

His question made Hannah look up from her letter. Was he truly interested in her friends or was he only desperate for any diversion?

"Yes sir. There were six of us. Rebecca, Marian, Grace, Leah, Evangeline and me. We met at a school in the north of England, a charitable institution for educating the orphan daughters of clergymen."

She referred to the Pendergast School in an offhand manner, yet her stomach seethed at the memories of that dreadful place. "After we left school my friends and I found employment as governesses. We have kept in touch by post."

"But you were not able to be reunited at your friend's wedding?" The earl sounded sincerely sympathetic and interested. "A good school was it? You seem well educated."

"Thank you, sir." There it was again—that dangerous flash of happiness in response to his praise. "We did receive a very…rigorous course of study. Yet I cannot truthfully call it a good place. If it had not been for the kindness of my friends, my time there would have been nothing but…misery."

A choking lump rose in her throat, which Hannah told herself was quite foolish after all these years. But suddenly her experiences at the Pendergast School felt all too fresh. Was that because she had locked those memories away for so many years, never speaking of them to anyone—not even the late countess, to whom she had been so close? Or had Lady Hawkehurst's recent passing stirred up painful memories of another loss?

Hannah blinked furiously, fighting back tears that threatened to fall.

The warm touch of the earl's hand on hers startled her almost out of her chair with a shrill squeak of alarm. Her head jerked up, and her gaze collided with his, so near that she could have lost herself in its dark, inviting depths.

"I am sorry to hear it." Besides the obvious sympathy, his voice rang with righteous indignation.

Was that why he had joined the cavalry, to battle oppressors and deliver the victims? He was too late for her and her friends. They had banded together to defend each other.

Yet she wondered if part of her was still held captive by her past, which needed saving.

"I know there is nothing I can do so long afterward," he continued, "except perhaps to listen."

The prospect of unburdening herself made Hannah feel as if she were standing on the high bank of a river, about to jump into unknown waters. In spite of her trepidation, the promise of freedom and refreshment compelled her to take the plunge.

Chapter Seven

Capable, managing Miss Fletcher harbored a painful past and had friends to whom she was fiercely devoted? Gavin had never imagined the two of them might have so much in common.

Ordinarily, he had a proper masculine aversion to tears. Clarissa had frequently exploited that weakness to get her way. Yet he sensed Hannah Fletcher would never use such tactics. She would go to any lengths to prevent her tears from falling. And if that failed, she would steal away to weep in secret so as not to burden anyone else with her private sorrow.

How could he be so certain of that? He had not known the lady for very long, and he'd had little liking for her until very recently. That uncomfortable question was followed by a stab of shame for having entertained uncharitable thoughts about his late wife. After all, Clarissa was the mother of his children, who were becoming dearer to him with every passing day. He had not been able to make her happy in life. The least he could do was treat her memory with respect and charity.

Was Hannah Fletcher thinking that, too, as she tensed at his touch and recoiled from his nearness?

"Sir, you should not be sitting up like that!" She sprang from her chair and practically pushed him back onto his pillows. "You might open your wound again. Does it hurt? Should I summon the doctor?"

Gavin shook his head. "Do not fret. I am quite well." The sudden movement had sent a dull spasm of pain through his muscles, but he had no intention of telling her so. "I forgot myself in my concern for you. Forgive me for stirring up such unpleasant memories."

Had he truly offered to listen if she wanted to talk about them? Gavin could scarcely believe it. Clarissa had often complained he never listened to her, and he could not deny the charge. It had been one in a long list of his shortcomings as a husband.

What made him so willing to listen to Hannah Fletcher and so curious about her past and her feelings? Had his tedious convalescence and the frustrating lack of news from France made him so desperate for diversion? Or could it be an effort to atone for his many mistakes with Clarissa? His wife was no longer there to confide in him, so he had turned to *her* confidante, Miss Fletcher.

The explanation soothed Gavin's stinging conscience.

"You could not have known." Hannah Fletcher was far quicker to excuse him than he was. "I should never have mentioned it. I should be grateful any place would take us after our father died. It might not have been an ideal situation, but I did receive an education that equipped me to earn a living and I was fortunate to make some very dear friends."

That seemed to remind Miss Fletcher of her letter, which had fluttered to the floor when she sprang from her chair. Now she stooped to retrieve it. "Shall I read you more from Rebecca's letter? Did I mention her new husband is a viscount? Perhaps you know him."

Gavin recognized a diversionary tactic when he encountered one. He had taken part in such maneuvers during the Peninsular Campaign. Their purpose was to distract the enemy from some point of weakness so it would not be recognized and exploited. He hoped Miss Fletcher did not consider him an enemy or suppose he would use any vulnerability against her.

"Us?" he asked in an offhand tone.

She did not appear to understand his question. "What about us?"

"Not *us*." He gestured from himself to her. "When you spoke of that charity school you said, 'I should be grateful anyone would take *us*.' I only wondered who you meant besides yourself."

"My sister." Hannah Fletcher scanned the letter, her gaze flitting back and forth across the page. "Rebecca says the ceremony was lovely. It was a double wedding."

"Older or younger sister?" Gavin interrupted the instant she paused for breath. "Where is she now?"

Miss Fletcher seemed to realize that her attempt at diversion was having the opposite effect. She looked up from the letter, meeting his gaze straight on. "Younger. She is now in the same place as your wife—with God."

The stern gray of her eyes seemed to insist he would

get no further information, while the soft blue silently pleaded with him to respect her privacy.

The latter had much more influence over Gavin. Quashing his curiosity, he turned his questions down a different avenue. "Who is this viscount your friend wed? Unless he served in the army, I doubt we are acquainted, but I may have *heard* of him."

Miss Fletcher's tense features relaxed into an expression of relief and gratitude. "Rebecca's new husband is Sebastian Stanhope, Viscount Benedict. His brother married the young lady who had been Rebecca's pupil for many years."

"Benedict?" The name distracted Gavin's thoughts from the subject of Miss Fletcher's past. "I know the gentleman only by reputation, but that is enough to have earned him my esteem. There is not a man in Parliament who has done more to support Britain's troops during this infernal war. I have long wanted to meet him and shake his hand."

"He sounds like the sort of gentleman who deserves as fine a wife as Rebecca." A smile of sincere happiness for the newlyweds lit Hannah's face.

The sight stirred something in Gavin. At the same time, he could not help but contrast her approval of Lord Benedict with her attitude toward him. Clearly she felt he had not deserved Clarissa. She was probably right.

Fortunately her next words took his mind off that demoralizing thought. "From what Rebecca writes, you may get your wish to meet her husband. Lord Benedict is taking her on a bridal tour around the country to visit each of her friends. They will be in Kent the week after next, and she hopes I shall have time to see her. You should be on your feet by then, sir. If it would not be too inconvenient, perhaps you could spare me for a few days to meet with my friend. I have not had a holiday for some time."

He should certainly be up and about by then, Gavin reflected. He would no longer need to rely on Miss Fletcher to keep him occupied. Somehow the prospect did not appeal to him as much as he expected.

"Of course, you must take as much time as you like to visit with your friend. You have shown exemplary devotion to my family in our time of need. You are more than due a holiday." Though he meant it with all his heart, Gavin could not stifle a strange empty feeling at the thought of Miss Fletcher going away, even for a short time.

"Where do Lord and Lady Benedict intend to stay when they come to Kent?" He wondered if the viscount might have friends or relatives in the area.

Miss Fletcher turned the letter over and continued to read. "Rebecca asks if I can recommend a good inn near Edgecombe. I must confess myself at a loss. Perhaps Mr. Owens would know. I shall ask him at my first opportunity."

"I have an idea," said Gavin. "Why don't you invite Lord and Lady Benedict to stay at Edgecombe? That way you and your friend will have ample opportunity to visit. I daresay her husband and I can find plenty to talk about."

Much as he had come to value Miss Fletcher's society, he missed the company of male friends.

"That is very kind of you to offer, sir." Miss Fletcher

shook her head. "But I could not presume to invite *my* friends to *your* house."

"Rubbish." Gavin waved away her objection. "Edgecombe has space enough to house an army. It is a waste to have so many rooms sitting empty when one or two might be put to good use. I am certain it would do the servants good to have a bit of company around the place."

"But Edgecombe is in mourning," she reminded him, with a hint of reproach that he could have forgotten. "Would it not be disrespectful to her ladyship's memory to entertain so soon?"

Would it? Even in death he could not seem to do right by Clarissa.

"I am not proposing a house party," he insisted. "Only a quiet visit by an old friend of yours. I am certain my wife would have approved, considering the staunch support you provided her when she needed it most."

In truth, he was not entirely certain Clarissa would have agreed. For all the reliance she had placed on Peter's governess, he'd sensed their *friendship* was rather one-sided. Gavin had no intention of letting that happen between him and Miss Fletcher. His family was already in her debt. Besides he would welcome her friends' visit as much for his own sake as for hers.

That, he realized, might be the best way to win her agreement. "Please, Miss Fletcher, I would consider it a great favor if you would permit me to offer Lord and Lady Benedict the hospitality of Edgecombe. It would allow you to visit with your friend while still remaining available to supervise the children's care. And I would very much like to make the viscount's acquaintance. If anyone knows what is happening in France, and can foresee the likely consequences, it is he. Discussing the situation with him might put my mind at ease."

She did not answer right away, and he did not try to rush her. Gavin sensed her conflicting inclinations battling for the upper hand.

"I know what you are doing," she said at last. "Trying to make it seem as if I would be obliging *you* by agreeing."

He tried not to look too guilty. "So you would."

"You are a very poor liar, Lord Hawkehurst." The way she spoke, with a silvery twinkle in her eyes and one corner of her lips arched, it was clear she meant the pronouncement as praise rather than criticism.

Gavin replied with a self-conscious grin, "Perhaps there are times when it is not such a bad thing to fail."

Odd, that had never occurred to him before, but the more he thought about it, the truer it seemed. "My father used to say I had no subtlety. I reckon he meant I am hopelessly honest."

"What else did your father say about you?"

Gavin shrugged as if to indicate he could not remember. Miss Fletcher had turned the tables on him—asking about parts of his past he would prefer to forget. Perhaps he owed her an answer to make up for his earlier prying.

It was more than that, though. Part of him *wanted* to open the door to his past just a sliver and let her peep inside. After all, she had seen him at his worst and weakest, yet still found enough good to alter her poor opinion of him.

* * *

Why should the earl share something so private and perhaps unpleasant from his past after she had refused to answer his questions about her sister with more than the barest crumbs of information? As her employer, he had far more right to inquire into her past than she did to quiz him about his.

Yet even as she recognized she had no right to an answer, Hannah could not help wanting one. It must be because his lordship had proven to be quite a different man than she had once judged him. Perhaps she felt it her duty to understand him better, as she had failed to do until recently. For good or ill, the events of his past had shaped him into the person he'd become, just as hers had.

The earl's earlier revelation about his reason for marrying had taken her by surprise and made her wonder what more there was to discover about him.

Only yesterday that curiosity had driven her to consult Mr. Owens. "I was not aware his lordship had an elder brother. I suppose you remember him well."

"Indeed, Miss Fletcher." The butler had beckoned her into the library to show her a fine portrait of a gentleman and two small boys. "That is the fifth Earl of Hawkehurst, his elder son Lord Edgecombe and the present earl."

The older boy looked to be the age of Peter and very like him in appearance. His father sat in a chair with his arm around the child's shoulders and a look on his distinguished features of affection bordering on reverence. The younger son wore the short gown of a three-year-old and sat on the floor some distance away, playing with a small spaniel.

"Lord Edgecombe was the apple of his father's eye. A clever young man who showed considerable promise in politics." Owens shook his head regretfully. "The earl took his death very hard indeed. He lingered long enough to see Master Gavin wed and an heir provided. I often thought if the earl had lived long enough to see how much the present Lord Edgecombe favored his late uncle, it might have given him something to live for."

Had Gavin Romney's father felt no reason to live for his younger son? Hannah wondered with more than a little indignation. But she had not dared ask Mr. Owens a question so critical of his late master.

Now she sat near the man who had once been that small boy playing with the dog. Had he not told her he understood horses better than people? Could that be because he'd had more affection from animals as a child than from his family?

"My father was never short of things to say," the earl mused after a long pause. "He was fond of observing that I had little aptitude for self-preservation."

Inwardly Hannah bristled. It reminded her of the criticism the Pendergast teachers had inflicted on their pupils under the righteous guise of seeking to improve them. She had not come in for nearly as much of it as their intrepid leader, Evangeline, or Grace, whose beauty inspired envy and spite in those who were not her friends. Hannah had tried to accept any criticism of herself in the spirit of improvement, but she'd bitterly resented disparaging remarks about her friends.

Now she hastened to defend Gavin Romney from his

judgmental father. "Humph! All that means is that you are brave and unselfish. A man concerned only with self-preservation would not have ridden into enemy fire to rescue his friend."

If she thought her words might raise the earl's spirits she was mistaken. Darkness crept into his gaze, and it had nothing to do with the color of his eyes. "A fine rescue. It did not save my friend's life, only put mine in jeopardy, which might have made orphans of my children. I thought you, of all people, would agree with my father that a poor sense of self-preservation is a serious failing."

Hannah opened her mouth but found it impossible to produce a reply. Did the earl suppose she was like his father—critical of everything he did, every choice he made? She longed to deny it. But looking back she could not help but wonder if she had given him some justification. Had her years at the Pendergast School and a lifetime of striving to improve herself made her judge others too harshly?

"I must admit, for the sake of your children, I wish you could be more cautious." That was not the only reason, though Hannah could not bring herself to say so. The thought of any harm coming to the earl chilled her. "But I cannot fault your courage or your willingness to risk your well-being for that of others. It is all part of what makes you the man you are."

She hoped her tone conveyed her belief that he was a very good man in spite of the mistakes and weaknesses that made him human.

"As for your friend," she continued, "his death was

no fault of yours. Do you suppose he would have been better off if you had left him on that field?"

The earl thought for a moment. His gaze seemed to turn inward, as if reliving the incident in search of the answer to her question. "The French were not taking prisoners that I could see. I suppose he would be dead either way."

That realization seemed to bring him some consolation, which pleased Hannah.

She fought the sudden urge to brush a lock of dark hair back from his brow as she might have done with his young son. "Thanks to you, Major Molesworth spent his last moments among his comrades, being cared for. And he died knowing you were willing to risk your life for him. Do not underestimate the value of such blessings."

His lordship mulled over her words. "I would never have thought of it in quite that way. You bring a fresh perspective to many things, Miss Fletcher. Now, may I beg you to reconsider my offer to invite Lord and Lady Benedict to Edgecombe? I mean it when I say you would be doing me a favor."

"Very well, then," Hannah agreed, still somewhat reluctant. She could foresee considerable awkwardness in having her personal friend as a guest in the house where she worked. The place of governess in any household was ambiguous at best, hers more than most due to her friendship with the late countess. "Since you seem quite determined."

"I am." The earl appeared pleased at having gotten his way. "Though my father would have called it willfulness. If you would be so kind as to fetch your writing box, I wish to dictate a letter of invitation."

Just then the mantel clock chimed.

"Is it that time already?" the earl cried. "I must say, my convalescence is passing faster than I ever expected."

He did not sound as pleased about that as Hannah expected.

His fortnight in captivity was more than half over. Gavin marveled at how swiftly it had passed. If he'd known how it would be, he would not have objected so strongly in the beginning.

Miss Fletcher's schedule had broken the endless stretch of hours down into more easily endurable divisions. He seldom had an opportunity to grow tired of one activity when it was time to move on to the next. Often he and Miss Fletcher would fall into conversation and forget the schedule entirely as minutes and hours flew by.

He had originally demanded her companionship in a mistaken belief that their mutual antagonism would challenge and amuse him. Instead he'd discovered they had more in common than he had thought possible. The visits with his small son and daughter had helped, too, much to his surprise. He was discovering their distinct personalities and noticing small changes in them as they grew. He was astonished to find he could handle an infant without sending the child into a frenzy of tears. And if the child did cry, he was capable of soothing it.

"It never occurred to me," he remarked to Hannah Fletcher as they played chess while waiting for the Friday post to arrive, "that caring for infants was a skill one could learn, practice and improve, like riding or shooting. I always assumed a person was either naturally good with children—as you are—or quite hopeless, as I thought I was."

Miss Fletcher moved her bishop forward. She was a much more cautious, thoughtful player than he. Sometimes that gave her an advantage. Other times his bold, decisive style of play brought him victory.

Now he sensed she was trying to suppress a self-conscious smile. Was it because she expected to win the chess match or because he'd said she was good with children? "Surely you have spent enough time with babies to see that nearly everything human beings do must be learned. I am no more *naturally* adept at caring for children than you or anyone else. But I have had a good deal of practice and learned from my experience how best to handle them. It is all a matter of application and a desire to improve."

"Are you certain of that?" Gavin moved a pawn forward to threaten her bishop. "Do you not believe a person may have special aptitude for certain things—music or languages or gardening?"

Or riding. Someone must have put him on a pony and taught him how to make it run and jump and stop again. They must have told him how to keep his seat and move with his mount so he did not bounce up and down like a sack of meal in the saddle. But it was so long ago he could not remember a time before he'd felt perfectly at home on horseback. Far more at home than he ever had in a schoolroom or attending a fashionable assembly.

Could he have acquired the skills necessary to excel in those situations, as well, if only he'd applied himself?

He had convinced himself it would be fruitless to try. Now he began to wonder if he'd been wrong.

Miss Fletcher studied the chessboard, pondering her next move and perhaps his question, as well. Gavin looked forward to hearing her answer. Her opinions often disagreed with his, challenging him to weigh them more critically and sometimes look at the world in a whole new way. To his surprise, he was beginning to enjoy it.

His opponent had just grasped the bishop's miter in her slender, deft fingers when Owens marched in bearing the day's post.

"Very good reports from abroad, my lord." The butler could not resist waving the newspapers in a gesture that ran contrary to his usual dignity. "Paris has surrendered!"

"It has?" Hannah Fletcher dropped the white bishop and knocked over several other chess pieces as she surged up from her chair to seize the post. "What a blessed relief!"

She scanned the newspaper and found what she was seeking at once. As Owens slipped out of the room, she began to read aloud so quickly her tongue tripped over some of the words. "We have at length the happiness to be relieved from the state of anxious suspense in which we have been held for the result of the expedition to Paris. Last night Lord Arthur Hill arrived with dispatches from the Duke of Wellington announcing the surrender of Paris on conditions on Monday last."

"I know Hill," Gavin interrupted. "Aide-de-camp to the duke. His father is the Marquis of Downshire. A sound young fellow." And a second son, like him and so many other British officers.

Miss Fletcher used his interruption to catch her breath. When he had finished speaking she took up reading where she'd left off, recounting the troop movements that had led Wellington to Gonesse and Prince Blücher to Versailles, while General Grouchy retreated to occupy the heights of Montmartre.

"At length on Monday at three o'clock the city was surrendered on a military convention—the troops laid down their arms—the provisional government dissolved and Louis XVIII was again recognized as their sovereign."

"That is all very well," said Gavin. He hated to sink Miss Fletcher's spirits, but he had to know the full story. "But have they printed the actual dispatches?"

Perhaps those would contain the information he needed to hear.

"I was just coming to that." Miss Fletcher read the dispatches, including the eighteen articles of surrender as signed at Saint Cloud by the commissioners designated by both sides. "Surely this *is* good news, is it not, sir? From the look on your face I am inclined to think otherwise."

"It is certainly better than no news." Gavin began to gather up the chessmen and return them to their box. "And it is official—not the fog of rumors and speculation we have been teased with for the past week. But to me the most significant news is to be found in what the report and dispatches *do not* say."

Miss Fletcher slowly lowered the newspaper, her

brow furrowed. "I beg your pardon, sir? I do not understand what you mean."

"Did you not notice one name conspicuous by its absence?"

The lady's eyes opened wide as the truth dawned on her. "Bonaparte. There was no mention of him at all."

Chapter Eight

No mention of Bonaparte. Why hadn't she seen it? Hannah wondered this the next day when the newspapers echoed his lordship's question.

"What is become of Bonaparte?" She glanced up at the earl between sentences to gauge his reaction. "His departure from Paris openly and with a great cavalcade is asserted without contradiction. A letter from Rouen dated the third instant says that he was arrested in his flight, but it does not state where or give any particulars. The fact is therefore doubted. It should be a singular incident in this diversified drama if he should be suffered after all to escape."

With every word she read the earl's jaw clenched tighter and his black brows lowered over his eyes like thunderclouds warning of an approaching storm.

"How could they let him ride away?" He pounded his fist on his mattress. "Much less openly in a great cavalcade."

His gaze slammed into Hannah's with such fierce intensity she could picture lightning flashing from his eyes. "Do you *still* think I am a vengeful fool for being determined to bring that man to justice?"

She flinched from the earl's outburst in a way she would not have ten days ago. Then she would have expected it, perhaps even welcomed the opportunity to vent her own feelings at him. But over the course of the past few days, something fundamental had changed between them. She thought they had come to understand and respect one another. Perhaps they had not become *friends,* but was it too much to hope they'd at least grown friendly?

"I never thought any such thing!" she protested. At least, not recently…

"Do you still believe I should leave the task to others better equipped than I?" This time he did not give her an opportunity to reply. "The allied commanders, perhaps, who have allowed Bonaparte to slip through their fingers?"

"Are you certain he has?" Hannah's old antagonism roused like a sleeping dog that had been suddenly kicked awake. "What if that letter from Rouen is correct and he has been arrested?"

The earl reached out and snatched the newspaper from her hands. After the briefest pause to find the report, he read the rest of it in a voice harsh with indignation. "It is worthy of inquiry how and by whom he is to be stopped. The Allies have no force in the road which he was to take—and it is not likely that he should throw himself into the hands of his enemies."

He slammed down the paper. "If someone does not take action soon, mark my words, Bonaparte is going to slip away to plot his next return. When he comes back, the Allies may not have the good fortune we did at Waterloo to turn back the tide. Who knows how many more young lives could be lost for the want of decisive action now?"

Hannah wished she could argue with his reasoning, but she found it impossible. She'd been so certain the allied commanders would make Bonaparte's capture their first priority, for precisely the reasons his lordship had stated. But it seemed she'd been wrong. Was the only answer for one determined man to pursue the former emperor in a quest for justice?

"This news is five days old!" the earl fumed. "Who knows where Bonaparte could be by now? There are plenty of ports within a five-day journey of Paris. If he slips aboard a frigate and sails away—"

"Surely the Royal Navy will be watching the ports." Even as she said it, Hannah knew she was clutching at straws. One look at the map of France on which they had been marking reports of Bonaparte's whereabouts showed hundreds of miles of coastline.

"The Royal Navy let him slip away from Elba!" the earl shot back as if she had been personally responsible for their lapse. "If Bonaparte slips though their fingers again and sails away for parts unknown, it will be a thousand times worse than before. At least on Elba his actions could be monitored to some degree. If he flees to America or the Indies, he could return at any time of his own choosing, perhaps at the head of a naval force raised from among our enemies."

The alarm and desperation in his lordship's voice was contagious. Deep in her bones Hannah felt what a terrible thing it would be for so many people if Napoleon

Bonaparte was not stopped now. But she could not bear to see Lord Hawkehurst return to France on a single-handed quest to track him down. In a few more days the doctor would declare him well enough to rise from his sickbed. That would *not* mean he was fit to ride and sail for long distances, eating and sleeping under who knew what conditions. Not to mention the danger he would face if he did corner the man who had brought Europe to its knees.

"I was wrong to assume others would capture Bonaparte without any help from you," she admitted, difficult as that was for her. "I often say if I want something done properly I can trust no one to do it but myself. I understand why you must feel that way about so vital a task."

"You do?" The earl sounded a bit suspicious to hear her agree with him.

At least he seemed calmer. Hannah was anxious to do anything to keep him that way. The last thing she wanted was for the earl to give in to his frustration and do something that might jeopardize his recovery.

"Of course I can." She retrieved the newspaper and set it out of his reach. She did not want him to read anything else that might set him off. "But the best thing you can do at present is continue to gather information and concentrate on recovering your strength."

As soon as she said it, Hannah realized she should have omitted one of those things.

"Information?" The earl indicated the map of France with a disdainful sweep of his arm. "That is what galls me. My information is so far behind Bonaparte's actual movements. He will have an even greater lead by the time I am fit to follow his trail. For all I know, he may already have set sail for parts unknown."

"That is possible." Hannah had far more sympathy with his self-appointed mission than when he'd first told her of it. But it was still at odds with the promise she'd made to his wife. More than ever, she wanted to keep him safe at Edgecombe with her and the children.

Not with *her,* Hannah's conscience chided, with *his children.*

"B-but," she continued, flustered by her inadvertent thought, "if Bonaparte has fled the Continent, I have no doubt you will be able to pick up his trail once you are well. Surely the worst thing you could do would be to start after him before you are fully recovered."

That was all she could do for the moment—plead the state of his health to postpone his going for as long as possible. Hopefully by then she could find some other excuse to delay him.

The earl gave a grudging nod. "You talk good sense as always, Miss Fletcher. But you must realize by now patience is not one of my virtues. I hope you know I am not angry with *you,* only with my situation. You are all that has made it bearable for this long…you and the children."

A bolt of dizzying happiness shot through Hannah. She told herself it was only relief that the recent cordiality between them had not been shattered after all. "I am pleased to have been of service, sir."

"Everything you have done in the past month has gone far beyond the duties for which you were engaged." Every trace of his earlier frustration had left the earl's voice. Instead the mellow warmth of appreciation infused it. "Perhaps it has been that way ever since you came to Edgecombe?"

His questioning inflection seemed to request an answer.

"Not at first." Hannah could not lift her gaze from her lap. "But over time her ladyship came to see how anxious I was to be of assistance. She began to rely on me and take me into her confidence. I believe she was rather lonely by herself in this big house."

Lonely and neglected by a husband who put his military duty ahead of his family life. Now that Hannah had come to know the earl better, she realized it was not as simple as that. She could not place all the blame for her ladyship's unhappiness on the earl. Yet more than ever, she pitied his late wife. How hard it must be to love someone who could not return the feeling.

"I know her ladyship appreciated your companionship and support. I wish I had done the same much sooner. Tell me, have we received a reply to my invitation from Lord and Lady Benedict?"

The abrupt change of subject caught Hannah off guard, as did his use of the word *we*. "N-not yet, sir. I only sent it the day before yesterday."

The earl could be excused for thinking it had been longer. The past few weeks had altered Hannah's perception of time. In some ways the hours and days flew by all too quickly. The end of his lordship's convalescence was approaching faster than she would have liked. On the other hand, so many things had happened and so much had changed—particularly her attitude toward Lord Hawkehurst—that his wife's death seemed a very long time ago.

* * *

He should never have spoken so sharply to Hannah Fletcher yesterday, Gavin chided himself as he waited for her to return from church and bring his infant daughter for another visit. Though it vexed him beyond bearing that Bonaparte had been permitted to escape from Paris, the situation was no fault of hers. If the allied commanders had done their duty with the capable dedication Miss Fletcher brought to every task she undertook, Gavin had no doubt Bonaparte would be safely under arrest by now.

When he had first told her of his mission, Miss Fletcher had not seemed to grasp its urgency. But lately he sensed a welcome change in her outlook. She might not *approve* of him leaving Edgecombe and the children long enough to bring Bonaparte to justice, but at least she seemed to understand the necessity.

His attitude had undergone some change, as well, he was forced to admit. Somehow he had grown to share Miss Fletcher's hope that someone else might accomplish the task he was prevented from undertaking. He had begun to picture himself remaining at Edgecombe, making a life with his young family, secure in the knowledge that Napoleon Bonaparte would not make another curtain call on the European stage.

Friday's news from Paris had shattered that fledgling hope and sent a slimy wave of shame washing over him. Poor Molesworth seemed to reproach him for his conflicted feelings about the vow he had made. His instinctive reaction had been to deny those reservations and recommit himself to his mission with greater determination. If he could have leaped from his bed and set off for France immediately it would have been much easier. Instead he was forced to cool his heels while unreliable, days-old news fed his frustration. Meanwhile his growing affection for his infant son and daughter threatened to tie him down with gossamer threads.

Part of him had regretted lashing out at Miss Fletcher even as he vented his frustration on her. He'd been certain she would strike back, or retreat into the kind of injured silence with which he was all too familiar and against which he had no defense. Instead she seemed to understand, which had soothed his explosive emotions. He could not imagine how he would have borne the past ten days without her. The time she spent with him sped by while her brief absences seemed to stretch on and on.

This one, for instance. It gave him far too much time to think.

He reflected on what he must do once he recovered and on the tug of reluctance he did not want to feel. After pondering the matter for some time, Gavin finally hit on a solution. He must tell Miss Fletcher not to bring the babies for any more visits. Surely he had proven he cared for his children. The more time he spent with them, the harder it would be for him to leave Edgecombe. Once he returned home with his vow fulfilled, he would have all the time in the world to renew their acquaintance. It was not as if they were capable of noticing his absence or pining for his company. They were far too young to have the slightest idea who he was.

By the time Hannah Fletcher arrived with her precious bundle, Gavin had resolved this would be his last visit with little Alice until he had accomplished his mission. Instead of allowing his feelings for her to hold him back, he would make them an incentive to succeed as quickly as possible so he could return to his family.

"Lady Alice is not asleep today," Miss Fletcher announced in a doting tone. "She wants to be wide-awake to see her dearest papa."

"About that..." Gavin instinctively opened his arms to receive the baby. Once he drew her toward him and gazed into her wide blue eyes, he could not remember what he'd wanted to say except, "Good day to you, sweet Alice. I declare, you have grown bigger since I saw you last."

Without warning, his daughter's solemn, delicate features blossomed into a great toothless smile that made his whole chest ache with tenderness for her. His mouth stretched into an answering grin that he knew must look positively simpleminded. But he did not care.

"Did you see that?" he cried, anxious to share the experience. "She smiled at me. Come and look, Miss Fletcher!"

"Her wet nurse told me she had begun to smile." Hannah Fletcher perched on the edge of the bed and leaned in close. "But I was not able to coax one out of her. I suppose you have been saving all your smiles for your papa, haven't you, Lady Alice?"

"Were you, indeed?" Gavin asked his daughter with a delighted chuckle. "Were you saving your smiles for me?"

It felt right to have Hannah Fletcher by his side to share this joyful moment. If it had not been for her, he would never have experienced one of his daughter's first smiles. Somehow he managed to tear his gaze away from the baby long enough to glance up at her. In her eyes he saw reflected the same protective, nurturing love he felt for his tiny daughter. No fine silks or jewels could have made her look lovelier.

The two of them sat there cooing and chortling like a pair of besotted fools rather than a fierce cavalry officer and an imperturbable governess. They gibbered and pulled faces—anything to coax another smile from his little daughter. When she did favor them with a wet, gummy grin, they went into transports of delight as if nothing had ever made them so happy. Gavin had to admit he'd never felt this kind of buoyant joy before.

He told himself it was entirely due to his sweet tiny daughter, though he had a faint troubling sense there might be something more to it. Alice was one of the first people close to him who did not judge and condemn his actions; she made him feel entirely accepted and loved. He wondered if that was a truer reflection of divine love than the stern, punishing patriarch he had envisioned for so long.

Yet even as little Alice kept a powerful grip on his finger with her tiny hand and on his heart with her bright melting smile, Gavin could not ignore a pang of conscience. Surely it could not be right for him to feel so happy such a short time after the death of his wife. Clarissa had left these two small treasures as a final gift to him. What had he ever given her to deserve them?

He tried to push that troubling thought from his mind, but it clung with stubborn tenacity. Fortunately his daughter provided a much-needed distraction. In the middle of one enormous smile her features clenched and she gave a violent sneeze. It seemed to startle her for her eyes flew open again, wider than ever, and her lips formed a perfect circle.

This tickled Miss Fletcher's fancy. She began to laugh in a free, hearty way Gavin could not resist. Soon they were both helpless with laughter, gasping for air, while the baby grinned at their foolishness. How soon would it be before Alice and Arthur learned to laugh? Gavin hoped he would be there to hear some of their first infant chuckles.

Meanwhile Miss Fletcher's vigorous laughter seemed to tire her. She subsided against Gavin, her arm pressed against his and her head resting on his shoulder. A sensation of deep warmth spread through him, kindled by her nearness.

Before he had a chance to savor it, the lady tensed and pulled herself upright. "I beg your pardon, sir! I forgot myself for a moment."

Gavin wanted to assure her that he did not mind having her so near—quite the opposite in fact. But he sensed that would be the wrong thing to say. Moreover, it was the wrong way to feel. He should be mourning his late wife, not thinking about how much he enjoyed the company of another woman.

"Think nothing of it, Miss Fletcher." He sought to make excuses for both of them. "I expect you are exhausted with the hours you keep looking after the children and me. I cannot blame you for nodding off, even with my engaging little daughter to entertain us."

Hannah Fletcher scrambled off the bed and backed away. "I must confess I am rather weary, though that is no reflection on your daughter's company...or yours."

Baby Alice seemed to sense the sudden tension between them. When Gavin glanced at her, she was no longer smiling. She waved her arms and made anxious little sounds as if to draw their attention back to her.

"I have been working you too hard." Gavin bounced the baby a little in an effort to soothe her. "Making you dance attendance on me all hours of the day. I have been miserably selfish, depriving my son of his governess because I lack the wit to keep myself occupied."

Recalling his eldest son brought him another pang of guilt. He had sworn he would not favor any of his children over the others, yet he had spent considerable time with the twins while ignoring young Peter.

He tried to make allowances for his behavior. Babies were so much easier to get on with. Bounce them, pull a face and they were content. It would take much more than that to win over his elder son, if it was even possible after all this time. That did not excuse him from trying. Keeping Peter from his beloved governess after he had so recently lost his mother was no way to begin.

"I have only four more days until I will be allowed up, and you have shown me how to pass the time." Gavin forced himself to say what he did not want to. "Perhaps you should return to your usual duties starting tomorrow. I can manage on my own until the doctor grants me my freedom."

He watched Hannah Fletcher's face, seeking to guess her reaction, though it had never been a skill at which he excelled. He had clearly not improved, for he could not decide whether she was disappointed, hurt or relieved.

Then she smoothed her features the way a housemaid would tug the wrinkles from a bedsheet, leaving a calm, bland visage and cool gaze that betrayed none of her feelings. "Perhaps that *would* be for the best, sir, if you are certain you can spare me."

It must have been relief he'd glimpsed in that first unguarded moment. Gavin's spirits sank though he told himself not to be so foolish. He was relieved, too—at least part of him was. This growing closeness with Miss Fletcher had the potential to become awkward. He should have seen that from the beginning. Their earlier animosity had blinded him to the fact that she was a woman. Now that he was aware of it—too aware, perhaps—it would be a relief to put some distance between them.

It *should* be a relief....

What could have gotten into her?

Hannah struggled to regain her composure, but never had it been so difficult. She should have known better than to sit on the earl's bed and make eyes at the baby. But when he'd invited her she hadn't thought of him as a nobleman and her employer. They had simply been two people drawn together by their affection for his children.

Did he truly believe she had leaned against him out of fatigue, or was he giving her an excuse to spare them both a great deal of awkwardness?

Baby Alice sensed the swift change in atmosphere for she began to fuss. Her faint bleats of distress grew louder. Though Hannah tried to avoid looking directly at his lordship, out of the corner of her eye she could see the child flailing her tiny arms. It came as no surprise when she began to wail in earnest.

It was all Hannah could do to keep from joining

in the doleful chorus. Though she agreed it might be better if she returned to her nursery duties, the prospect dismayed her deeply. She told herself that was because she feared how Lord Hawkehurst might react to any fresh news from the Continent. Besides, her plan to foster his affection for the children had shown great promise. She could not stand to give it up while it might still bear fruit.

As Alice's cries grew louder, Hannah knew she should offer to take the baby, but she did not want to make the earl doubt his fledgling skills as a parent. Besides, she was reluctant to get too close to his lordship, her hands and arms brushing against his. Such innocent contact roused feelings she wanted no part of. Or did she?

Apparently the earl did not need her help after all. He lifted his squalling daughter to his shoulder and began to rub her back.

His deep voice, which could sound so harsh and commanding, was muted to a tender murmur. "Dear me, what is the matter? Did we exhaust your good humor?"

Watching him soothe his tiny child stirred something deep in Hannah's heart. "We probably overexcited her. She is accustomed to taking a nap at this time of day. Shall I take her back to Mrs. Miller?"

"In a moment, perhaps." The earl coaxed two soft belches out of the baby. "Surely you would not want me to give up too soon."

Hannah struggled to hold herself erect when her bones felt like butter in the sun. She forced her gaze away from the touching sight of father and child. Of course she wanted the earl to persist at the tasks of fatherhood even when they did not come naturally. She wanted him to see that he could improve with practice and not take temporary setbacks as a sign of failure.

Baby Alice seemed willing to teach her father those vital lessons for she gradually quieted. Finally the earl announced with a faint ring of pride, "I believe she is asleep now. Give her a little more time, then you may take her."

Hannah could not let all her efforts come to nothing when his lordship had made so much progress. Hoping to take advantage of his good humor, she ventured to ask, "May I still bring the babies to visit you, sir?"

He considered for a moment. "Of course, if you would be so kind."

"I should be happy to, sir." Happy that her heedless lapse of judgment had not spoiled her plans regarding Lord Hawkehurst and his children? Hannah wondered. Or happy she would still see him for a while each day?

She had no business feeling anything remotely like that for the earl, Hannah's sense of propriety warned her. How had he come to mean so much to her in such a short time? Was it seeing him interact with the babies that called forth the softer emotions she tried to conceal behind a mask of brisk resourcefulness?

If she was going to spend time with him from now on, she would need someone present besides the babies to keep her from forgetting herself again. "What about Peter, sir? That is…Lord Edgecombe…may I bring *him* to visit, as well? I believe it might do him good."

"I thought you did not want Peter to see me laid up like this." The earl's reluctance showed as plain as his sweeping black brows. "In case it might upset him."

Did he guess that her motives were not entirely for the benefit of his son? "I did at first, sir. But you are so much better now I doubt your condition will cause him any worry."

His lordship considered her suggestion. Hannah wished she knew what he was thinking.

"If you reckon it would be for the best, Miss Fletcher. I trust your judgment when it comes to the welfare of my children."

That was one of the nicest compliments he could have paid her.

"However," he continued, "I fear it will be uphill work for me to win my elder son's regard. It is a simple matter to be a good father to the little ones. With them, I am starting off with a fresh slate. They do not have years of absences and awkwardness to overcome. Peter has been his mother's darling all this time, and I sense he does not think well of me."

Hannah tried to tell the earl he was wrong, but he dismissed her protests with a rueful shake of his head. "I do not blame the boy, but neither can I figure how to remedy the situation. I only know I do not want him to think I favor the little ones over him."

"The way your father favored your elder brother?" The instant those words slipped out, Hannah clapped a hand over her mouth in horror.

What was it about Gavin Romney that made her speak and act without thinking after a lifetime of strict discretion? He had proven more forgiving than she'd expected of such lapses, but she did not want to test the limits of his tolerance. For the children's sake, she could not afford to risk her position at Edgecombe.

She began to sputter an apology, but the earl cut her off. "You divined my very thought, Miss Fletcher. My brother was the apple of our father's eye. He could do no wrong while I could never do anything right. Father always claimed I did not try hard enough, though nothing could have been further from the truth. Finally I stopped trying for I knew it was no use. I would never measure up to his standards."

Had it been the same with his wife? Hannah clamped her lips together to keep from asking more impertinent questions. She wished she could stop herself from even entertaining the thought. How could she be so disloyal to her ladyship's memory?

Disloyal or not, it might be true, a stubborn little voice inside her insisted. The countess had appeared so devoted to her husband and distressed when her feelings were not returned in equal measure. Hannah had sympathized with her litany of complaints about the earl and believed them all to be true. Now she wondered if any demonstrations of affection, no matter how lavish, would have satisfied her ladyship.

Worse yet, Hannah wondered whether her sympathy and indignation had only encouraged Clarissa Romney's dissatisfaction with her marriage.

Chapter Nine

After Hannah Fletcher departed with the sleeping baby, the remaining hours of Sunday seemed easily ten times longer to Gavin. He could have sworn some invisible force was holding back the hands of the clock. He tried to occupy himself by rereading the newspapers and tracing Bonaparte's movements since Waterloo. But it was difficult to separate the golden needles of fact from the haystack of rumor and speculation.

If only he could have talked it over with Miss Fletcher, he felt certain the picture would have come into clearer focus. But that was impossible because he had sent her away. Had he overreacted to their accidental contact and the unexpected feelings it provoked?

There could be any number of innocent reasons why he felt closer to her than he had any right to. Most likely it was because they had been forced to spend so much time together. Pairs of soldiers sent out on patrol often came to rely on one another and develop a close camaraderie.

Or perhaps the feelings he imagined were prompted by the presence of his infant daughter. All the firmness and severity he had cultivated as a cavalry commander deserted him when he held that small, soft creature in his arms. His heart grew as malleable as warm wax, which she proceeded to wrap around her tiny finger. Was it any wonder such a state should make him vulnerable to unexpected fancies? Perhaps it was best to keep a cautious distance.

Gavin roused from his musing to realize he had spent far more time thinking about Hannah Fletcher than Napoleon Bonaparte.

The next morning was just as bad. The time crept by with aching slowness. Yet whenever Gavin sought to pass it, his wayward thoughts returned to Miss Fletcher like a flock of stubborn homing pigeons. When they did, his conscience never failed to reproach him.

He looked forward to the early afternoon hours which would bring the post and a visit from little Arthur. He longed for those events as eagerly as any embattled regiment had ever looked for reinforcements. When at last he heard Miss Fletcher's firm, brisk footsteps approaching, his heart bounded with the expectation of deliverance.

She entered the room, cradling his tiny son against her shoulder. In her left hand she clutched a newspaper and a letter. Seldom in his life had Gavin beheld so welcome a sight.

"I have received a reply from Lady Benedict," she announced with barely suppressed excitement.

A fortnight ago, Gavin would not have believed her capable of such feelings. Since then he had glimpsed several unexpected facets of her character. She also possessed many fine qualities he had perceived but failed to appreciate. She was honest, practical, responsible and hardworking. But the lady had a softer side, which she tended to keep well hidden. Perhaps because she feared it would make her vulnerable? Though she strove to appear placid, Gavin had discovered she could be stimulating company with an engaging sense of humor. Now he was pleased to find she was capable of almost childlike eagerness.

The contagious feeling communicated itself to him, banishing the frustrated boredom of the past hours. "What does Lady Benedict say? Do she and her husband accept my invitation? When will they arrive?"

"I will not know until I read her letter." A winsome smile softened Miss Fletcher's tart reply. "Since that will be difficult to do while holding a squirming baby, I must ask you to take your son."

She transferred the child to Gavin's waiting arms, then seated herself beside his bed. She tugged off her bonnet and opened the letter.

Meanwhile, Gavin greeted his small son. "How do you do today, Arthur? I hope you are in good cheer."

Though he could not understand his father's words the child answered by bursting into a wide grin. His eyes sparkled with innocent pleasure in Gavin's company.

"I see you have learned something new!" Gavin gave a delighted chuckle. "You did not want your clever sister to get ahead of you, I expect."

His enthusiastic response made little Arthur smile even wider. He wriggled in Gavin's arms and crowed happily.

"Have you seen what he can do?" Gavin held his son up for Miss Fletcher's inspection. "Isn't he a clever lad?"

She glanced up from her letter as if reluctant to stop reading. But a smile tugged up the corners of her lips in response to the baby's. "What would the men of your regiment say if they could see their colonel now?"

He tried to resist her teasing tone but found it quite impossible. "The bachelors among them might reckon I *have* gone mad from being confined to quarters for so long. But the men who are married with young ones of their own would surely take a more charitable view."

Gavin addressed his next words to his son. "Give Miss Fletcher another smile and turn her to mush so she will not make fun of your poor, doting papa."

The baby obliged, with precisely the effect Gavin had predicted.

Hannah Fletcher cooed and chucked Arthur under the chin. "You are going to grow up to be a charmer— I can see that."

"What *does* Lady Benedict write?" Gavin asked, now that Miss Fletcher had begun to read the letter.

She winked at the baby then glanced back over her friend's missive. "Rebecca asks me to thank you for your kind invitation and says they would be grateful to accept your hospitality. She also wishes you their sincere condolences on the passing of your late wife. She hopes it will not be too inconvenient for you to entertain guests while Edgecombe is in mourning. The rest is private news I will not tire you with."

Miss Fletcher seemed a trifle flustered. Gavin wondered what Lady Benedict had written that might affect her so.

"I am pleased to hear my invitation has been accepted." He kept his gaze fixed on his infant son. "I look forward to meeting your friend and her husband. When do they expect to arrive?"

"Rebecca writes that they should be here on Friday, if that will be convenient."

"Perfectly." Gavin raised his voice to carry over the babbling of his small son. "With the doctor's approval, I should be out of this wretched bed and able to receive them properly."

"You will still be here, then?" Miss Fletcher asked. "Not gone to the Continent?"

Gavin could not tell whether the prospect pleased or dismayed her. "I doubt it would be wise to set out on a long, uncertain journey the day after I am allowed out of bed. Besides I need reliable information, and I hope Lord Benedict can provide it. Speaking of which, can I prevail upon you to check whether the newspaper has anything useful to report?"

He knew he should save the paper to occupy him after Miss Fletcher and his son went away, but he enjoyed hearing her read the news to him in her clear, melodious voice.

"Of course, sir." Miss Fletcher opened the newspaper and searched for the reports he wished to hear.

"Well…?" he prompted after several minutes of paper rustling without a word out of her. "Have they anything at all to report?"

"Not about the subject of most interest to you," she replied. "There is only a single sentence in the Brussels Mail column. 'It is not known what is become of Bonaparte.'"

How could one man create such havoc and then disappear without a trace? Gavin could barely suppress a growl of helpless vexation. What made him imagine he could catch the man when no one else in Europe seemed to have the slightest idea of his whereabouts? Gavin could picture his father sneering at the very idea.

"Is there anything else about the situation in France?" he asked.

He found it harder to keep his attention on the baby, who was no longer smiling and becoming agitated. Perhaps wee Arthur was picking up on *his* mood.

When Miss Fletcher did reply to his question, her voice sounded husky. "There is nearly an entire page given over to returns of the killed, wounded and missing from Waterloo and the other battles. The numbers are almost impossible to comprehend. They go on and on."

"I can imagine it." Gavin held the baby to his shoulder, hoping it would soothe the wee fellow as it had his sister. "I saw many of them fall—men and horses. Does it give a total reckoning for Waterloo?"

"The total killed for British and Hanoverian troops combined was two general staff, one colonel, four lieutenant colonels, six majors, forty-eight captains, twenty-eight lieutenants, sixty cornets or ensigns, five staff, two quartermasters, one hundred and seven sergeants, thirteen drummers, one thousand eight hundred and nine rank and file and one thousand four hundred and ninety-five horses."

In a hollow tone she read off the numbers missing, which were roughly equal to the number dead, then the number wounded, which was five times higher.

In spite of Gavin's efforts to soothe his small son,

the baby began to wail as if he understood the devastation those stark figures represented.

"Something I cannot fathom," Hannah Fletcher concluded in a horrified murmur, "is how fifteen hundred men can go *missing*."

Gavin shrugged. This deadly reckoning of war's cost had long ago become routine to him. But the massive casualties of that one battle and Miss Fletcher's sickened reaction made it seem intensely personal. "They were unaccounted for after the battle. Some may have deserted their ranks or been taken prisoner, others may have gotten separated from their regiments somehow but turned up later. Most will be dead, I'm afraid."

He did not tell her how wounded soldiers might crawl away under cover to die, their bodies only discovered long afterward. Or how a direct hit from artillery could leave almost nothing to identify. The numbers were enough to appall her on their own.

"It isn't only for Molesworth's sake that I must prevent Bonaparte from ever doing this again." His son's cries provided a fitting accompaniment to Gavin's fierce declaration. "It is every one of the men those casualty numbers represent."

Perhaps it was a good thing he had become so attached to his children. Leaving them to undertake his final mission would be a sacrifice, but only a tiny one compared to what those men had given for king and country. He could not let it have been for nothing. If it meant he must miss some of the babies' early accomplishments, he would make it up to them later, during the years of peace those brave men had won.

Would seeing those casualty returns help Hannah

Fletcher accept what he must do? Gavin hoped so, for he felt he would have a much greater chance of success with her staunch support.

Those grim numbers in the newspaper plagued Hannah as she returned little Arthur to his wet nurse and then headed back to Edgecombe. The sky had grown overcast, and now the black-bottomed clouds spat large drops of rain on her. It felt as if the heavens were weeping for all those slain at Waterloo. Hannah was inclined to join in, venting some of the grief she had been obliged to stifle so she could fulfill her promise to Lady Hawkehurst.

It was not only her dismay over those appalling casualties that made her throat tighten and her eyes sting. It was also her fears for his lordship. She had made such excellent progress fostering his paternal feelings for the babies. When he spent time with the twins, he seemed content to sit and cuddle them, not itching to be off in pursuit of Napoleon Bonaparte.

But hearing those dreadful numbers of soldiers killed had revived the earl's determination to take up his quest. Hannah was relieved that he seemed willing to delay his departure until after Rebecca's visit, but that would only buy a little extra time. If no one else apprehended Bonaparte by the time the Benedicts departed, there would be no stopping Lord Hawkehurst.

Much as she longed to find a way, for the sake of her young charges, she could not deny the need to prevent a repeat of Waterloo in another year. The allied commanders had failed to capture the former emperor, and Hannah wondered if one resourceful, resolute man might succeed where unwieldy armies had failed.

But must that man be Lord Hawkehurst? As Hannah entered the big house and hurried up to the nursery, she fancied she could hear the late countess questioning her loyalty. Was it not enough that the earl had put king and country ahead of his family while his wife was alive? Must he abandon his three motherless children to go off on a dangerous mission from which he might never return? There must be something more she could do to persuade him where his priorities should lie.

Hannah squared her shoulders and tilted her chin. She could not let her ladyship down, nor the children she had come to care for as if they were hers. Gavin Romney was a much better man than she had appreciated until recently. She knew he wanted to be a good father to his children. He had needed her help learning to handle the babies. Now perhaps he needed her help to understand how very much his children needed him.

When she entered the nursery, Hannah found Peter with the nursemaid, folding scraps of paper into little boats and other shapes.

"Aren't you clever?" Hannah ruffled the child's hair affectionately. "Did Maisie show you how to make those?"

"Only the boat," Maisie said, beaming with pride in her young master. "He figured out all the others by himself."

That gave Hannah an idea. She picked up the remaining paper and addressed her young pupil. "Why don't you choose three of your best ones and bring them to show your father? I am certain he would like to see them."

The child looked over his creations with a frown of concentration. At least Hannah *hoped* that was the cause of his expression. "I thought Papa could not see me because he is too tired. You said he must have a very long rest and you needed to look after him."

It took Hannah aback to hear her excuses parroted so accurately. Sometimes young Lord Edgecombe could be rather too clever for his own good. She considered what to tell him and decided the truth would be best, now that he seemed to be recovering from the shock of his mother's death.

She pulled up a chair and sat down beside him at the nursery table. "Your papa did need to rest, but not only because he was tired. He was injured, you see, and he needed to get better. But he is almost well now and I believe he finds the time long with little to do. I believe he would enjoy a visit from you."

The child pursed his lips and turned his paper boat over and over in his hands. "Do I *have* to go and see him, Miss Hannah?"

How should she answer that? Hannah did not want to force the child to do something against his will. On the other hand, it would not be a good thing for the earl and his son to be kept apart much longer. The sooner they began to build a proper relationship, the better it would be for both of them.

"I think it would be a very kind deed for you to visit your papa," she replied after several minutes' consideration. "Remember how much you enjoyed having company when you were ill in bed last winter?"

She rose and held out her hand to the child. They could discuss his reservations on the way. By the time it was all settled, they would have reached his lordship's chamber.

"That's because it was Mama who came to see me." With a reluctant air, the boy slid off his chair and gathered up three of his folded paper creations from the table. "Papa never visited me at all."

Hannah thought back. "That's because he had been summoned to London, remember? I'm certain he would rather have stayed home to visit with you, but there were urgent army matters that required his attention."

She began walking toward the door. Though she did not insist Peter accompany her, he followed.

"Papa is always doing army things," the child grumbled as he trailed her down the thickly carpeted corridor hung with imposing family portraits. "Mama said he should not have gone to London when I was ill. She said he cares more about war and fighting than he does about us."

Hannah spun around as if someone had seized her from behind. Why had her ladyship said such a terrible thing to her young son? Even if she had believed it, how could she have told the child something that was certain to hurt him and poison his chances of one day growing close to his father?

She recalled how desperately Lady Hawkehurst had hoped the end of the war would mean the beginning of an idyllic family life with her husband. But while the earl had returned to Edgecombe in body, his spirit had remained elsewhere. Uncommunicative and preoccupied, he had sought any excuse to escape the house.

Lately Hannah had begun to understand why, but back then she'd encouraged his wife to confide in her, providing sympathy and indignation to a long litany of complaints. Had they sometimes spoken within earshot of the child, trusting that he was too young to understand? Perhaps he had grasped more than they had ever suspected.

Overcome with remorse for the harm she might have done through her thoughtlessness, Hannah sank to the floor before her young pupil. Was it too late to undo the damage?

"Peter, you know how devoted I was to your mama, but I do not believe your father cares more about war and fighting than he does about you."

"Why did Mama say it, then?" The child regarded her with a grave, doubtful expression, his head cocked to one side. "She wouldn't tell me lies."

"Of course not." The last thing Hannah wanted to do was turn Peter against his late mother. "But sometimes when people get angry or frightened or have their feelings hurt, they may say things they would not say if they were quite happy. When they feel better, they might admit they…exaggerated. I know it must be difficult for you to understand now, but when you get older…"

Her explanation trailed off. Was there any way she could convey such a complex idea that a child might understand?

"Is it the same as when I was ill and you had to put that poultice on me?" asked Peter. "I didn't like it so I said you were nasty and I wished Mama would send you away. I meant it just then but after I was sorry and wished I hadn't said it."

Out of the mouths of babes, indeed.

"That is just what I meant." Hannah reminded herself not to underestimate his powers of reason in the future. "Regardless of what anyone has told you about your father, I hope you will give him a chance to prove himself. I do not believe he *likes* fighting and war, but he knows it is sometimes necessary to protect our country and its friends."

She rose and beckoned the child on, hoping that his innocent wisdom would guide him to give his father the benefit of the doubt. If the earl could win *her* regard after the way she had misjudged him, surely he could forge a bond with his young son if he tried.

"Now that the war is over," she continued, "I believe your papa wants to devote himself to you and Arthur and Alice."

It was certainly what he *ought* to do and what she wanted him to do. There were times she had watched him with the babies and felt certain it was what he wanted, too. Yet he had such stubborn, limiting ideas about what he could and could not do. Sometimes his fear of failure seemed to prevent him from trying things Hannah firmly believed he could accomplish. Though he had any number of good reasons for wanting to apprehend Napoleon Bonaparte, she wondered if the earl felt he had a better chance of succeeding at his final military mission than he did of raising three young children.

She had helped him experience some success with the babies. Now if she could bring him and his eldest son together, perhaps he would realize that fatherhood was his most important mission.

When they reached the earl's bedchamber, she peeped in. "Excuse me, sir. I have brought Lord Edgecombe to visit. He has something he would like to show you."

Lord Hawkehurst reclined on a pile of pillows, studying the newspaper, his dark brows knit in a severe expression. Hannah could hardly blame him, considering the news, but she hoped his look would not frighten his young son. In her experience, children that age viewed everything in relation to themselves. If someone was angry or upset, it must be their fault.

"Has he, indeed?" The earl set his newspaper aside and made an obvious effort to welcome his son…a bit too obvious, perhaps. His tone of forced heartiness rang false. "Well, bring him in and let me see."

Peter peered around the edge of the doorway but made no move to enter. Hannah was reluctant to push him. Had the child ever been inside his father's bedchamber or seen him in his nightshirt?

Perhaps the most helpful thing she could do was approach Lord Hawkehurst, to demonstrate that there was no reason to be afraid of him. She marched toward the bed and tried to ignore the fluttery sensation inside her that had nothing to do with fear. Was she only anxious that this meeting between father and son would go well or was it something more?

"Maisie showed him how to fold paper into little figures." She raised the sheaf of paper and waved it to fan her cheeks, which had suddenly grown warm. "He is very skillful. I thought you might care to give it a try to pass the time."

"Folding bits of paper?" The earl gave a derisive

laugh, which ceased abruptly when Hannah shook her head and nodded toward the door, where his son hung back. "I…er…suppose it might be amusing, though I am not certain I possess the necessary dexterity."

Who had first told him that and made him believe it? Hannah could guess. "I imagine it takes considerable dexterity to handle a horse and wield a weapon at the same time."

"Coordination, perhaps." The earl made it sound like nothing of which to boast. "Wielding a pen takes far more skill, which I never properly mastered."

"I can make my letters," piped a small voice from the doorway.

With a swift jab of shame, Hannah realized that she had almost forgotten about the child.

She turned to him with an encouraging smile. "You are making fine progress with your penmanship."

There was still room for improvement, but Hannah refused to dwell on that. Her young pupil did very well for his age. She had no intention of planting any seeds of doubt about his abilities in his impressionable mind. She had seen what poisonous fruit they could bear in later years.

The earl's voice rang out, addressing his son. "You are a fortunate boy to have such a kind governess. When I was your age, mine was a perfect ogre in skirts."

"She was?" Peter's eyes widened.

His father gave a rueful nod. "According to her, I was the greatest dunce in three counties and too lazy to improve my shortcomings."

What would Peter make of all that? Hannah wondered. It helped her understand why the earl had once resented the privileged position she had assumed in his household. He must have viewed her as another *ogre in skirts,* determined to think the worst of him no matter how hard he tried. She wished his opinion of her had been further from the truth.

"Miss Hannah says everyone makes mistakes." Peter edged over the threshold. "She says mistakes can help us learn sometimes."

Inwardly Hannah shuddered at how prim and naive that sounded.

The earl gave no sign of sharing that opinion. "Then Miss Hannah is wise as well as kind. Does that mean if you show me how to fold paper I should not allow my mistakes to discourage me, but try to learn from them?"

His lordship's praise, and his use of her Christian name, made Hannah's heart swell, while his question to his son humbled her. She had intended to show *him* how to draw closer to the boy. Yet even after they'd gotten off on the wrong foot, the earl had kept trying until he began to find his way. She prayed his effort would yield the success he deserved.

In reply to his father's question, Peter nodded. "That's right."

As Hannah stood rooted to the spot, the child walked past her toward his father's bed. "Would you like me to show you? It isn't as hard as you think. It may be easier for me because my fingers are smaller, but you mustn't mind about that."

The remark might sound patronizing coming from a young boy to his father, but it was kindly meant. It brought a lump to Hannah's throat and a smile to her lips at the same time.

"These are some of the ones I made." Peter spread his handiwork on the bedclothes. "Maisie showed me how to make this boat. She floated hers in the nursery basin, but I didn't want mine to get wet. Next I made this little box. And this one is supposed to be a hare."

"I thought so by the long ears." The earl glanced from the small paper objects to his son.

Pride and pleasure in the child's company seemed to battle fear that he might put a foot wrong again and spoil the promising beginning they'd made. Hannah hoped he would heed his son's advice about learning from mistakes rather than letting them keep him from trying.

Chapter Ten

As he waited for the doctor to arrive and examine him, Gavin concentrated on the piece of paper he was endeavoring to fold into the shape of a bird. It was not an easy task for it required more patience, dexterity and concentration than he possessed. He'd persisted just the same and tried to follow his young son's advice not to mind about that. His first efforts had been laughably bad, but he refused to let that deter him. It was not the product that mattered, after all, only the activity to occupy his attention and pass the time.

On both those counts it had succeeded.

Unlike reading the newspapers, which frustrated and agitated him, paper folding had a calming effect on his mind. And while it absorbed his attention, the time passed. Not as swiftly as when he was in Hannah Fletcher's company perhaps, but quickly enough. It also kept his thoughts from dwelling on his son's governess quite so much.

A brisk knock sounded on his door, making his heart beat faster as he called out permission to enter.

But when the door swung open, it admitted only the

butler and Gavin's physician. "Dr. Hodge to see you, my lord."

"Thank you, Owens." Gavin dismissed the sudden fall of his spirits by reminding himself the physician's arrival might set him free at last. "Good day, Doctor. I hope you will have good news for me."

Putting aside his half-finished paper bird, he carefully turned onto his good side and tugged up his nightshirt to facilitate the examination.

"If I do, you shall have yourself to thank for it." The doctor unwound the bandaging that bound Gavin's wound. Then he rummaged in his satchel for tweezers and a pair of long-bladed scissors. "If I were a wagering man, I would have staked good money against you following my orders for a fortnight's bed rest."

With considerable care the doctor cut and tugged out the stitching thread that had held Gavin's torn flesh together while it knit. "How on earth did you manage to stay still for so long? Did Miss Fletcher have you placed in a strait waistcoat? I would not put it past her. She strikes me as a very determined young woman."

For some reason the doctor's comment about Miss Fletcher stung Gavin worse than the removal of his stitches. "Determination is a fine quality. Precious little would get done in the world if it were not for determined people and even less would get changed."

"True." The doctor sounded amused. "I take it Miss Fletcher did not have you restrained or you would not be defending her with such vigor."

"Of course she did not have me restrained!" Gavin snapped. "And I am not defending her, vigorously or otherwise. I was only making a general observation."

"I see." Doctor Hodge gave the most exasperating chuckle.

"I will admit, Miss Fletcher managed to impress upon me the need to follow medical advice if I wish to recover my health."

"The lady must have been most persuasive." The doctor snipped off the last of Gavin's stitches. "I wish she would speak to some of my other patients who are not inclined to heed me."

Though he knew the doctor was only jesting, perhaps to distract him, the thought of Hannah Fletcher assisting another man did not sit well with Gavin. "You should cultivate your own powers of persuasion. Miss Fletcher has quite enough to occupy her here at Edgecombe."

Once again the doctor chuckled. Gavin could not fathom what the man found so amusing. "Does this mean I am allowed to leave my bed at last?"

"It does." The doctor began to pack away his instruments as Gavin pulled down his nightshirt. "In fact, you may rise now, if you wish, to test your strength and balance."

Gavin did not need to be asked twice. He was eager to be active again. Twitching aside the covers, he surged to his feet only to sink back onto the edge of the bed when the room began to spin and his legs gave way beneath him.

"Go easy now." The doctor rushed around the bed. "I said you could get up. I did not invite you to run a steeplechase. Your legs will be weak from disuse, and you will need to become accustomed to standing upright again."

Before Gavin could reply, a knock sounded on his

door. The habit of a fortnight made him call out for the person to enter before he realized this might not be the best idea at the moment.

He had no opportunity to withdraw the invitation before Miss Fletcher strode in.

"I beg your pardon, sir!" she cried when she spotted him sitting on the bed in his nightshirt. She turned her gaze toward the mantel as if she spied something of absorbing interest there. "I heard the doctor had come and I was anxious to hear what he thinks of your recovery."

She had come to check up on him. Two weeks ago, Gavin would have resented her meddling. Today he could not for he knew Miss Fletcher had his welfare and his children's at heart. Besides, if it had not been for her, he might have ignored the doctor's orders and prolonged his recovery.

"Dr. Hodge says I am doing well." Gavin climbed back into bed to spare them both any further embarrassment. "He gives you all the credit for making me follow his advice, and I daresay he is right."

"I only told you what you should do and why." The lady seemed uncomfortable accepting his praise. "You were the one who had to comply with the doctor's orders in spite of how disagreeable you found it."

"Not nearly as disagreeable as I expected," he countered. That was entirely thanks to her, though Gavin was reluctant to say so in the doctor's presence.

Instead he changed the subject to one he should have raised earlier. "Tell me, Doctor, how soon do you think I will be fit to travel?"

His question brought an anxious frown to Hannah

Fletcher's face, which he regretted, though he could not let it stop him.

The physician considered for a moment. "That will depend upon the type and length of journey you wish to make. I would say you might manage a carriage ride to London in a week or so."

"What about returning to the Continent by ship then traveling on horseback?"

The doctor shook his head. "Not for quite some time unless you wish to set back your recovery."

Hannah Fletcher's frown dissolved into a grateful smile, which she directed at the doctor. Gavin resented her smiling at another man, though he knew he had no right to.

He did not waste his breath disputing the advice he'd been given. He knew the other two would only unite against him. It did not help that part of him shared Miss Fletcher's obvious relief at the doctor's warning.

What kind of man did that make him? What kind of soldier? What kind of friend?

"If you will excuse me, then." Gavin politely dismissed them both. "Miss Fletcher, would you be so kind as to show the doctor out?"

"Of course, sir." She sounded a trifle suspicious that he had not argued with the doctor's advice. "May I be of any other service?"

He nodded. "Kindly send along one of the footmen to help me dress. Once I am back on my feet, I must see about engaging a proper valet."

"As you wish, sir." Hannah Fletcher seemed so much more formal and servile in her manner than she had only a few days ago. To his consternation, Gavin found himself looking back on that part of his convalescence with unaccountable wistfulness.

Would his lordship continue to follow the doctor's advice now that he had been allowed to rise from his sickbed? Hannah peered out the nursery window for the twentieth time, hoping to catch a glimpse of Lord Benedict's carriage.

The earl had not objected when his doctor told him it would be some time before he could safely travel to the Continent. Nor had he questioned precisely how long "some time" might be. Those were encouraging signs, surely.

Perhaps she had managed to persuade Lord Hawkehurst that he was capable of being as good a father as he had been a soldier. With that assurance, he might not feel quite so compelled to take on sole responsibility for capturing Bonaparte. He might also realize what an unacceptable risk such a mission could pose to the welfare of his children.

Much as she hoped that was the case, Hannah found it impossible to savor her victory. She could not forget reading how much money and how many men it had cost to defeat Bonaparte for a second time. What if he *did* return again? She feared her mind would never be quite easy on the subject until the general had been captured and brought to justice.

A tug on her skirt jolted Hannah from her disquieting thoughts. She glanced down to find Peter staring up at her with an expectant air. "Do you see your friends yet, Miss Hannah?"

She was about to say no when a flicker of movement drew her gaze back out to the lane. A fine travel-ing coach had just turned off the road, heading toward the house.

"I do see them." She spoke in a breathless rush. "They are coming! We must go down to greet them."

"Me, too?" A wide grin lit up the boy's solemn lit-tle face.

"Of course." Hannah seized him by the hand and they headed off at a brisk pace. "Lady Benedict will be pleased to meet you, I'm sure. She likes children."

That was not the only reason Hannah wanted her young pupil with her when she met her friend again after so many years. She hoped Peter's presence would smooth over any awkwardness during their meeting. In truth, she was not certain how she ought to behave to-ward Rebecca now that her old friend had become the wife of a viscount.

It was kind of Lady Benedict to want to visit the friends of her youth. But would she soon realize there was now a wide gulf separating them?

Peter's mama had found a way to bridge that gulf, Hannah reminded herself, though lately memories of the countess provoked an ache of guilt inside her. Per-haps she should treat Rebecca the way she had Lady Hawkchurst —never too familiar or presuming upon their prior acquaintance, but with the deference befit-ting her friend's new station in life.

Bringing Peter along to their first meeting would be a subtle way of acknowledging her position in the earl's household.

As they descended the great staircase to the entry

hall, the child asked, "Should we find Papa and tell him the guests are here?"

The question caught Hannah off guard. Would Lord Hawkehurst want to be on hand to greet the Benedicts? Though he had extended them the hospitality of his house, they would be coming to visit *her,* not him.

"I'm not sure where we might find your father now that the doctor has allowed him out of bed." That was true and as good an excuse as any, though it gave Hannah a pang to speak of it. How accustomed she had grown to knowing where to find the earl at all times and being free to visit him as often as she could find an excuse.

As she and Peter reached the foot of the stairs, his lordship came striding toward them from the direction of his study. "I hear our guests have arrived. Owens proposed a formal reception with all the staff lined up to greet Lord and Lady Benedict, but I abhor such stuffy ceremony. I hope they will not feel slighted by a small family welcome party."

Several things struck Hannah at once. The first was how well the earl looked. No one would ever guess that less than three weeks ago he had collapsed from loss of blood and been close to death. After spending so many days and nights sitting by his bedside, she had forgotten what it was like to look up at him. He appeared taller than she remembered—his shoulders broader. The rest and nourishment of his convalescence seemed to have agreed with him. The chiseled hollows of his face had filled out nicely. Hannah could not recall ever having seen him so smartly dressed and groomed.

No doubt his fine appearance was meant as a compliment to Lord and Lady Benedict, but that made it a roundabout compliment to her, as well, which she appreciated. So much so that she found herself lost for words.

"F-family?" she managed to stammer.

For an instant Lord Hawkehurst looked almost as disconcerted as she felt, but he quickly recovered his composure. "You are the twins' godmother, after all. That makes you rather a member of the family. Don't you agree, son?"

Peter gave a vigorous nod. "Mama often said Miss Hannah was like part of the family."

The child's innocent mention of his mother and her kindness shook Hannah. She had no business being here, taking the late countess's place.

"Just so," said the earl with a forced smile. "Now we had better go greet our guests before they decide they are not welcome at Edgecombe."

"We cannot have that," Hannah agreed, giving Peter's small hand a squeeze.

Now that the moment had come to meet one of her friends in the flesh again after so many years, she found herself as anxious as she was eager.

Lord Hawkehurst threw open the great front door and beckoned her out. Clinging tightly to her young pupil's hand, Hannah emerged into the summer sunshine.

The viscount's carriage had just come to a halt. A footman in formal livery scrambled down from his perch to open the door and unfold the steps for his master and mistress to descend.

Lord Benedict climbed out first, made a brief bow toward the Edgecombe party, then turned to help his bride alight. Hannah approved the gentleman's looks.

He carried himself with distinguished bearing and his features were balanced in pleasing proportions. When he held his wife's hand and led her forward, Lord Benedict's face radiated affection and pride in her.

To Hannah's relief, she recognized her friend at once. Though dressed in a flattering gown of blue-green muslin and a smart hat trimmed with matching ribbons, Rebecca still had her full, dark brows, generous mouth and features that conveyed an ideal blend of strength and softness. It took every ounce of self-control Hannah possessed to remind herself that her friend was now the wife of a peer.

"Welcome to Edgecombe, Lord and Lady Benedict." She dropped a proper curtsy but could not suppress a smile of fond familiarity.

"Hannah Fletcher!" Rebecca swooped toward her with no thought for rank or decorum.

The next thing Hannah knew, she was being embraced and kissed with the vigorous affection of a long-lost sister. Any worries about proper deference were swept away by a powerful wave of joy. She held her friend close, repeating her name as if it were the most beautiful word in the language. Her eyes misted with tears of happiness, and for once she let a few of them fall. She heard an answering sniffle from Rebecca.

At last they drew back to find the three gentlemen regarding them with indulgent puzzlement.

Peter was quick to articulate what they all must be thinking. "Why are you weeping, Miss Hannah? Did your friend hurt you when she hugged you so hard?"

"Not in the least." Hannah chuckled at the child's question as she dashed away her tears with the back of her hand. "I will explain it to you later, though I am not certain any man can properly understand."

It was not only seeing her friend again, so little changed, that overwhelmed her with emotion. It was also the unexpected assurance that Rebecca's elevated position need not spoil the closeness they had once shared.

"Speaking of men—" Rebecca drew Hannah toward the viscount "—allow me to present my husband. He could not have given me a more cherished wedding gift than this opportunity to see you and my other dear friends again. Sebastian, this is Hannah Fletcher, of whom I have told you so much. My friends and I owe her such a debt. We would all have suffered a great many more punishments at school if she had not helped us with our studies and made certain our beds and possessions were always kept tidy."

"It is a pleasure to meet you at last, Lord Benedict." Hannah swept him a curtsy that was a token of sincere respect. Any man who had been such a staunch advocate of Britain's military forces and also made her friend so happy deserved her wholehearted approval.

"That will not do, Miss Fletcher." The viscount held out his hand to her. When she clasped it, he bowed low over her hand. "You must call me Sebastian for I look upon you and your friends as much my sisters-in-law as dear Hermione."

The affection for Rebecca that shone in his eyes seemed to reach out and encompass her, too. In spite of that, Hannah was still not certain she could bring herself to address a viscount by his Christian name.

"You are very kind." She returned his smile with

greater warmth than she had ever extended to anyone upon their first meeting. "Now allow me to present your host, Colonel the Earl of Hawkehurst and his son, Lord Edgecombe."

"A pleasure." Lord Benedict and the earl bowed to one another, then shook hands. "I cannot begin to thank you for your generous offer of hospitality."

"It is an honor to welcome you and your wife to Edgecombe." Lord Hawkehurst bowed over Rebecca's hand. "As Miss Fletcher can attest, I have long desired to make your acquaintance. I believe we shall have many matters of mutual interest to discuss during your stay."

Peter had hung back, watching the adults' introductions, perhaps still a bit troubled by seeing his governess in tears. Now, at a nudge from Hannah, he stepped forward and bowed to the guests as she had shown him.

Rebecca stooped to the child's height. "It is a pleasure to meet you, Lord Edgecombe. I have heard such fine reports of you from my friend's letters. To hear her tell it, there is no better or cleverer boy in Kent, if not the whole kingdom. I look forward to learning the truth of that for myself."

It was difficult to tell who looked more pleased to hear Hannah's praise relayed—her young pupil or his father.

The boy cast Rebecca a shy smile. "Do you have any children?"

Hannah stifled a little gasp, then cast the earl a look that begged him not to mind his son's innocent question.

Rebecca and her husband exchanged a fond, private

glance. She replied, "None yet, but we would very much like to someday."

"We have twins," Peter announced. "They are quite nice. Perhaps Papa and Miss Hannah could tell you where they got ours and you could get some from there, too."

Lord Benedict laughed heartily at that, and the earl pretended to join him, though Hannah sensed he was not amused. Meanwhile her cheeks blazed at the way Peter's remark implied the babies belonged to his father and her. It was all very well to consider her a member of the family, but she was not, nor would she ever be. Poor Lady Hawkehurst had asked her to watch over the children, not to take her place in their lives.

Gavin had hoped that having her friend to stay at Edgecombe would make Hannah Fletcher happy. Her rapturous reaction to Lord and Lady Benedict's arrival convinced him the visit would be a great success. But as the four of them dined together that evening and the conversation flagged, he wondered if he had been mistaken or if he'd done something wrong.

Miss Fletcher had scarcely said a word since they sat down, except brief answers to direct questions. She had resisted the invitation to dine with him and their guests until he pointed out how ridiculous it would be for him to entertain *her* friends while she ate in the nursery. Only when he suggested they all dine with his son in the nursery had she relented. But now every time the footman took a dish away or brought another she cringed as if she feared he might strike her.

For the life of him, Gavin could not make out what

he had done to offend her. If she and Lady Benedict were not going to keep up the usual table talk, he had plenty he wanted to say to the viscount. He'd planned to wait and raise the subject after the ladies retired to the drawing room. But the awkward pause in conversation needed to be filled, and he had no skill whatsoever at small talk.

"Lord Benedict, I have been almost as anxious for your arrival as Miss Fletcher. Tell me, are you any better informed than the newspapers about the whereabouts of that infernal Bonaparte?"

As he awaited the viscount's reply, Gavin took a bite of tender roast veal. After a fortnight of invalid food and many weeks of army rations before that, he savored the well-prepared, flavorful dishes. From the foot of the long dining table, he noticed Miss Fletcher's expression darken, but he chose to ignore it. If she objected to this avenue of conversation, she was free to speak up and direct it elsewhere.

Lord Benedict gave a wry chuckle. Gavin had never met a man in such perpetually good spirits. His happy disposition did not match the reports Gavin had heard of him over the years.

"I must confess I never pay much attention to the press, so I have no idea what they may or may not know. However, I did speak with an acquaintance of mine from the Foreign Office while we were in London. There is some consternation that Wellington and Blücher did not demand custody of Bonaparte as a condition of the surrender of Paris."

Gavin gave a vigorous nod of agreement.

"To be fair," the viscount continued, "the military

situation is still unsettled, and many of the French do not want King Louis back on the throne at any price. Wellington may have felt that having the Allies seize Bonaparte would put spark to the tinder. I am inclined to trust the duke's instincts in such matters."

"As am I," Gavin replied with less than complete conviction. "But to risk Bonaparte getting away altogether…"

"Every French port is being patrolled to prevent that from happening," Lord Benedict assured him. "Every ship of His Majesty's navy is on full alert."

Hannah Fletcher did not say a word but concentrated on her dinner as if trying to make herself invisible. Yet Gavin sensed her agreement with the viscount.

"So I have been frequently reminded." He cast a significant glance in her direction.

She pretended not to notice.

"There are reports that Bonaparte is in Rochefort seeking passage on frigate," Lord Benedict added.

The frustration Gavin had been trying so hard to keep in check threatened to boil over. "If his whereabouts are known, or even suspected, why can a select detachment not be sent to intercept him before he slips away?"

Was he angrier with the allied commanders' puzzling lack of action or with himself for accepting the doctor's advice so tamely? Had he seized on any excuse to remain at Edgecombe, where he had begun to feel truly *at home* for the first time he could recall?

"Do you not trust the Royal Navy?" Lord Benedict inquired in a bantering tone. "I assure you they are anxious to redeem themselves after allowing Bonaparte to slip away from Elba. I believe they will do everything in their power to prevent him escaping again."

"I hope so." Gavin wanted to believe the viscount, for it might silence his nagging conscience.

Since nothing he'd heard from Lord Benedict so far had set his mind at rest, Gavin decided he should steer the conversation in a different direction—one the ladies might be happier to follow.

He glanced at the viscount's wife, whose attractive looks also suggested warmth of heart and strength of character...very much like her friend Hannah Fletcher. "I understand one of your school friends is married to a naval officer. Have you been to visit her yet?"

Lady Benedict shook her head. "We have begun with the nearest first and plan to venture farther afield as we go on. Edgecombe is only the second stop on our bridal tour. Our first was to Grace Ellerby in Berkshire. I was delighted we were able to secure an invitation to Lady Maidenhead's Victory Ball from her."

Gavin thought it rather premature to celebrate victory with Bonaparte still at large. Out of consideration for Miss Fletcher, he refrained from voicing his opinion.

Glancing toward her friend, Lady Benedict shook her head. "I did not recognize Grace when I first saw her wearing a hideous old cap and spectacles. But when she joined us for the ball she was a vision of loveliness."

"I still say there is something very odd going on with Miss Ellerby," the viscount declared as a footman exchanged his well-cleaned plate of veal for a dish of Dover sole in caper sauce.

"Odd in what way?" Gavin asked.

"Let us just say your hospitality is very welcome

after the rudeness of her employer, Lord Steadwell. I had hoped to pay him my compliments, but he would not receive us."

"Steadwell?" Gavin muttered the name to himself for it had a familiar ring. "Rupert Kendrick—he was a few years ahead of me at school. He seemed a decent enough fellow back then."

He recalled a quiet, rather gangly lad who had been much kinder to the younger boys than most. Another reason Rupert Kendrick stuck in his memory was because he had so clearly preferred his home to their school, quite the opposite of Gavin.

"Steadwell has a reputation for diligence in the House of Lords." Viscount Benedict seemed puzzled by the baron's recent behavior toward him. "I could usually count on his vote for any legislation in support of our military forces."

Lady Benedict paused over her fish. "I doubt Lord Steadwell was reluctant to receive *you,* my dear."

Her husband scowled. "What do you mean by that?"

The lady gave a faint smile of regretful resignation. "You know, and do not pretend otherwise. Not everyone is as blind to rank and position as our present host. Some people deplore the idea of a viscount marrying a governess. You cannot deny when we first met, you would have been one of them."

Lord Benedict squirmed in his seat. "Well, I was a daft fool who let one unfortunate experience sour my opinion on a number of matters. Thank goodness you came along to show me the error of my ways. If that is Lord Steadwell's problem, I hope he gets an undeserved opportunity to correct his error, as I did."

The viscount's words made Gavin wonder if he had been given similar opportunities to make things right. With his comrades in arms, who had sacrificed their lives when they should have been done with war. With his young children, who might have been deprived of their mother because of his actions.

If so, he should be grateful for those opportunities... and he was. He only wished he could do right by them both, rather than trying to accomplish one at the expense of the other and tearing himself apart in the process.

Chapter Eleven

"Weren't you rather hard on your poor husband at dinner last night?" Hannah asked Rebecca the next day as the two women strolled down to see the babies. Peter scrambled along ahead of them.

"Perhaps a little," her friend conceded with a mellow, musical chuckle. "I fear it may be a failing I picked up at school, being too quick to criticize. Fortunately Sebastian has learned to put up with my faults as I have with his. We do not love each other any less for them. As fine a man as he is in so many ways, he often forgets that other people may have reasons for behaving in ways of which he does not approve."

Hannah nodded in sympathy with the viscount. "I share his difficulty."

She lowered her voice so the child would not overhear. "When I first came to Edgecombe, I formed a very poor opinion of his lordship. He was away at war while the countess was here and so kind to me. I came to blame him for all her unhappiness, without knowing or caring why he acted as he did."

"Do not expect me to reproach you." Rebecca

reached for her friend's hand and gave it an affectionate squeeze. "I was the same when I met Sebastian. I believe I wrote you about him after our first meeting when he mistook me for Hermione."

Hannah nodded. "And you did not correct his mistake."

"Not one of my finer moments." Rebecca grimaced. "It amazes me that we ended up in love and so happy together after such an unpleasant beginning to our acquaintance."

"But you *are* happy?" Hannah asked. "You both certainly appear to be."

"Happier than I ever expected." Rebecca's smile sparkled like rays of summer sunshine through the leaves. "Happier than I deserve, perhaps, but it is a blessing I shall never take for granted. I only hope all my friends can find such happiness of their own someday."

Was *she* happy? Hannah had been far too busy to stop and ask herself that question. Surely she could not be happy so soon after the death of dear Lady Hawkehurst. But when she examined her heart, Hannah was surprised to find herself considerably happier than she ought to be under the circumstances. Perhaps it was seeing her friend again after all these years that had lifted her spirits. But Rebecca's talk of her love for Lord Benedict made Hannah fear it might be something more.

Fortunately they arrived at the tenant cottages before Rebecca had a chance to notice her preoccupation. Because the day was so warm, Mrs. Miller and Mrs. Wilkes were happy to let Hannah and her friend take the twins outside in the shade of a towering oak tree.

While Peter poked about nearby searching for acorns and other small treasures of nature, the women cuddled and cooed over the babies. The little ones responded by gurgling, smiling and otherwise contriving to steal Rebecca's heart.

"I have never been around infants much." Rebecca abandoned the proper decorum of a viscountess to rub noses with little Alice. "Hermione was an only child and half-grown by the time I became her governess. I envy you having charge of these two little darlings. I can hardly wait to have one of my own."

"You will be a wonderful mother." Hannah held Arthur to her shoulder and patted his back. "I wonder how long it will be before Marian and her captain announce a happy event. I wish I could go with you to visit her."

"Why don't you?" Rebecca's eyes sparkled with excitement. "I'm sure Lord Hawkehurst could spare you for a week or so if you asked. And think what a surprise it would be for Marian to see us both."

Much as the idea appealed to Hannah, she shook her head without great regret. "I am needed here at Edgecombe. A certain young gentleman has had too many upheavals in his life of late. My presence has been the one constant, and I cannot take that from him. Besides, I fear I would grow sick with longing for the little ones if I had to go more than two days without seeing them."

There was another reason she could not bring herself to leave Edgecombe now, even for a week. What if the earl received a reliable report of Bonaparte's whereabouts? If she was not here to prevent him, he might ride off to Dover in spite of his physician's warning.

"It is all very well to be so devoted to the children

you care for," Rebecca said as she rocked little Alice in her arms. "I would expect no less of you. But do you never yearn for a home, a husband and little ones of your own?"

Hannah dismissed her friend's question with a shake of her head. "There are already two from our group married, which is twice the number our teachers predicted. If any more of us make it to the altar, it will likely be our beauties, Grace or Evangeline."

Rebecca laughed, prompting a delighted squeal from Alice. "Grace will never attract a husband in that hideous cap and spectacles, and I am not certain Evangeline would accept a proposal if she received one. You know how independent she is. But I always thought you would make some fortunate man an excellent wife. You must not leave it too late, though, or you will lose any chance of making a match."

Hannah's friend checked to make certain Peter was not too near, then lowered her voice. "Once the earl's children grow a little older, perhaps when he remarries, you should come to stay with us in London. Then I can introduce you to some suitable gentlemen."

Rebecca's offer made Hannah's heart race and her stomach feel quite hollow. Which dismayed her more, the thought of leaving Edgecombe to seek a husband or the notion of Gav—*Lord Hawkehurst* marrying another woman to take the place of his first countess?

"That is very kind of you, Rebecca, but I cannot think of leaving Edgecombe as long as his lordship needs me." In truth, she could not imagine leaving Edgecombe, or the earl, under any circumstances without a shadow of despair threatening to blight her future.

There was only one man she conceived of marrying with any prospect of happiness.

That thought possessed Hannah so suddenly she almost dropped Arthur. She'd had hints of the nature of her feelings for the earl before. But she had thrust them from her mind, hoping they were only foolish fancies bred of fatigue or a reaction to her grief. Seeing Rebecca's love for her husband and their joy in each other's company, Hannah was now forced to recognize her feelings for what they truly were.

Suddenly she understood why people spoke of *falling* into a romantic attachment. She had never intended such a thing to happen, never believed it possible. But the emotional ground had shifted beneath her heart, plunging it to a frightening depth. Perhaps if she had experienced such feelings before she might have recognized the danger signs and been able to stop herself before it was too late.

Rebecca might not have taken their teachers' harsh predictions to heart. But Hannah's prior experiences had disposed her to believe they were right in claiming she would never be good enough to attract a husband. To protect herself from the pain of their inevitable rejection, she had avoided men her own age and focused on the faults of those she did encounter. Like Aesop's fox and the sour grapes, she had convinced herself she was not missing anything by remaining unwed. Could that be why she had formed such a poor opinion of the earl and concentrated on the problems in his marriage?

"Hannah?" Rebecca's anxious voice called her back from her troubling realizations. "Are you quite well? You've gone so pale. I hope I have not upset you. I know how much a part of the family a governess can feel, especially when the father is widowed. But children grow up far too quickly, as I discovered with Hermione. Once these little ones do, even after all your loyal service, you would be expected to go elsewhere and begin again in a new household."

Much as Hannah wanted to pretend that would never happen, she knew better. "I am well aware of what being a governess entails. Edgecombe was not my first position."

She had been employed by another family before coming here, some distant relations of Lady Hawkehurst. Though she had grown fond of her pupils, she'd scarcely heard from them after they'd outgrown the need for her services. Peter had been such a dear little fellow and the countess so welcoming that she had not minded putting her earlier attachments behind her. The thought of that happening with the Romney children, and their father, shook her.

"At least promise me you will think about my offer," said Rebecca. "You need not decide right away. The earl's second countess may not be so congenial, especially when she learns you were close to his first wife. Then you might not be so sorry to leave Edgecombe as you would be now."

"What makes you certain his lordship will remarry?" Hannah heard her voice growing sharp, quite against her will. That, and perhaps her preoccupation, made Arthur begin to fuss.

"Of course he will remarry." Rebecca cast her friend a puzzled glance, as if bewildered by her sudden irritation. "For the sake of his children, if nothing else. It would be a shame if such a fine man remained alone for the rest of his life."

From wondering how she could ever leave Edgecombe, Hannah began to question how she could bear to *stay,* feeling the way she did about Gavin Romney. Her situation could only get worse if he did as Rebecca predicted and took a new wife.

"It was good of you to invite me riding while the ladies have some private time," said Lord Benedict as he and Gavin made a leisurely circuit of the estate. "I suspect there are subjects they might wish to discuss without a gentleman listening in."

"The pleasure is mine." Gavin inhaled a deep breath of warm summer air scented with leather and horseflesh. "I have been looking for an excuse to get back in the saddle. I cannot recall the last time I went so long without riding."

"Does it bother your wound?" asked the viscount. They had talked about Gavin's experiences at Waterloo after dinner the previous evening.

"Only a twinge now and then," he confessed. "Though I would consider it a great favor if you would not mention that to Miss Fletcher. She seems determined to swaddle me in cotton wool."

"You may depend on my discretion," Lord Benedict assured him. "Rebecca tells me Miss Fletcher was very close to your late wife. Perhaps she feels obliged to look out for your welfare as the countess would have wished."

Was that why Hannah Fletcher had gone to such pains to care for him—because it was part of the vow she'd made to Clarissa? The thought did not sit well with Gavin.

His face must have betrayed his feelings for Lord Benedict cried out, "Forgive my confounded thoughtlessness! It was not my intention to distress you by speaking of your wife while your loss is so fresh. I do not know how I would bear it if any harm should come to Rebecca. You have taken such pains not to dampen our spirits with your grief, yet I should have considered how you must be feeling."

Gavin could not let the poor man reproach himself so severely over an innocent remark. "Do not fret. Your mention of my wife did not cause me the grief you suppose. I wish it did. Hard as that would be to take, at least it would be a clean wound that might heal properly in time."

The words had barely left his mouth before Gavin regretted not holding his tongue. How could he expect a man who clearly adored his new bride to understand the complicated, burdened relationship that had been his marriage to Clarissa?

The last thing he expected was for Lord Benedict to reply with a sympathetic murmur, "Even tainted wounds *can* heal if treated with the proper medicine."

Gavin wondered if he had misheard.

Marking his puzzled look, the viscount explained, "Rebecca is not my first wife. After my previous marriage I neither expected nor wanted to try my luck again. I am grateful that Providence decided otherwise."

"Then you do understand."

The viscount nodded. "I contracted my first marriage

for all the wrong reasons. Thankfully, I made my second for the only reason that truly matters."

How well Gavin knew about wedding for the wrong reasons. It was like trying to construct a house on a flawed foundation. The higher one built and the longer the house stood, the more likely it was to collapse.

They came to a narrow stream shaded by towering elms. The horses waded into the water and dipped their heads to drink.

Sebastian patted his mount's neck. "I was a besotted young fool the first time—taken in by looks and vivacity. She did not care for me, only for what I could give her. Unfortunately, men in our position seem to attract such women."

Perhaps so, but Gavin knew the troubles in his marriage had been quite the opposite of Lord Benedict's. He sensed it was not a subject about which the man confided in many people.

"When I first met Rebecca," the viscount continued, "I was trying to break the engagement between my brother and her former pupil. I was convinced any marriage between two people of unequal fortune must be doomed to failure."

"Yet you married a governess." Judging the horses had drunk enough, Gavin urged his to move on at a sedate walk.

Lord Benedict gave a rueful chuckle as his mount followed Gavin's. "Only after she refused me for interfering in the happiness of Claude and Hermione. Our present joy is a blessing I hardly deserve, yet I am all the more grateful for it on that account."

Like the blessing of his life and his beautiful children? Gavin wondered. Those gifts had been purchased for him with the lives of others. He was grateful for them, without a doubt. But that gratitude was tainted with bitter guilt.

"Forgiveness was the key to making peace with my past," Lord Benedict continued. "Once I tried to understand what made Lydia act as she did, anger and resentment gradually loosened their hold upon me until I was able to break free. Even if I had not succeeded in securing Rebecca as my wife, I would be far better off than I was before she taught me that priceless lesson."

Pleased as Gavin was that matters had worked out so happily for two such fine people, he felt once again that their situation was the opposite of his. There was nothing for which he needed to forgive Clarissa. The fault for *her* unhappiness lay with him. Again and again he had failed her as a husband. It hardly mattered whether that was because he was not cut out for marriage, as he liked to believe, or because he had not tried hard enough, as Hannah Fletcher would claim. Either way, the result had been the same. And now it was too late to atone, even if he could have found a way.

Hard as it might be to forgive others, Gavin feared it would be far harder to forgive himself.

The days of Rebecca's visit passed in a swift blur of pleasure for Hannah. Because Lord Hawkehurst and Lord Benedict got on so well together, the ladies had plenty of opportunities for long, intimate chats. They shared memories of their girlhood at the Pendergast School. Harsh as life there had been, they now found themselves remembering the rare happy times and the supportive camaraderie of their circle of friends that had made the difficulties bearable.

"I am not certain how I would have gone on after Sarah died if not for you and the others," Hannah admitted one evening after dinner as they waited for the gentlemen to join them in the drawing room. "I felt as if I had gained a whole family of sisters who needed me."

Rebecca reached over to squeeze her hand. "Sarah was a dear child. I must confess, I rather envied you having someone to look after. Someone who had been with you for a very long time and would remain close to you always. When you lost her, I began to think I was better off without such close attachments to lose."

Hannah understood her friend's conviction. It had ruled her own heart for many years. Yet when she thought of Rebecca denying herself the possibility of love, it seemed wrong somehow.

The unhealed grief that throbbed in her heart, fresh and raw, warned Hannah of the terrible power love could wield. "I should have taken better care of Sarah so she did not sicken and die."

Eager as ever to defend a friend, Rebecca shook her head in vigorous denial. "You did as much for her as anyone could in that awful place. Sometimes even our very best efforts are not enough to prevent bad things from happening. I am certain Sarah would not have wanted you to reproach yourself or think of her with guilt and regrets."

She might have said the same thing to any of her friends in such a situation. But it was easier said than done to absolve herself of her long-held sense of responsibility for her sister's death. Her father had commended Sarah to her care when he'd sent them to live with Aunt Eliza. If only she had made herself indispensible to their aunt, she and Sarah might not have been sent away to school. Once there, she should have done more to keep her delicate sister warmer and better fed, so Sarah might have survived the epidemic of typhoid when it had broken out.

"Lady Hawkehurst reminded me of Sarah," Hannah mused as she gazed around the elegantly decorated room that had been one of the countess's favorites. "She relied upon me quite as much as my sister did. But in the end, I could not save her either, poor lady."

Thoughts of the earl's late wife brought Hannah even more regret now that she recognized the true nature of her feelings for him. After the countess's death, she had become like a mother to the dear little twins. Now, with her friend visiting Edgecombe, it was as if she had also assumed the role of lady of the house.

She'd never intended to do that. Indeed, she had resisted the earl's invitation to join him and the Benedicts for meals. But he had insisted with considerable determination, arguing that Rebecca had come to see *her,* not him. He had even threatened to dine in the nursery if she refused to eat with them. Hannah knew he was stubborn and unorthodox enough to make good on that threat. Reluctantly, she had taken his wife's place at the foot of the great dining table.

Though the cook had outdone herself for Lord and Lady Benedict's visit, every bite Hannah took was tainted with the bitter taste of self-consciousness. What were they saying about her down in the servants' hall? Were they gossiping about the time she had spent with

Lord Hawkehurst during his recovery? Wondering whether she had taken advantage of that opportunity to insinuate herself with the earl? Speculating whether she had set her cap for him?

How would she ever be able to look any of the servants in the face again? Not that any of them could think worse of her than she thought of herself. There were moments she forgot herself and actually enjoyed pretending to be part of the foursome to which she did not belong. An outsider seeing them together might mistake them for two married couples—*happily* married couples at that.

Though she knew it was a betrayal of the countess to wish that were true, Hannah could not seem to suppress her wayward feelings for his lordship. Whenever he was nearby, all her senses seemed to grow more acute and focus entirely on him. When he spoke to her or her name passed his lips in conversation, it jolted her pulse from its usually sedate rhythm into a skittish jig. The briefest glance from him seemed to pierce her like a ray of shimmering sunshine.

"Hannah!" Rebecca's voice reached her as if from a distance. "My dear, you must not brood about such things."

Her friend's words gave Hannah a fright until she realized Rebecca was referring to their earlier conversation. "I'm certain there was nothing more you could have done for poor Lady Hawkehurst. Knowing you, I suspect you did far more for her than most people would. It is clear to me that her husband is vastly grateful for all your service to her and their children. His generous invitation to Sebastian and me is proof of how much he feels he owes you."

Though she knew Rebecca meant to reassure her, Hannah could not suppress a chill that rippled through her. Gavin—*Lord Hawkehurst* had been so obliging to her of late, so considerate and good-humored. Of course, his change in manner must be motivated by gratitude and not…anything else. She would be a fool to imagine otherwise. Such thoughts made it impossible for her to speak, lest her voice might betray something of her traitorous emotions.

Rebecca seemed to believe she understood her friend's feelings. Rising from her chair, she crossed to sit beside Hannah and slip a comforting arm around her shoulders. "I know you must miss her ladyship dreadfully. A governess can grow very attached to the family that employs her. Hermione became almost like a daughter to me. But now that Marian and I are both wed, I am certain there will be more opportunities for us to visit you and the others. Sebastian was not certain it would be right for us to call on you so soon after your loss. But I believed it was just the time when you might most need the companionship of an old friend. I hope I was not wrong and that we have not intruded upon your grief."

"Certainly not!" Hannah could not stand to have Rebecca think she was out of spirits on account of the Benedicts' visit. "It has been a great comfort to spend time with you again. And I believe it has been good for his lordship to have your husband here. It has prevented him from going off in search of Bonaparte before he is well enough to withstand such a journey."

But what would happen when the Benedicts left Edgecombe? Hannah had hoped Rebecca's husband would persuade Lord Hawkehurst to leave the task of apprehending Bonaparte to the Royal Navy. But she was not certain he had succeeded.

The muted thunder of hurrying footsteps made both women glance toward the door in alarm. An instant later the gentlemen burst in.

Their sparkling eyes and eager smiles allayed any fears.

"We've got the blighter!" Lord Benedict waved an open letter as if it were a flag of victory. "The captain of *HMS Bellerophon* prevented Bonaparte from fleeing Rochefort by frigate. He has taken the general's whole party aboard his ship and set sail for Torbay to await further orders!"

A powerful wave of relief swamped Hannah, along with a twinge of disbelief. After everything that had happened, she found it hard to accept that the worst would not befall her after all. Gavin would not be compelled to abandon his young children and chase off on a dangerous mission that might go on for months, even years. He would stay at Edgecombe, fully recover his health and learn to be a family man rather than a warrior.

She and Rebecca surged up from the sofa.

"What marvelous news!" Rebecca flew toward her husband. "This terrible war will truly be over at last."

Carried away by the unexpected joy of the news and their great love for one another, Sebastian and Rebecca fell into one another's arms and exchanged a jubilant kiss.

The same tide of emotion caught Hannah in its powerful grip and bore her toward Gavin. He rushed to meet her as if propeled by some force stronger than his own will. The closer they drew to one another, the more everything but his face seemed to fade away, until all Hannah could see were his shining dark eyes and the incandescent breadth of his smile.

Her arms rose and fastened around his neck as his slipped around her waist. For a moment, her heart and breath seemed suspended and the world outside the circle of their embrace stopped. It felt so natural to be in his arms, as if this was the haven for which she'd searched so many years without success, only to wander in by accident and find a welcome fire burning in the hearth. A subtle movement on his part urged her to tilt her head and slant her lips toward his.`

She was about to oblige him when her sense of prudence was roused at last.

Had she lost all judgment *and* morals? Bad enough for her to lean against his lordship when they were playing with the baby, but to forget herself in so brazen a fashion was inexcusable!

"Forgive me, sir!" She pulled back abruptly and felt Lord Hawkehurst do the same, though she fancied she felt his lips graze her ear in passing. "I was so elated to hear the news, I rather..."

"As did I, Miss Fletcher," the earl cut off her explanation.

His tone bristled with barely concealed annoyance. No doubt he had intended a much more decorous expression of his pleasure at the news—a friendly clasp of hands, perhaps, not an ardent embrace from his son's governess when they both should be in mourning for his late wife.

Chapter Twelve

Gavin could not recall when he had ever been so vexed with himself or when he had let his emotions carry him away as he had last evening.

After weeks of being on tenterhooks, not knowing what had become of Bonaparte and fearing the worst, news of his capture by the Royal Navy had lifted Gavin on a racing billow of euphoria. A crushing burden had been lifted from his spirit, freeing him to soar.

His first impulse had been an urgent need to share the news with Hannah. She was the only one who truly understood how much this mattered to him and why. He knew she would share in his elation that his vow to Molesworth had been fulfilled without him having to leave Edgecombe and his children.

He had not meant to take her in his arms, but at that moment it seemed the only suitable expression of his feelings. So much joy must be shared or it would burst his heart. Perhaps he might have come to his senses sooner, but seeing the Benedicts' embrace demolished any possibility that it might not be a good idea.

Now, in the stark light of an overcast morning, Gavin

could see matters more clearly. Hannah had taken refuge in the nursery, tending to his son, and the Benedicts had not yet come down to breakfast. So Gavin sat alone, consuming the last of his breakfast with very little notice of what he was eating. His thoughts were entirely occupied with the previous evening and the vigorous embrace to which he had subjected his son's governess.

He assured himself it had not been altogether unwelcome. He could not have borne the thought of Hannah feeling that he had imposed on her. Even though his memories of their embrace were rather jumbled, he was certain she had put her arms around his neck. Had it been an instinctive movement, triggered by his swift approach, or had her accustomed restraint also been swept away by her reaction to the astonishing news?

Thank goodness *she* had come to her senses in time to prevent him kissing her, as he'd been about to do. Still, when they'd pulled apart, making an awkward effort to dismiss what had happened, Gavin could not ignore the shocked looks on their guests' faces. Not that he blamed them. What gentleman of honor would embrace his son's governess when he should still be in mourning for his late wife? Gavin knew what his father would have said about that.

He would have reproached himself far worse if he had not recalled his conversation with Sebastian. It helped to know he was not alone in his experience of a troubled marriage, even if the circumstances had been widely different. The viscount's words of hard-won wisdom kept running through Gavin's mind—*Even tainted wounds can heal if you find the right medicine.*

He knew it was true. In spite of the guilt, grief and

worry that had plagued him these past weeks, some of the lingering hurts from his childhood had eased thanks to the warm understanding of Hannah Fletcher.

His feelings for her were unlike any he'd entertained for a woman before. Indeed, they were emotions of which he had long believed himself incapable. He wanted to confide in her and share experiences with her. He wanted to protect her from harm and unhappiness. She had suffered too much of both already. He wanted to ease the ache of old wounds, as she had done for him.

Though his conscience reproached him for having such feelings when he should be mourning Clarissa, a hopeful whisper in the depths of his heart reminded Gavin that his period of mourning would pass eventually. If he bided his time, guarded his tongue and restrained his actions, then the day would come when he could acknowledge his feelings and begin to make Hannah aware of them. In just a few short weeks, she had gone from detesting him to tolerating and understanding him. Given enough time and effort on his part, what further progress might he make in winning her affections?

A slight movement drew Gavin's gaze to the dining room doorway, where Lady Benedict stood watching him. His military instincts put him on his guard and made him wonder how long she'd been there.

"I beg your pardon, Lord Hawkehurst. I did not mean to disturb you." She approached the table as Gavin rose to his feet. "May I join you? My husband will be down shortly. He felt he ought to draft a reply to the letter he received last evening, and I could not persuade him that he might write better on a full stomach."

"By all means." Gavin hastened to draw out a chair for the lady. "I welcome your company. We have had little opportunity to talk to one another since you arrived. I must confess I sympathize with your husband's desire to get paperwork out of the way as quickly as possible."

The footman brought Lady Benedict coffee and a plate of food, then refilled his master's cup.

Under ordinary circumstances, Gavin might have fled from the necessity of making table conversation with a member of the fair sex. But he found Lady Benedict forthright yet kind. Besides, if he was not able to talk *with* Hannah, the next best thing might be to talk *about* her with someone who knew her well.

Lady Benedict smiled at him over the rim of her coffee cup. "I have said it before, but it bears repeating how much I appreciate you extending us your hospitality. It has given Hannah and me so much more time together than if my husband and I were lodging elsewhere. My visit with Grace Ellerby was rather disappointing in that regard. I had no opportunity to talk with her in private. Lord Steadwell's daughters were always with us, and though they are dear girls, there were subjects I did not feel free to raise in their hearing. Besides, I had a feeling Grace was always looking over her shoulder, afraid or ashamed that we might be seen together. I am delighted to find Hannah so much happier at Edgecombe…in spite of your terrible loss."

Clearly Sebastian could not have told his wife about their conversation regarding his marriage. Gavin was glad of that. He did not mind another man knowing the true state of his marriage, especially one who could understand and sympathize. But it troubled him to think of

Lady Benedict knowing what a poor husband he'd been. Her warm manner toward him suggested that Hannah had never complained about him, even in private letters to her oldest friends. That showed admirable discretion and raised his regard for her even higher.

"I do hope Han…er…Miss Fletcher is happy at Edgecombe. I hate to think how we would have managed without her these past weeks. My family owes her a great debt, and I am pleased if I can repay a small portion of it by whatever means. But since your company has been such a welcome diversion for me, as well, you must not feel your presence is the least imposition."

"Thank you." The lady inclined her head to acknowledge his reassurance. "It does not surprise me to learn that my friend has made herself invaluable to you. When we were at school, Hannah was the one on whom we all relied. I am glad she has found a position where her abilities and devotion are properly valued. As you may have gathered, ours was not an easy childhood."

Gavin nodded. He had heard enough to suspect that was an understatement.

"Hannah's memories of the Pendergast School are made even darker," Lady Benedict continued, "by the loss of her dearly loved sister."

"She mentioned a sister." Gavin leaned forward in his chair, eager to learn anything new about Hannah. "How did the child die?"

"Typhoid." Lady Benedict sighed. "Brought on by the wretched conditions of the place. Seven pupils died that winter, enough to raise questions and bring about a few reforms, which did not last. I wanted to tell you of it because your late wife reminded Hannah of her sister.

I believe she was nearly as devoted to the countess as she was to little Sarah. As a consequence, she has taken her ladyship's death harder than you might realize."

No wonder she had been so protective of Clarissa. Gavin wrapped his hands around his coffee cup and inhaled the rich, bitter aroma. No wonder she had detested him.

"I wish there was something I could do to ease her grief and make up for what she suffered in the past." He jammed his lips together, not daring to say anything more on the subject in case he betrayed the true nature of his feelings for Hannah.

Lady Benedict smiled as if that had been precisely what she wanted to hear. "That does you great credit, Lord Hawkehurst. I wish the same, which is why I would like to bring Hannah to London with me one day and try to find her as good a husband as she deserves."

The lady seemed to expect him to be as excited about her plans for Hannah as she was. Instead, Gavin felt as if she'd hurled a cup of scalding coffee in his face.

"London? Husband?" He bridled at the very idea. "But Miss Fletcher belongs here at Edgecombe! You said yourself she is happy and valued here."

The lady appeared bewildered by his response. "For the moment, she is, but we must think of her future. If you owe her as much as you say, surely you would not wish to deny her the opportunity to secure a home and family."

When Lady Benedict put the matter that way, it did sound cruelly selfish. Of course he did not want Hannah to grow unhappy and unfulfilled looking after *his* children rather than having a life of her own.

"She is reluctant to leave your children, even when it might mean sacrificing the opportunity to have her own," Lady Benedict continued. "Once life at Edgecombe settles down, I hope you will have a word with Hannah and urge her to accept my offer."

How could he let Hannah Fletcher walk out of his life? Where would he ever find someone who cared for his children the way she did?

Fortunately, Gavin was spared the necessity of answering when Lord Benedict strode in.

"Sebastian, dearest, I trust you finished your letter." His wife changed the subject abruptly. "What a good thing you write so much faster than I do. Otherwise I fear you might not have broken your fast until dinnertime."

Sebastian rounded the table and came to a halt behind his wife, resting one hand on her shoulder in a light caress. "I am pleased to see you were not obliged to dine alone, my love. I dashed off my note in a trice so I would not be parted too long from you."

As the couple chatted away fondly, Gavin could not suppress a spasm of envy. Not that he begrudged the newlyweds their happiness. Nor would he have taken a particle of it from them if he could. This was the first truly happy marriage he had observed at close range, and he could not help wanting a measure of that rare domestic felicity for himself.

Then he recalled what Lady Benedict had said about taking her friend to London to find her a husband. Perhaps he would *not* have the time he needed to win Hannah Fletcher's affections after all.

* * *

"Thank you so much for coming to see me!" A week after the Benedicts' arrival at Edgecombe, Hannah clasped Rebecca in a lingering embrace as if she could not let her friend go.

The truth was a great deal more complicated.

Of course she had been delighted to see Rebecca again, so little changed in essentials since their school days. It had been most welcome to have another woman to talk to and exchange confidences with. Hard as Hannah tried to deny it, their time together made her realize that her relationship with Lady Hawkehurst had not been the sort of mutual attachment she had experienced in her youth.

Rebecca and the others had relied on her for all manner of practical assistance, which she had been happy to provide. But they had given her unique gifts in return. Rebecca's steadfast loyalty, Leah's diverting antics, Grace's sweet sympathy and more had been hers to call on whenever she needed them. Indeed, they were often supplied before she ever had to ask. That anticipation of her needs was perhaps the most precious gift of friendship she'd received.

Now that she thought of it, Hannah could not recall the countess ever asking how *she* felt, expressing concern for *her* well-being or encouraging Hannah to confide in her. Lady Hawkehurst had frequently expressed her appreciation for everything Hannah did for her. She had paid her son's governess the compliment of confiding in her. Hannah had never expected anything more. But reflecting on her ladyship's actions, she wondered if the other woman's feelings for her had been as fond as she'd believed.

Or were those memories being poisoned by her feelings for the lady's husband? If she could persuade herself to care less for her ladyship's memory, perhaps she would not feel so wretchedly disloyal.

As she and Rebecca broke from their parting embrace, Hannah stole a covert glance at the earl. She had not been able to look him in the face since she'd hurled herself into his arms. That was another reason she was sorry to see Rebecca and Sebastian leave. The Benedicts had provided a buffer between her and the earl, so their awkwardness with one another was not painfully obvious.

Lord Hawkehurst looked as sorry to see her friends go as she was. Could it be for the same reason? Hannah hated the thought that she might have destroyed the easy fellowship that had developed between them while he was bedridden.

"Thank you again for the fine hospitality of Edgecombe." Lord Benedict shook the earl's hand heartily. "I hope you will allow us to return it by visiting Stanhope Court one day. Since it is in the Cotswold Hills, I fear the riding there is not so good as you are accustomed to."

The earl flashed a grin that Hannah sensed was rather forced. "Much as it pains me to admit, there is more to life than riding and soldiering. Miss Fletcher helped persuade me of that. We…that is…*I* should be happy to accept an invitation to Stanhope Court. It sounds like a fine place, and I should very much like to meet your brother and his wife."

His lordship's slip of the tongue reminded Hannah why she was *not* sorry to see Rebecca and Sebastian leave.

While they had been guests at Edgecombe and the earl insisted she spend the evenings with them, it had been dangerously easy to think of herself as part of a congenial foursome. From there it was but a short step to feel as if she and Gavin Romney were somehow a couple.

That was unpardonable presumption on her part—it had led directly to the liberty she'd taken by embracing the master of the house. Though he'd pretended to excuse her lapse of propriety, the earl's coolness toward her since then made it clear he might *forgive* her familiarity but he would never *forget* it.

Once the Benedicts were gone, Hannah hoped she could forget her friends' easy affection for one another, their obvious delight in one another's company and their playful banter. Happy as she was that Rebecca had been blessed with such wedded bliss, it made her long to experience something similar. Perhaps she should consider Rebecca's generous offer to help find her a husband.

But that was impossible. She had responsibilities toward the earl's young children. The prospect of leaving Edgecombe held no promise of happiness whatsoever. Yet, as Rebecca had reminded her, she would be forced to leave one day. By then she would be too old to attract a husband or start a family.

"Who will you visit next?" she asked her friend. "Marian in Nottingham or Leah in Norfolk?"

Lord Benedict answered for his wife. "Neither immediately, I fear. First I must return to London to learn what is to be done with Bonaparte now that he is in British custody. I support a plan for his exile to Saint Helena. The island is very remote, in the middle of the South Atlantic, easy to defend against any misguided attempt to liberate the fellow by force."

The earl nodded in agreement. "By far the best place for him, in my opinion, as well."

"Unfortunately not everyone feels as we do." Lord Benedict looked very severe when he frowned. "There are influential people of the Whig persuasion who firmly believe Bonaparte was better than the Bourbon kings. They fail to realize a man need not be born to the throne to become a despot. I fear they will argue against the necessity of preventing him from returning to power by whatever means. Until the matter is settled I feel I must be on hand to make my voice heard on behalf of all those who fought and beat Bonaparte's forces twice. They must not be obliged to repeat it again."

"Indeed they must not." The earl shook his head grimly. "I should go with you to add my voice in favor of confinement on Saint Helena."

Hannah was hard-pressed to stifle a cry of opposition. The earl must not go away so soon! What if the journey proved too much for him? What if Napoleon managed to escape custody and Lord Hawkehurst decided to take up the chase? She could not dare to risk either of those things.

"You should remain at Edgecombe," Lord Benedict insisted, and Hannah could have hugged him. "To mourn your wife and look after your family. Reason may prevail and neither my voice nor yours will be needed to argue the point."

The earl raised his eyebrows. "Reason prevailing in politics—that would be a novelty. Promise me that if you need additional support you will summon me at once."

Lord Benedict nodded. "You may depend upon it."

Hannah reached for Rebecca's hand and cast her friend a beseeching glance. She hoped Rebecca would recognize a silent plea to keep her husband from sending for the earl.

Her friend turned toward the earl and dropped a curtsy. "Farewell, Lord Hawkehurst. Your generous hospitality in the midst of your time of mourning speaks volumes of your respect for Miss Fletcher. I hope you will think over the matter of which we spoke and do what I requested."

The earl bowed over her hand—rather stiffly, Hannah thought. "I shall give your request my most careful consideration, Lady Benedict."

A short while later, as they waved after the Benedicts' departing carriage, Hannah asked, "What is this request of Rebecca's that you are going to give such careful consideration?"

"Nothing of any consequence." The earl turned and strode off in the direction of the stables.

His curt dismissal of her question assured her he was not telling the truth. Whatever her friend had asked of him, Hannah sensed he had no intention of doing it.

In the days after their guests' departure, Gavin tried to persuade himself Lady Benedict's request was of no consequence. Otherwise it would mean he had lied to Hannah—a transgression he could not bear to make.

But no matter how strenuously he argued, he was forced to admit it was of vital importance to him and the children whether he urged Hannah to accept her friend's invitation to London.

For the sake of Peter and the little twins, he could not think of urging their governess and godmother to leave Edgecombe. A fine way that would be to compensate the poor little creatures for the loss of their mother and his deficiencies as a father. With Hannah's help, he was beginning to make progress in that area, but without her he was not certain that would continue. Indeed, he feared the loss of Hannah from his household might make it harder for him to become the kind of father she wanted him to be.

Was that part of what had poisoned his father's relationship with him—the loss of his mother? That possibility brought Gavin the first stirrings of sympathy he had ever felt toward his distant, judgmental father.

But how could he deny Hannah the opportunity to have a home and family of her own? Lady Benedict's argument kept returning to reproach him for his selfishness. Now that he recognized her many fine qualities, how could he stand in the way of her being loved and cherished as she deserved? Besides, was his concern for the well-being of his children merely an excuse to keep the lady here so he could enjoy her company without risking his heart?

Gavin wished he could deny the accusation. Since that was not possible, he sought a diversion from it.

He had thought once he was allowed out of bed, he would be able to keep busy. Instead he found himself unaccountably restless. Even riding could not hold his interest for too long. After giving the matter some thought, he wondered if he might be missing a sense of purpose in his life. For years his cavalry duties had provided an urgent purpose. His vow to Molesworth had promised to fill that void. But with the war over and Bonaparte in custody, what was left for him to do?

Tend to his children, of course, he remembered with a pang of shame. Raising them would become his new mission. If he was not certain how to go about it, he would consult Hannah Fletcher for advice.

That prospect eased his restlessness and filled him with fresh energy. He set off at once for the nursery, where he found Hannah working with young Peter on his penmanship.

"Your hand is far better than mine at your age." Gavin looked over a practice sentence the child had written. "Better than it is now, I daresay."

His son seemed pleased by the compliment. "Perhaps you just need more practice, Papa. Would you like to join me? Miss Fletcher can show you how to form your letters properly."

He and Hannah exchanged a glance over the child's head, both of them struggling to suppress a grin. It was the least awkward interaction they'd had since their embrace. It gave Gavin hope that they might be able to recapture their earlier ease with one another.

"That is a tempting invitation." He gave his son a tentative pat on the shoulder and was rewarded with an approving smile from Hannah. "But I fear I might set you a bad example. Besides, my habits of bad penmanship may be too deeply ingrained for any amount of practice to correct."

How his father would have doted on young Peter, so grave, studious and neat-handed. Here was a boy who could be molded into a proper aristocrat, perhaps even a courtier—not a boisterous, outspoken lout who was only good for cannon fodder.

"Is there something the matter, sir?" Hannah's brow creased, and her eyes shadowed with concern for him.

Only that he feared becoming a good father would be harder than commanding a cavalry regiment. For instance, where would he find common ground with the son who was so much like his father and brother and so little like him?

He shook his head in response to her question. "I am quite well, thank you. I was only thinking since it is such a fine day I might pay a visit to Arthur and Alice. I wondered if the two of you would care to join me."

Peter jumped from his chair. "Can we, please, Miss Hannah?"

His son's pleading gaze made Gavin realize they might have one thing in common at least—their love for the babies. That was as good place to start as any, surely.

Hannah gave a rueful chuckle. "You have had such a long break from your studies the past few weeks, another hour or two can do no harm."

Peter gave a cheer. Perhaps the boy was not *always* so grave and quiet, Gavin reflected, only subdued by the loss of his doting mother and anxious around the father who was still rather a stranger.

"I know it isn't far." Peter addressed his governess, yet Gavin sensed a request coming that was meant for him. "But can we take the pony cart? I haven't ridden in it since Papa began to feel better."

The last thing Gavin wanted was for his young son to associate him with the loss of favorite amusements.

"You enjoy the pony cart, do you?" he asked and received a vigorous nod in reply. "Have you ever ridden on a pony's back?"

This time Peter shook his head and heaved a sigh. "Mama said I was not big enough. She said I might get thrown off and hurt."

"Not big enough?" Gavin scoffed. "Why, I was riding before I could—"

A pointed look from Hannah silenced him. Perhaps it was not a good idea to dismiss his late wife's concerns in front of their son. "That is…your mother may have wanted you to be properly taught to ride. She loved you a great deal and did not want to take any risks with your safety."

If Clarissa had lived, might the two of them finally have established a bond in their love of the children? He would never know.

"Could you teach me to ride, Papa?" This time his son addressed Gavin directly.

He smiled. "I reckon I could. And since it is only a short distance to the Millers' and the Wilkeses', this would be an excellent opportunity for your first lesson."

The child jumped up and down, clapping his hands, then cast a wary glance toward his governess as if afraid she might disapprove and forbid the riding lesson.

Gavin had more faith in her affection for his son.

Hannah did not disappoint him. "That sounds like a fine idea. You have grown a good deal in the past two months. I believe your mama would think you are big enough to learn to ride. And who better to teach you than your papa?"

Peter's face glowed with happiness. He threw his arms around his governess's waist and squeezed tight. "Thank you, Miss Hannah!"

She stiffened for a moment at the child's unbridled show of affection. Gavin wondered if it reminded her of *his* recent embrace.

She quickly recovered from her surprise and ruffled his son's hair. "Your father is the one you should thank. It was his idea, after all, and he will be teaching you."

The boy let go of her and approached Gavin with an air of uncertainty. "Thank you, Papa."

A covert nod from Hannah told Gavin he ought to stoop to his son's level, which he did. "You are quite welcome. I expect I shall have an easier task teaching you to ride than you had teaching me to fold paper."

Peter grinned as if he knew that was true but did not want to gloat. Though the boy made no move to embrace him, Gavin still felt he was making progress in learning to be the kind of father his son needed. A soft glow in Hannah's eyes told him she agreed.

"Shall I come along?" she asked. "Or would you gentlemen prefer to be on your own?"

"'Course you must come, Miss Hannah." Peter's tone suggested that the answer should be obvious. "The babies will want to see you."

"I agree, Miss Hannah." As Gavin rose, he savored the opportunity to address her by her Christian name, as his son did. "We need you with us."

He cast a silent plea for her assistance. He would feel more confident of his parenting efforts if she were there—like the boost it gave troops heading into battle to know there were reinforcements ready to come to their aid. Peter clasped hands with his governess, then held out his other hand to Gavin, who was happy to take it. Together they headed off to the stables, where Gavin ordered a small, gentle pony saddled.

The next several hours passed swiftly and enjoyably. Gavin was pleased to discover that although his son did not have his natural aptitude for riding, the child clearly loved horses and was eager to learn. Little Alice and Arthur had recently begun to laugh and engaged everyone with their infectious chortles and gurgles. Gavin wished he had more opportunity to chat with Hannah, but he was obliged to keep his attention fixed on Peter and the babies. In spite of that, he was aware of her presence and her warm approval of his efforts.

They returned to the house hungry for tea. Gavin wondered what Hannah would say if he asked to remain in the nursery and eat with her and Peter.

That thought fled his mind when the butler bustled toward them, holding out a letter. "For you, sir. From Lord Benedict, I believe."

Reluctantly Gavin let go of his son's hand, took the letter and broke the seal. As he scanned the viscount's spiky scrawl, he muttered the words under his breath.

"Are they coming back to visit again?" asked Peter. "Is that what it says?"

"I hope it is not bad news," said Hannah.

"Not…exactly." Gavin tried to make light of it so as not to worry his son. Yet coming on the heels of this very pleasant day, the news definitely cast a shadow. It reminded him of the price others had paid so he could enjoy a peaceful afternoon with his children. "But there is a matter with which Lord Benedict could use my help. I may have to go away for a little while."

His effort to sound casual could not have succeeded, for his son's expression grew anxious and Hannah's downright stormy.

"You're going back to the war, aren't you?" Peter demanded. "Mama was right. You do only care about fighting!"

"Hush now." Hannah dropped to her knees and wrapped her arms around the child. "We talked about this, remember? I'm certain your father will not go anywhere if you do not want him to."

How dare she make such a promise on his behalf? Gavin glared at her, and she glared back, even as she stroked his son's hair and murmured words of gentle reassurance. How could such a caring, nurturing woman have such a core of iron? The contrast puzzled Gavin until he recalled how gentle mother animals could turn positively vicious in defense of their young. Hannah Fletcher might not have borne his children but he sensed that no one would love them more or fight for them more fiercely than she.

"I am *not* going to war." He strove to sound certain but not harsh. "The war is over. I want to prevent another one from starting, so I will not be called away from Edgecombe again. I am only going up to London, and I should not be away for long."

Though Hannah continued to comfort his son, Gavin glimpsed a flash of fire in her eyes. He knew he would not be going anywhere if she could prevent him.

Chapter Thirteen

"How can you think of going away now?" Hannah tried to ignore the look of shock on the earl's face when she stormed into his bedchamber after only a cursory knock.

It was a grave breach of propriety for her to come here. But she'd grown so accustomed to it while he was bedridden that she scarcely gave the matter a thought. Besides, what she had to discuss with him was more important than propriety. "You heard your son—he is afraid you are going off to war again and may never return!"

Once she spit out the words that had been burning on her tongue ever since he'd received that cursed letter, Hannah realized they were not alone. The earl turned toward a young footman, who was folding garments into a traveling case. "Perhaps you can finish that later, Matthew."

Before Matthew could reply, his master reconsidered. "On second thought, keep on with your work. Miss Fletcher and I will talk in the drawing room instead."

"Very good, your lordship." The footman returned

to his task, but not before Hannah spied a glint in his eyes that suggested her confrontation with Lord Hawkehurst would soon be the subject of gossip below stairs.

As the earl stalked down the corridor with Hannah hurrying to keep up, he muttered, "Why did you have to make such a fuss about this and fret my son? I am only going to London for a few days…and perhaps to Plymouth."

"Why must you go anywhere at all?" It bewildered Hannah to find herself so vexed with the earl again after her feelings toward him had undergone such a dramatic change.

Earlier in the day she had watched him with his children, trying so hard to do what did not come naturally. Her heart had warmed toward him more than ever. Yet the moment he'd mentioned the possibility of going away, outrage had reared within her, fueled by a deep pain she did not understand.

"What did Lord Benedict say in his letter?" She found herself angry with the viscount, too. Why must he trouble a wounded soldier with news that could only distress him and perhaps set back his recovery?

The earl did not reply until they reached the drawing room. Then he rounded on her with hands clasped behind his back and his features clenched in an intimidating scowl. "Lord Benedict writes that the situation with Bonaparte is far from settled in the way we would wish. Some radicals argue that if a man is to be imprisoned he is first entitled to a full trial by jury. They want a judge to issue a writ of habeas corpus. If a writ is served, who knows how long a trial and appeals might drag on, with *the defendant* on British soil the whole time?"

He began to pace back and forth. "Sebastian is also troubled by reports from Torbay. Boatloads of gawkers are crowding around the *Bellerophon* while Bonaparte puts on a show of charm for them. He is a dangerous man, even without an empire or an army behind him. He has a nefarious ability to bend others to his will. Sebastian reports that Bonaparte has written to the Prince Regent as one brother monarch to another—of all the infernal impudence! He claims it was never his intention to surrender to the Allies, but only to seek asylum in Britain. So far his letters have been intercepted, but who knows what might happen if one reaches its destination? The prince is so capricious and easily influenced. I would not be surprised if he took pity on Bonaparte!"

The earl would never rest while the man responsible for so many British deaths remained free on British soil. Hannah had no doubt of that. And London was not such a long journey. Yet she could not escape the distressing certainty that if Gavin Romney left Edgecombe, he would never return.

"Surely the government would never permit such a thing," she argued. "Your place is here, and your first duty must be to your children. They have already lost their mother. What if some harm were to befall you?"

"In London?" He gave a rumble of derisive laughter. "Even my fusspot of a physician admits the journey there will do me no harm. Besides, the will of the government is only as strong as that of its members. So many representatives from both houses of Parliament have gone to the country for the summer. Sebastian says every possible voice is needed to press for Bonaparte's immediate transportation to Saint Helena."

Hannah was running out of reasonable arguments, which made her desperate. "Are you certain that is not simply an excuse to get away from Edgecombe and your children?"

"It is no such thing!" He flared up at her. "And I resent your accusation."

Hannah held her ground, though inwardly she winced. Was she deliberately trying to destroy any friendly feeling the earl might have for her? If so, she seemed to be succeeding…which pained her almost more than she could bear.

Abruptly the earl stopped pacing and inhaled a slow, deep breath. When he spoke again, his tone was not angry, but bewildered and concerned. "Why can you not see reason? Do you think so little of me that you believe I would abandon my children or put myself in harm's way when they need me?"

His dark eyes ached with misery. How many people who'd mattered to him had condemned him as a failure because he had not conformed to their expectations? Hannah could not stand to become another on that list. Yet how could she let him go without a fight when part of her was so deeply convinced he would never return?

"It is not that." Suddenly her knees felt too weak to sustain the weight of emotion pressing on her heart. She sank onto the nearby sofa.

"What is it, then?" The earl sat down beside her, angled toward her. "I promise you I will not be absent an hour longer than necessary. In the meantime, I know the children will be in safe hands with you to watch over them."

"My father promised that Sarah and I would only

have to stay a little while with our aunt after our mother died." The words spouted from her mouth, yet Hannah felt as if she were listening to someone else—someone she could not prevent from speaking. "Then, after our father died, Aunt Eliza promised we would only have to go away to school for a little while. Yet she would not take us back even when Sarah fell ill."

She should not be telling him these things! Hannah clamped her lips together to keep from saying anything more. Yet even as she chided herself for burdening the earl with her long-forgotten troubles, she could not deny the deep sense of relief and rightness it brought her to confide in him. For the first time, she realized what a painful impression those long-ago events had left on her. Was it possible they continued to influence her decisions and actions the way his lordship's past did to him?

"I see." His brief utterance was infused with a tender blend of understanding and consolation.

Out of the corner of her eye, Hannah saw him lean toward her. Did he mean to offer her the comfort of his arms? Much as she wished he would and much as she longed to accept, she knew it was too great a risk. What if she lost control of her tightly bound emotions? Her tongue had already run away with her. What might be next?

She flinched, as if from approaching danger, though it was her own feelings that alarmed her more than any possible action of his.

When she started, the earl drew back abruptly. He reached for her hand and clasped it as a friend might. "I am sorry you had to endure such difficulties, Hannah... Miss Hannah...Miss Fletcher. I hope you will not think ill of me for saying I understand what might have led your father to act as he did. The responsibility for two young daughters must have seemed daunting to him. He may have feared he could not look after you properly."

Might that be true? Hannah wished she could believe his explanation; it would be balm to her heart, which still ached from the memory. But it was not that easy.

She shook her head. "It was *my* fault. If I had done a better job keeping house and minding Sarah, Father would not have been obliged to send us away to Aunt Eliza. But the chore girl was such a lazy slattern and she would not listen to me. The dinner burnt night after night, then Sarah fell and got a great bump on her head."

There, she was doing it again!

Clearly the earl's nearness made it impossible to keep her guard up. Hannah forced her mouth shut and tried to rise from the sofa.

But he refused to release her hand. "How old were you then—nine…eight?"

"Six." The word slipped out in spite of her determination to hold her tongue.

"Six years old and trying to keep house?" His lordship's voice was husky with pity for the child she'd once been. "I do not wonder that your father sent you away for your own good, so you would not be burdened with such heavy responsibility for your young years."

Hannah tried to wrest her hand from the earl's grasp, but she could only manage a token effort. The steadfast strength of his touch was too comforting to resist.

But she could not meekly accept what he had said, even though she recognized a ring of truth in it. "I did not mind the responsibility. I would rather have done every scrap of housework myself than be sent away. I had to work at Aunt Eliza's house anyway and make myself useful so she would not begrudge our presence."

This sudden inability to maintain her guard frustrated Hannah. One tiny crack in the dam of her accustomed reserve was letting emotion gush out, enlarging the fissure as it burst forth. But that release eased the pressure she had long felt inside—pressure that had grown almost intolerable during the past few weeks.

She must stop talking about herself and her past. It would only make the earl defend her father, with whom he clearly sympathized. Perhaps he might even persuade her that neither she nor her father was to blame for what had happened. She needed someone to hold accountable, someone on whom to vent her long-buried anger. It was easier to blame herself than her father. But she could not bear to think of Peter or the twins growing up with that kind of burden in the years to come.

"I am not saying what your father did was the right thing." His lordship's mellow murmur grazed over the hurting places in her heart like a consoling caress. "I only meant I am certain he did not do it to punish you, but rather to protect you as best he could. He may have been mistaken, but I believe he acted out of love for you and your sister and tried to do what he thought was right."

Was the earl talking about her father, Hannah wondered, or was he seeking to defend his own choices, of which she disapproved? If she returned to their original subject, it might get him away from this one, which stirred up too many intense, painful memories.

"Even if what you say is true, I had no way of understanding at the time. What was I to think except that Father sent us away because my efforts had fallen short?" Hannah risked a brief, sidelong glance at the earl to find his rugged features set in a pensive look.

Clearly she had struck as tender a nerve with him as he had with her. In any event, he did not have a ready reply, which gave her the opportunity to emphasize her point.

"If you go away, I fear Peter will feel as I once did—that he is somehow to blame. And if any harm should come to you, what would become of him and the twins? Who would care for them without being tempted to enrich themselves upon the estate? My friend Marian Murray had two young pupils who were orphaned, and even their modest inheritance attracted an unscrupulous aunt. Fortunately, their cousin, Captain Radcliffe, adopted the girls and wed Marian to ensure they would be looked after when he was obliged to return to his ship."

That was the *reason* Marian and her captain had wed. But Hannah had read enough of her friend's letters praising the reserved but gallant captain to know Marian loved him dearly. The arrangement had benefitted Marian's beloved pupils, who had become her adopted daughters.

"That is the perfect solution!" The earl continued to clasp Hannah's hand as he slid off the sofa to kneel before her. "Say you will marry me, Miss Fletcher, and neither of us will need to fear for my children's future. If you agree, I shall fetch the special license back with me from London."

A marriage proposal from the earl? Hannah wondered if she had fallen asleep and dreamed this.

He sounded so eager—almost as if he wanted her because he cared for her, not simply as a convenient guardian for his children. But she knew his regrettable history of marrying for the wrong reasons. And she had seen how bitterly unhappy such a marriage could make a woman who was reckless enough to let herself care for him.

This was the perfect solution to so many of the difficulties that had been plaguing him, Gavin realized as he blurted out his proposal and waited for Hannah's answer. Why had he not thought of it sooner? Captain Radcliffe was clearly a clever fellow, as was Lord Benedict, to secure such admirable wives.

He would never be able to find a better mother for his children than the governess and godmother who was already so devoted to them. If he made Hannah his wife, then she would have no need to worry about ever leaving Edgecombe to find a husband and start a family of her own. Secure in the knowledge that she would have the authority to care for the children no matter what happened to him, she could stop fretting at the prospect of him stirring a step from home. And he would not have to worry about losing her from his life.

He had no illusions that she cared for him as he had come to care for her, but this would give him all the time he needed to win her affections. He would do what she had so wisely advised—keeping at it, trying harder and harder until he finally succeeded. He might not possess natural ability as a husband and father, but he'd made considerable progress at the latter. Surely he could do the same with the former if he put forth sufficient effort.

Not that it would be an *effort* to make Hannah feel she was cherished and valued. He could scarcely wait to begin!

All those thoughts rushed through Gavin's mind as he knelt waiting for Hannah to consider his proposal and realize what excellent sense it made for her and him and the children. But the expectant silence stretched on longer than it should if his offer had found favor with the lady.

Gavin searched her face for some sign of how she intended to respond. Her expression appeared rather vacant, as if she had received a piece of shocking news and could not decide what to make of it.

That was his fault, of course. He'd been so carried away by his sudden flash of inspiration that he had not stopped to consider how unexpected his proposal would be for her. But surely once she recovered from her surprise, the advantages of such an arrangement would become obvious to her.

"You need not answer right away," he ventured when he could bear the suspense no longer. "I expect you will want to take some time to think the matter over and reach a decision."

His words seemed to shake Hannah from her bemused silence.

"Not at all." She shot to her feet, pulling her hand from his grasp, which had gone slack. "I cannot marry you, Lord Hawkehurst, not even if I had a week or a month to consider your offer. I hope you did not think I was angling for a proposal just now when I mentioned my friend's marriage. Nothing could be further from the truth. I only meant to point out the vulnerable position in which you could place your children if you endanger your health by chasing off after Napoleon Bonaparte."

Her vehement, defensive refusal stung Gavin much more than he'd expected. Could she give him no hope at all—no opportunity to change her mind?

Had she considered all the advantages he could offer her—a substantial fortune and everything it could buy, a fine estate, servants, not to mention a position in society that would outrank even her friend, Lady Benedict?

Of course she had not considered any of those things, he realized with a flash of admiration, because they meant little or nothing to her. She only cared for those things that truly mattered—devotion, loyalty and faith. Perhaps a tiny scrap of pride, as well?

He could not begrudge her that because at the moment *his* pride hung in tatters. He had offered Hannah Fletcher everything he possessed only to have it hurled back in his face.

Gavin scrambled up from the floor. Such a pose of supplication did not suit him. "Of course I did not think you were angling for a proposal. If I had imagined you were, I should never have offered. It only occurred to me what an excellent arrangement it might be for all concerned. But if you disagree…"

"I do." Hannah thrust the words at him the way she might have brandished a weapon to ward off an attacker.

But he was not trying to do anything that might hurt her, quite the opposite in fact.

Hannah shook her head. "Can you imagine the gossip it would cause if you wed your son's governess when you should still be in mourning for his mother?"

She wrapped her arms protectively around herself and took a step back from him.

Gavin flinched from that low blow. "I did not realize you cared so much about what other people say."

He certainly did not. As long as he could face the tribunal of his own conscience, nothing others said had any power to trouble him. But Hannah's reference to mourning Clarissa did unsettle his conscience.

What did it say of him as a husband that he had proposed to another woman so soon after her death? He wasn't certain which was worse—that or the fact that he had seen nothing wrong with it until Hannah confronted him. She cared more about his late wife than he did. What could induce her to accept a man she must consider incapable of loving a wife or making her anything but miserable?

"I *do* care about others' opinion of me." Hannah took another backward step, putting more distance between them. "Is that so wrong? You refuse to care what anyone thinks of you so you will not be hurt by their disapproval. But in order not to care about their opinions, you cannot allow yourself to care about *them.* That is no way to live."

Her sharp insight touched a very sensitive place within him. It did more than *touch*—it flayed the spot raw then rubbed salt into the wound. How could he have deluded himself that it would be possible to win the heart of a woman so capable of hurting him? If he failed, as he feared he might, she could make his life a torment that would make his troubled marriage to Clarissa seem like a love feast by comparison. He should be grateful Hannah Fletcher had not only rejected him but revealed her true colors into the bargain.

"I would rather be indifferent to the opinions of others," he growled, "than be so desperate for their approval that I would debase myself, turn a blind eye to all their faults and never do anything I might enjoy for fear of losing their regard. If that is what you call love, I want no part of it!"

Her features twisted in a stricken look that pierced Gavin as painfully as that shot at Waterloo. Only this time it seemed to strike closer to his heart. How could he have said such things to Hannah after all she had done for him and his family? How much worse would it hurt if she had let herself care about him and his opinion? Though it proved his point, Gavin could not take the slightest crumb of satisfaction.

No wonder she had refused to wed him. Prudent as she was, Hannah would not want to run the risk of caring for a man who might only hurt her, as her father had done by sending her away. From watching his marriage to Clarissa, she would have seen how capable he was of making a wife unhappy. He wanted to tell her how sorry he was for what he'd said and to beg her forgiveness. But a stern voice from the darkest recesses of his heart insisted it might be better for her to despise him than give him more power to hurt her.

Hannah made a visible effort to marshal her composure and somehow succeeded. Gavin's admiration for her grew and with it his bitter regret that he had shown himself so unworthy of her regard. Part of him wished she would rage and abuse him severely enough to do the very thing of which she had accused him. If Hannah could destroy his feelings for her, then her rejection might not inflict so deep a wound.

But when she spoke, her voice conveyed more pity than anger. Even his pride could not resent her pity, for it was kin to affection, however distant. "Is that how you feel about your children, too? Are you afraid to become close to them in case they might turn against you the way you did against your father? Is that why you would rather pursue a course of vengeance against Bonaparte in spite of the hazards it might pose to your family?"

Gavin wanted to deny her accusations in the strongest possible terms, but he was not altogether certain they were untrue.

Hannah seemed to take his guilty silence as confirmation of what she had said. "Is that why you proposed to me—so you would be free to abandon your children with a clear conscience? If it is, then you must be very desperate indeed. Fortunately, I am not so desperate to secure *your* approval that I would be willing to assist you. Not for a fortune or a title or anything material you could offer me. There is a great deal I would do for you if you asked me, but I will not make it easy for you to desert your children."

He had no intention of deserting his children, but it was no use trying to persuade her of that when she was so determined to doubt him. Could there be any clearer sign that she had no regard for him and never would? Gavin tried to tell himself that was better for her and perhaps even for him. But it did nothing to ease the wretched ache in his chest.

"Please do not go." Her full lower lip began to quiver.

Gavin found himself overwhelmed with longing to still it with a kiss.

Perhaps Hannah sensed that, for she caught her trembling lip between her teeth and brought it under control without any assistance from him. "Leave Bonaparte's fate in the hands of God. Concern yourself with what will become of your children instead. I know you doubt your ability to be an ideal father, but an imperfect parent is better than none."

Her voice broke on that last word, and Gavin sensed her tightly bound composure would soon shatter, as well. Though reason and prudence warned against it, he could not deny the instinctive urge to comfort her. His feet seemed to move of their own accord, bearing him toward her. His arms rose, aching to enfold her.

But she refused to accept anything from him—even comfort. Before Gavin could reach her, she spun around, bolted through the door and fled. He had just enough sense—or perhaps cowardice—to keep from going after her.

Even if Napoleon Bonaparte's future had been settled entirely to his satisfaction, Gavin knew he would still want to get away from Edgecombe for a few days. He needed to distance himself from the volatile feelings between him and Hannah and decide how to proceed.

He feared he had made it impossible for the two of them to live under the same roof, going forward. And if one of them must go, he had no doubt which of them the children needed more.

Chapter Fourteen

Had she made a terrible mistake by turning down Gavin's proposal? Since the earl had asked her to marry him, Hannah supposed it must be permissible to think of him by his Christian name.

After fleeing the drawing room, she tossed and turned in her bed that night, tormented by second thoughts. Perhaps if he had worked up to the subject a bit more deliberately, rather than springing his proposal on her, she might not have refused so ungraciously. But she'd been so taken aback by the suddenness of it and he had already aroused her antagonism with his plan to go away to London.

At first she could only assume he had taken her mention of Marian Murray's situation as a broad hint that he ought to propose to her. It grieved Hannah that he could believe her capable of such disloyalty to his late wife. Yet her conscience reproached her for the feelings she had developed for him so soon after her ladyship's death.

Even his denial could not dispel the sickening shame that fueled her hostile reaction to his proposal. If he had given the slightest indication that his offer was motivated by any emotion more tender than desperation, her heart might have gotten the better of her reason. It might have led her to accept with as little thought for the consequences as he had shown by proposing to her in the first place. But he had made it clear that his only concern was for convenience. He wanted a reliable, capable woman to bring up his children while he went chasing off after Bonaparte or whatever other excuse he might use in the future to abandon his family.

If she did not care for him, and could be quite certain she never would, then Hannah might have been able to give him the answer he claimed to want. But how could she consign herself to a marriage like the one that had destroyed the happiness of his late wife? She had seen what it did to a couple when one loved but the other could not or would not return the feeling.

Despite his accusation that she martyred herself in a pathetic effort to secure approval and affection, Hannah could not reconcile herself to a future of such unhappiness. Nor could she stand to become another reason he might use to avoid spending time at Edgecombe, as if he needed any more.

What was that sound? In the dark silence of the sleeping house, Hannah thought she heard something. She sat up in bed and strained to catch it again. Were her ears playing tricks to distract her from her turbulent thoughts?

Perhaps she ought to check on Peter, just to be certain. At least it would give her something to do besides lie there with her mind going in a dozen disturbing directions at once. Anxious not to make any noise that might disturb other light sleepers in the house, Hannah rose, pulled on her dressing gown and lit a candle. By its flickering flame she crept out into the wide corridor and padded off toward the nursery. The closer she approached, the clearer she could hear an urgent whisper of voices.

Easing open the nursery door, she peeped in and called softly, "Is anything the matter?"

"We didn't mean to disturb you, miss," replied the nursemaid, who perched on the edge of Peter's bed. "The young master woke from a bad dream and I haven't been able to settle him."

The girl gave a weary yawn. "He's been asking for you. Perhaps you might have more luck getting him back to sleep."

Hannah felt tired, too, but it wasn't anyone else keeping her awake. "Go back to bed, Maisie. I shall see what I can do."

Taking the nursemaid's place at her young pupil's bedside, Hannah snuffed the candle and reached out until her hand encountered the child's silky hair. She gave it an affectionate ruffle. "Now, what is all this fuss about a dream that you had to wake poor Maisie?"

Peter gave a moist sniff that tugged at Hannah's heart. How often, when she and Sarah were children, had she held and comforted her sister in the night?

"I dreamed you were going away, just like Mama and Papa. I didn't want you to, but you said you m-must!"

"It was only a dream." Hannah's brisk governess manner melted as she gathered the sniffling child into her arms. "I am right here and not going anywhere, so you mustn't fret."

Was that true? her conscience demanded. Would Gavin Romney continue to employ her after the ungracious manner in which she'd refused him and the impertinent remarks she'd made about his character and conduct? He had given as good as he got in that regard, but he was the master of the house while she was little better than a servant. He would be perfectly within his rights to dismiss her. Even if he did not, there was still her lurking fear that he might come to harm and his children's guardians would hire someone to take her place.

"Shh." She held the child in her arms, pressing her cheek against his hair. The prospect of being parted from Peter alarmed her even more than the dream had frightened him. While his fears were only a fancy of his sleeping mind, hers might be all too real. "Try to go back to sleep, and you might have a more pleasant dream next time, perhaps one about riding horses with your father."

"We will *only* go riding in my dreams," Peter replied in a plaintive murmur, "now that Papa is going away again."

"He says he will not be gone long." Hannah held the child close, determined that no one would take her from him. "The two of you can go riding again when he returns."

"You said Papa would not go away if I did not want him to. But he is going anyway. How do you know he will come back?"

How indeed? Hannah wondered. But she could not upset the child further by sharing her doubts with him. "I should not have been so quick to speak for your father. He told you the truth when he said he was obliged to go to London. We must trust that he meant it when he said he would only be gone a short while."

Could *she* trust Gavin to keep his word? Her feelings for him insisted that he was a man of honor and truth who did not go back on his promises. But experience had taught her that those she cared for could not always be trusted to keep their word. Especially when it came to staying or leaving. Was that why she'd felt so certain Gavin would never return to Edgecombe—not because *he* had given her any cause to doubt him but because she was incapable of trusting those she most cared for?

"I suppose we must give Papa a chance." The child sounded wary, as if he sensed that giving his father that opportunity would leave him vulnerable to disappointment.

"You are very wise for your years," Hannah said as she eased him down onto his pillow.

Thinking back on Gavin's proposal, she wondered if she had been hasty and selfish in her response. There was far more at stake here than her personal happiness. She had the children to consider. How would it affect them if she were to leave Edgecombe? Peter's nightmare would come true. And who could tell what it might do to the little ones to lose a close attachment at such an early age?

If their father was resolved to provide them with a governess for a mother, he surely would, for he was a vastly determined man. The next governess he hired then offered to marry might not think twice about securing such an advantageous match, even without love.

But could a person like that be trusted to place the needs of the children above every other consideration?

Who was she to judge anyone else? Hannah's conscience demanded. Had *she* considered the children's needs when she'd hurled Gavin's marriage proposal back in his face? Her heart had been full of fear for her own happiness. But how could she ever be truly happy if she was separated from the children? If she must be unhappy either way, should she not choose the path that promised the happiest future for three little people she cared for very much? Besides, if Gavin did as she feared and abandoned his children to her care, his absence might cause her less misery than if they continued to live under the same roof while she cherished feelings for him that he could not return.

With a decision made out of reason and love rather than fear and selfishness, the knot of tension inside Hannah began to ease. The repetitive stroking of Peter's hair and the slowing of his breathing helped, too. Her thoughts settled into deeper channels, and she soon caught herself nodding off. Certain the child had fallen back to sleep, Hannah left her snuffed candle and groped her way back to her own room.

First thing in the morning she would go to the earl and beg his pardon for the things she had said in the surprise of the moment. Perhaps he would have reconsidered his mad notion to marry her by then, but she hoped an abject apology might prevent him from dismissing her.

She fell asleep to the rhythmic ticking of her small mantel clock and woke to it again some hours later.

"Past nine? Oh, dear me!" Hannah bolted from her bed and dressed with excessive haste.

She flew down to the breakfast room to find it empty of all but a faint aroma of coffee.

"Jane," she called to the head parlor maid as she bustled by. "How long ago did Lord Hawkehurst take his breakfast?"

"Ages, miss," Jane replied. "Must have been all of two hours. I overheard his lordship say he wanted to get on the road to London before the sun rose too high."

"A wise decision." Hannah tried not to let her distress show. It would not do to add fuel to any gossip about her and the earl. "What I had to say to him will keep until he returns."

When might that be? she wondered as she headed back to the nursery, prepared to comfort Peter if he was upset by his father's departure. Would she have the opportunity to apologize to Gavin? Would she ever get the chance to speak to him again?

Could he stand to face Hannah Fletcher again after the fool he'd made of himself and the insulting things he'd said to her? Each mile his coach traveled away from Edgecombe, Gavin's sense of relief grew while his spirits sank.

Being cooped up alone in the carriage box for hours on end was almost as bad as being bedridden for a fortnight. There was nothing to distract him from his nagging regrets as Hannah had done so well during his convalescence.

What had made him suppose she would countenance a marriage proposal so soon after his wife's death? He should have waited at least until he returned from London. That would have proved he had no intention of abandoning his children…or her. It would have given her no reason to assume he only wanted to wed her so he could desert the children in future.

A deliberate, prudent man would have waited, but he was neither of those things. He was a man of action and impulse, always speaking and doing first, leaving the thinking until later. He had seen an opportunity to keep Hannah at Edgecombe long enough to win her heart and he had seized it.

His father, a prudent, deliberate man if ever there was one, would have reproached him for his impulsiveness. But Hannah might have looked at the positive side, calling him spontaneous and decisive. Would she ever recognize his positive qualities after this? Or had he demonstrated how few of those he possessed, especially qualities that might make him a tolerable husband?

After their disastrous interview, he'd hardly slept a wink. Now fatigue propeled his thoughts along darker paths, spiraling downward. What if his abrupt, clumsy proposal made Hannah too uncomfortable to remain at Edgecombe? What if it provoked her to accept Lady Benedict's invitation and leave his household altogether?

Much as he had come to care for his children, Gavin knew they needed her far more than they needed him. He'd begun to believe that, with her support and guidance, he could become the kind of father Peter and the little ones needed. Without her he had little confidence—only crippling doubts.

By the time his coach neared London, Gavin had become convinced he'd failed his children, just as he had failed their grandfather and their mother. Perhaps this was Providence's way of saying he ought to concentrate on making use of his natural gifts rather than trying so hard to do something at which he might never succeed.

"When we reach the city, take me to Berkeley Square," he ordered his coachman during their final stop for fresh horses. "Number forty-three, the home of Lord Benedict."

He wanted to let Sebastian know he had come to town to offer whatever assistance he could in keeping Bonaparte off British soil. He would support any effort to have the man detained somewhere secure until he no longer posed a threat to peace in Europe.

As it turned out, the viscount had still not returned home when Gavin arrived, but Lady Benedict made him heartily welcome. "Have you a place to stay in London, Lord Hawkehurst?"

Gavin shook his head. "The family used to have a townhouse, but it was so seldom used while I was away at war, I sold the leasehold. I mean to stay at the Cavalry Officers' Club if your husband wishes to reach me."

"That will not do at all," the lady insisted, in a manner that reminded Gavin of her friend Hannah. "You must stay with us. That way I can make certain you rest and eat properly and do not fall ill again."

When he tried to protest that he did not wish to inconvenience them, Lady Benedict refused to listen. "It is the least we can do after my husband summoned you to town when you are barely recovered from your wounds and still in mourning. Hannah would never forgive me if I let any harm come to you while you are here."

"I expect she would blame me more than you." Gavin avoided Lady Benedict's discerning gaze, fearful that she might glimpse more than he cared to reveal. "But if you are determined to make me your guest, I must accept your kind hospitality with my thanks."

"Excellent!" Her ladyship rang for a servant and ordered rooms made ready for Gavin, his coachman and footman. While she was at it, she ordered food and tea for him, as well. "This will be a welcome opportunity to repay a little of the kindness you showed us during our stay in Kent. Forgive me for saying so, but you look rather more tired and unwell than you did then. I hope our visit did not overtax your strength."

"No indeed," Gavin assured her. "I felt quite well while you were at Edgecombe, but the long carriage ride has tired me more than I expected."

"Men." Lady Benedict gave an indulgent chuckle. "I have yet to meet one who did not underestimate any obstacles to his particular plans or exaggerate them for a task he was reluctant to undertake."

Gavin could not deny her observation. Its critical edge was tempered with humor. "Is that fault entirely confined to men, do you suppose?"

Her chuckle blossomed into a peal of hearty laughter. "I believe you have me there, sir."

"What is all this frivolity?" Lord Benedict demanded in a tone of mock severity as he strode into the room. "There are momentous events afoot these days, you know."

When Gavin tried to rise to greet him, Sebastian waved for him to remain seated as he extended his hand.

"All the more reason we need a little laughter to lighten the gravity," Lady Benedict observed with a fond smile at her husband.

The way they looked at one another, Gavin suspected his host and hostess would have exchanged a kiss if he had not been present. Once again he felt a pang, not of envy but of longing for a happy marriage like theirs, where each loved the other equally. Had he *underestimated* the obstacles to a union with Hannah Fletcher or had she *exaggerated* them?

"How did your discussions go today?" Lady Benedict asked her husband. "Has General Bonaparte's future been settled yet?"

Sebastian sank onto the sofa beside her with a frustrated sigh. "There are some who recall the civilities he showed them years ago in Paris. They claim the government has no right to imprison any man without a trial, particularly if he did not intend to surrender to Captain Maitland, as he now claims."

"There can be no question the man has a dangerous degree of charm," said Gavin, "if it continues to work for him after all these years."

Sebastian nodded grimly. "That is the other problem. If he is packed off to the South Atlantic, who can be trusted to oversee his exile while remaining impervious to that charm? I fear Bonaparte will turn the full power of it upon his custodian until the poor fellow lets his guard down at an inopportune moment."

Gavin wished Hannah could understand the perilous nature of the situation as the viscount clearly did.

Then perhaps she would not imagine he was using it as an excuse to abandon his children.

"That is why I am so delighted to have your support," Sebastian continued. "The men who argue for Bonaparte's rights have never seen the carnage he wrought. Perhaps you can make them understand the danger he could still pose."

"I shall endeavor to assist you in any way I can," Gavin replied, though he could not dispel a host of doubts about his ability. He had no great powers of persuasion he could call on. As an officer and a peer of the realm, he was accustomed to giving orders, not arguing or cajoling.

At that moment, servants appeared bearing refreshments.

"I told Lord Hawkehurst he must stay with us," Lady Benedict informed her husband as she poured tea for the gentlemen. "He has been most obliging to accept my invitation."

"Well done, my dear." Sebastian exchanged a doting smile with her as he took the cup she offered him. "Already you are proving invaluable to me in my work."

Gavin and Sebastian discussed their strategy further until Lady Benedict insisted their guest must retire to rest from his journey. Gavin was grateful to get to bed for he felt weary and ached after the long drive. Perhaps Hannah had not been foolish to fret about his health after all.

Thoughts of her hovered in his mind as he drifted toward sleep. Was there any way in the world he might persuade her to stay on at Edgecombe now that he had put her on her guard with his ill-considered proposal?

He feared she would never be willing to remain there while he was in residence. What option did that leave him?

The next day Gavin and Sebastian ventured forth to Whitehall to speak with anyone in the cabinet who might give them a hearing.

"Does it matter what the Whigs have to say about the disposition of Bonaparte?" Gavin knew his father would have gloried in this sort of political activity. He felt out of his depth and rather sullied by the whole process. "The Tories are the party in power."

"True." Sebastian shrugged. "But several of the cabinet ministers are married into Whig families—the Lennoxes, the Burkes, the Leveson-Gowers. Who knows what they may be hearing on the subject around their dinner tables?"

"Lord Bathurst is my best ally," he continued. "We worked together to support Wellington during the Peninsular War. As Secretary of War and the Colonies he will have more influence in this matter than anyone but the Foreign Secretary, who has gone to France."

With some difficulty, they secured an audience with Lord Bathurst, who looked rather harried. "Lord Hawkehurst, an honor. I was well acquainted with your late father."

"I hope you will not hold that against me." The words burst from Gavin's mouth before he could prevent them.

Fortunately the other two gentlemen laughed in a way that suggested they had not enjoyed the most congenial relationships with their fathers either.

"There are some who favor imprisoning Bonaparte

in Dumbarton Castle," Lord Bathurst explained, "like General Simon, who also broke his parole."

Sebastian shook his head. "That would play into the hands of those who wish to see him stand trial."

The Colonial Secretary did not argue that point. "Others propose Fort Valetta on the island of Malta."

"Too near France," Sebastian objected. "Having Bonaparte there would invite no end of schemes to liberate him."

"What about Saint Helena?" asked Gavin. "I have heard it mentioned as a possible place of confinement, and I believe a better situation could not be found. It is remote, difficult to escape and easily defended."

"True enough," Lord Bathurst acknowledged. "But there is one difficulty, and it is not inconsiderable."

"What?" Gavin and Sebastian demanded in chorus.

"As a port of supply for Orient-bound ships, Saint Helena is under direct control of the East India Company, which has always been most jealous of its prerogatives."

Though inexperienced in politics, Gavin knew Lord Bathurst spoke the truth. As the uncrowned, unelected ruler of much of the Orient, with revenues that would have ransomed a hundred kings, the East India Company answered to almost no one. What other commercial enterprise held a seat in the British Cabinet?

"In that case," he declared, "we must appeal directly to the president of the Board of Control."

"Be my guest." The Colonial Secretary did not look as if he fancied their chances of getting anywhere. "Perhaps Lord Buckinghamshire will pay more heed to you than he has to me."

Gavin and Sebastian had even more difficulty getting in to see that gentleman than they had with Lord Bathurst. But at last he consented to give them a brief audience.

"Gentlemen." Lord Buckinghamshire looked them over with the air of a man who had better things to do with his time. "How may I assist you?"

Since he seemed in a hurry, Gavin did not beat about the bush. "You may oblige Britain and all of Europe by giving over control of Saint Helena to His Majesty's government as a place of exile for Napoleon Bonaparte."

"Not that again." His lordship's expression hardened. "It is quite out of the question. The island is a vital port of resupply on the route to the Indies. Need I remind you of the fortune brought into this country by the East India trade? Where do you suppose the money came from to finance the war against Bonaparte in the first place? There are other locations he might be kept that will not inconvenience the company."

"None as remote and secure." Gavin could feel his temper rising. He was so far out of his element, cooling his heels outside stuffy offices in Whitehall and trying to talk sense to men who cared more about safeguarding their privileges than about peace. "Surely the company can abide a little inconvenience to prevent another war."

"There is always a war going on somewhere." His lordship picked up a document from his writing table and began to read it—no doubt a signal that he considered their interview over. "Commerce continues and even thrives on conflict. I advocate letting Bonaparte go to America, where he can pay his own expenses rather than living off British hospitality. Now if you will excuse me, I have urgent business to which I must attend."

The curt dismissal lit a fuse to Gavin's temper. He leaped from his chair, strode to the table and snatched the paper out of his lordship's hand. "What could possibly be more urgent than preventing another Waterloo? Have you no heart, sir, or no conscience?"

Lord Buckinghamshire shrank from Gavin and called for a guard, but Sebastian dragged him away before anyone came.

"At least you managed to get the man's attention," the viscount muttered in a rueful tone after Gavin had calmed down and tried to apologize for his behavior. "It is my fault. I should never have summoned you to town while you are still recovering your health and the battle is still so fresh in your mind. There is a reason good soldiers seldom make good politicians."

Gavin could imagine his father pointing out all the things he'd done wrong. What had made him think he could do anything but a great deal of damage by interfering in an area about which he knew so little?

"Perhaps it would be better if you return to Edgecombe and complete your recovery," Sebastian concluded. "Your children need you far more than I do."

Did they? Gavin wondered as he prepared to leave the Benedicts'. He was not naturally disposed to fatherhood any more than he was to diplomacy. Sooner or later he was bound to make mistakes for which *they* would pay the price. Perhaps he had already with his ill-considered proposal to Hannah Fletcher. The children might fare better without him, just as Sebastian would.

Deeply entrenched beliefs argued in favor of that, but

a soft voice of newborn confidence insisted otherwise. It reminded him that the children might blame themselves if he left. It reassured him that choices and effort mattered more than natural ability. Surely the things he cared most about deserved his best effort—not once, but repeatedly until he got them right.

With that in mind he set out to the home of Lord Buckinghamshire. The gentleman had not yet returned for dinner, but his wife expected him at any moment and invited Gavin to wait.

"What in blazes are you doing here?" his lordship demanded when he caught sight of Gavin in his sitting room.

"Oh, don't fuss, Robert." The countess gently chided her husband in a way that reminded Gavin of Hannah, as so many things did. "The young man only came to beg your pardon, and I believe you ought to hear him out. Goodness knows, *you* have made more than one unfortunate remark in the heat of the moment."

Right before Gavin's eyes, the formidable politician transformed into a biddable husband. "Just as you say, my dear. Go on then, Hawkehurst, what do you have to say for yourself?"

What did he have to say that would not make a bad situation worse? Gavin wondered. Attacking his lordship and questioning his motives had done no good. It was no use trying to be subtle and diplomatic, for he was neither. He was a blunt but truthful man burdened with the consciousness of too many failures and the fear of committing more.

"I was wrong to speak to you as I did, sir. The truth is I was angrier at myself than you. And I did not want you to live with the regrets I will carry for the rest of my days."

Lord Buckinghamshire looked surprised by that admission. "What sort of regrets?"

"That I did not do everything in my power to prevent Bonaparte from returning to make war a second time," Gavin replied. "Last year when it seemed peace had been secured and the Allies permitted Bonaparte to retire to Elba, I doubted he would be content to remain there. Yet I did nothing to persuade anyone to place him under more secure confinement. I had excuses for my inaction, but they all seem hollow now. I should have come to London and pestered every minister who would give me a hearing. I should have gone to Vienna and made a nuisance of myself at the Peace Conference. If I had, perhaps…"

He paused to gather his composure, which threatened to desert him.

"Perhaps…" Lady Buckinghamshire prompted in a sympathetic tone.

"Perhaps I would not feel that some of the bloodshed at Waterloo is on my hands. Perhaps I would not feel responsible for the death of my dearest friend. Today with Lord Benedict, I may have gone about it all wrong and it may have done no good. But at least this way if Britain must fight Bonaparte a third time, I will know I did everything in my power to prevent it."

The deep scowl with which Lord Buckinghamshire greeted his appeal told Gavin he had only made the situation worse.

Strangely, that knowledge did not crush him. At Waterloo, he had tried his best to save his friend and just now he had tried equally hard to honor his vow. Something told him Molesworth would not condemn him for having fallen short. Nor would Hannah Fletcher.

Before Lord Buckinghamshire had a chance to blast him again, Gavin bobbed a respectful bow. "That is all I came to say, sir. I hope you will think on it and pardon me for trespassing upon your privacy."

With that he strode away and returned to the Benedicts' townhouse, where he found Sebastian in the entry hall conferring with his butler.

"May I impose upon your hospitality for one more night?" Gavin asked. There were matters he needed to consider carefully and decisions he needed to make. Another chat with Lady Benedict might go a long way toward bringing him clarity.

"You are welcome to stay with us as long as you wish." Sebastian glanced over his shoulder. "But I must tell you—"

Before he could get the words out, the sitting room door swung open and Peter appeared. "I thought I heard your voice, Papa. Miss Hannah and I came up to town for a visit. We didn't know you were staying here. Are you surprised to see us?"

Surprised? As Hannah and Lady Benedict appeared behind his son, Gavin felt as if all the muscles in his face had fallen slack. Peter and his governess were the last people he had expected to see in London. But more confounding than the shock of their sudden appearance was the questions it raised.

What did Hannah mean by bringing his son to town? Had she changed her mind about his proposal? Or did she intend to haul him home by the ear, like a runaway schoolboy? Perhaps she did not intend to return to Edgecombe at all, but had come to seek sanctuary with the Benedicts until Rebecca could find her a husband.

If his abrupt, ungallant proposal had forced her to leave Edgecombe, it would be a failure for which he might never be able to forgive himself.

Chapter Fifteen

Coming to London had been a fool's errand. The dumbstruck look on Gavin's face when he saw her and Peter left Hannah in no doubt of that.

The biggest risk she'd ever taken appeared likely to be her worst disaster. Having experienced the bitterness of failure, she should not have been so quick to condemn Gavin for his fear of it. Part of her wished she could return to the moment of her decision and make a safer choice.

With obvious effort, Gavin mastered his voice to answer his son's question. "I am very surprised to see you in London. I hope you had a pleasant journey."

Clearly, he wanted to know why she had come here and brought his son. Hannah feared a hostile confrontation like the ones they'd had after his return from Waterloo and more recently when she had refused his proposal. What could she tell him? She scarcely recalled the reasons she'd given herself. Whatever they'd been, she now realized they were only excuses to see him again.

In reply to his father's question, Peter gave a vigorous nod. "The road was bumpy in places, but there were lots of things to see. When I grow up I will come to London as often as I can. But I will ride my own horse—a big strong one."

Rebecca strode forward and offered the child her hand. "I expect your long drive will have given you an appetite. Shall we visit the kitchen and ask Cook to make us some tea and sandwiches?"

Hannah knew her friend well enough to recognize an effort to give Gavin and her a few moments to talk in private. Though she dreaded it, she knew that postponing the confrontation would not make it any easier.

"Why don't you come with us, Sebastian?" Rebecca beckoned her husband.

"What about Papa and Miss Hannah?" asked Peter as he took Rebecca's hand.

"It might be better if they wait up here for us." Rebecca led the child toward the servants' stairs. "Cook gets cross if her kitchen is too crowded."

As Peter and the Benedicts disappeared below stairs, Hannah heard her friend laugh merrily at some remark of the child's. The butler had gone upstairs, perhaps to have rooms prepared for the unexpected guests. Gavin and Hannah stood in awkward silence for a moment. She considered suggesting they retire to the sitting room but decided it would be presumptuous of her as the most recently arrived guest. Instead she turned and headed back into the room, leaving the earl to follow or not as he wished.

The sound of his firm, quiet tread behind her sent her heart into a skittish jig. Hannah reminded herself not to let hurt or anger make her say things she would regret; rather, she must trust the Lord to show her the way.

"You did not need to drag my son all the way to London," Gavin said as he closed the door behind them. "I was going home tomorrow anyway."

The consciousness of her folly slammed Hannah hard. She should have waited patiently and faithfully for his return. That might have shown Gavin that she did not mean any of the hurtful things she'd said during their last encounter. Instead her actions proved she did not trust him to keep his word or do the right thing for his family. He would think she judged him as harshly as his father had.

She spun around to face him. "Then you have succeeded in your mission?"

She should have known he would and believed he would return to Edgecombe afterward just as he had promised. Hard as Hannah chided herself, she could not quench a stubborn ember of hope. If the situation with Bonaparte was resolved to his satisfaction, Gavin could come home to Edgecombe and his children. Freed from the burden of guilt, he could begin life anew, like a penitent who had embraced salvation.

Before that ember could catch, Gavin doused it with a resigned, regretful shake of his head. "I'm afraid not. My father was right—I have no skill in politics or diplomacy. I should have left that part of the fight to men like Sebastian who are better equipped to wage it."

An overwhelming need to bolster his confidence propelled Hannah toward him, only to be stopped by the consciousness that she had forfeited any right to draw close to him. "I am sorry. It was a worthy undertaking, and I should never have suggested otherwise. You must not reproach yourself. No one could have cared more or tried harder. I am certain Major Molesworth would be satisfied of that."

To her surprise, Gavin replied, "I believe he would. I am not certain I will ever be entirely free of the guilt I feel over his death, but nothing anyone can do to Bonaparte will bring back a single one of my fallen comrades. If I let my pursuit of him divert me from my children, it would be a victory I refuse to grant him."

His rueful admission made Hannah's throat tighten. Would he ever have come to that conclusion if she had forced him to stay at Edgecombe? Or might part of him have blamed his family responsibilities for preventing him from discharging this final duty?

"I did not come here because I doubted *you.*" Hannah forced herself to seek and hold his gaze. Though it risked betraying her feelings for him, she was determined to persuade Gavin of her sincerity. "I came because I was afraid I might have driven you away from Edgecombe and your children with my unkindness. I should never have said what I did. I should have believed you when you promised to return, only…"

She stopped herself from making any excuses for her behavior. "I understand if you would rather I not stay at Edgecombe. The children need their father far more than any governess, no matter how capable."

It was not easy to say those words. Her throat grew tighter with each one as she thought of parting from Peter and the dear babies. Everything she had worked and schemed to accomplish—nursing Gavin back to health, forcing him to spend time with his children—

had all served a selfish purpose, to keep them with her at any cost. Now she realized that, hard as it would be to lose them, *their* well-being and future happiness mattered far more.

If she expected some sign of relief from Gavin that she was making it easier for him to do what he must, Hannah was disappointed.

His face fell, just the way his little son's did when some calamity occurred. "Do not leave us, I beg you!"

He reached out and grasped her hand. Prudence warned Hannah to pull away, but she could not. Besides, all her attention was concentrated on his words, which were quite the opposite of what she'd expected to hear.

"I know it is selfish of me to stand in the way of you finding a husband and starting a family of your own, but I am only asking for a little time, for the children's sake. With your help, I believe I can be good father to them. But on my own…"

"Of course you can be a good father, with or without my help!" The words burst out of her with fierce conviction. "You *are* a good father. If I have said or done anything to suggest otherwise, I was wrong. If you and the children need me, of course I will stay. I only offered to go because I thought you must still be angry with me. And I was afraid you would find it too awkward having me in your household after…after…"

Hannah could not bring herself to say that he had made her an offer of marriage. It would sound too preposterous. Had she misunderstood him, perhaps, or only imagined it? Besides, if she spoke those words, Hannah feared her voice would betray her regret that she had not been able to give him a different answer.

"After I made a fool of myself," Gavin growled.

Hannah sensed he was not angry with her but with himself. Once again, he was his own severest critic, as he had been trained from an early age.

The impulse to defend him from that harsh inner taskmaster overran all the barriers she'd erected around her heart to protect it. "You did nothing of the kind. Once I recovered from my surprise and had an opportunity to reflect on what you'd said, I realized it was quite heroic of you to be willing to take such measures for the sake of your children. I should have known it was a sign of how much you care for them, to sacrifice your chance of future happiness with a wife you could love."

Gavin tried to interrupt at that point, but Hannah refused to let him get a word in. If she stopped now, she was afraid she might never find the courage to continue. "I should have been honored and touched that you would think me worthy to be a mother to those dear children. You have *nothing* to reproach yourself for. I only wish I could say the same for myself."

She was forced to pause then for she had no more breath to continue. Like the trained warrior he was, Gavin did not hesitate to seize the initiative.

"Heroic?" he scoffed. "Sacrifice? I cannot let you think so much better of me than I deserve. The truth is, I took advantage of a noble excuse to do something I wanted to for purely selfish reasons. When you mentioned the captain who married your friend, I thought what a clever, fortunate man he was. I thought if I could persuade you to marry me for the children's sake, it would give me all the time I needed to…win…your heart—as you have won mine."

It was too plain and honest a declaration of his feelings for Hannah to misunderstand. Part of her wanted so desperately to believe it, even as old dark doubts insisted it could not be true. She had done nothing to win or keep Gavin Romney's regard because she'd never thought she would *want* it. Instead she had misjudged him and browbeat him, defied and doubted him. How could he possibly care for her after all that?

And if he did, against all odds, how could she accept what the countess had longed for in vain?

Could he not succeed at anything? Gavin reproached himself as Hannah's blue-gray eyes filled with tears. Her free hand rose to her lips in an abortive effort to contain the sobs that burst from her lips in response to his bald, clumsy declaration. He had been on the brink of salvaging his earlier mistake and securing Hannah's presence at Edgecombe for a while at least. Then he'd sabotaged his efforts by blurting out his unwelcome feelings.

"Forgive me!" He groped in his pocket and produced a handkerchief, which he offered her in a gesture of remorse. "I know it is far too soon to be proper, and you had such a poor opinion of me for so long. I do not want to burden you with obligations or expectations. But I am no good at concealing my feelings or pretending they are anything different."

Hannah was weeping too hard to speak, but she shook her head. Was she trying to tell him to stop because the subject was so distressing?

Just when his sense of failure threatened to overwhelm him, Gavin remembered the only other time he had witnessed Hannah give way to tears. When she had been distressed, telling him about that abominable school, her sister's death and her father sending her away, she had somehow managed to keep her composure. Only in a moment of intense happiness, when she'd been reunited with her dear friend after a separation of many years, had her restraint given way to open weeping. Was it too much to hope that the tears she was shedding now might be a sign of happiness rather than anguish?

"Come sit down." He helped her toward the sofa. "We can talk more when you are calmer."

Her tears had already begun to ease. When they sank onto the sofa, she did not protest his nearness. That emboldened Gavin to slip his arm around her shoulders. Hannah did not object to that either.

"I c-cannot think what c-came over me," she said at last. "I have soaked your poor handkerchief, and I must look a fright."

"Not to me," Gavin replied, his own voice husky with unaccustomed emotion. "Would I be presuming too much to hope you might return my feelings someday?"

For an instant, a look of fear came over Hannah. But she seemed to wage a quiet battle within herself and emerge victorious. "Not at all. It is I who should not presume that a man like you could care anything for me. Especially after the rude way I refused you and the terrible things I said. It is a wonder you want anything to do with me after that."

She looked away as if ashamed. Gavin could not allow that, for there was something he must tell her, and he needed her complete attention.

With the sort of gentle touch he might have used to caress the babies, he brought the knuckle of his forefinger to rest beneath her chin and nudged her to look directly at him. "You do not need to be perfect for the right person to love you. They will always see the best in you, regardless. Like that bit of the Bible you quoted to me, about sheep going astray."

For a moment he thought Hannah might cry again, but she collected her composure. "Do you still believe all those things you said about the Lord setting impossible standards and judging our failures?"

Gavin shook his head with a rueful grin. "I'm not certain I did even then. Getting to know my children, learning to be a proper father, has made me better able to understand the kind of love that can forgive anything and never fail."

Now it was his turn to fight down a lump in his throat. Suddenly the idea of joyful tears was not nearly so mystifying.

Hannah took advantage of his silence to speak. "If I did not care for you, I would have accepted your proposal without a qualm for the sake of the children. But I was afraid, selfishly afraid, that I would become another unhappy countess, wanting more from you than you could give me."

On the verge of the greatest happiness he could imagine, Gavin had never been more conscious of his unworthiness. "Poor Clarissa. I wish I could have made her happy. Perhaps if I'd tried harder…"

Hannah shook her head. "There are some things that all the effort in the world cannot change. I see that now. The past is one of those things. I have carried mine with me for far too long, like a heavy work basket. I put so much energy into guilt and regret, yet they could not change a single moment of my past. All they did was spoil the present and threaten my future."

Her advice made excellent sense to Gavin, especially since he knew what it had cost her to learn those hard lessons.

"If God can forgive us," Hannah continued in a soft, musing tone, "who are we to deny *ourselves* forgiveness?"

"You are right, of course. But some truths are easier to believe here—" Gavin touched his forefinger to his temple "—than here." He tapped his chest. "But if you were there to remind me of it often enough, perhaps it would sink in at last."

An endearing blush spread up Hannah's tearstained face. Her generous lips arched in a self-conscious smile. "Does that mean what I think it means?"

"If you think it means I never want you to leave Edgecombe, except for an occasional visit with your friends, you would be correct." Gavin found it hard to stop grinning. "But I spoiled my last proposal by offering it too soon and for the wrong reasons. I may not be able to change the past, but I *can* learn from my mistakes. If I do that, they will not truly be failures after all."

"I like the sound of that." Hannah beamed her approval. Suddenly the darkened London sitting room seemed full of country sunshine.

"I mean to take my time." Gavin relished the prospect. "I want us to become much better acquainted. I want to prove to you what a good father and husband I can be. Not perfect, by any means, but to the very best of my ability."

Hannah hesitated for an instant, then raised her hand to caress his cheek. "Your best effort will be more than good enough for me."

He believed her—not just in his head, but in the most doubtful depths of his heart. "I promise you, I will be entirely circumspect. I will say nothing more of what is in my heart until after I have observed a proper period of mourning for Clarissa. I owe it to her and to our children to respect her memory."

"We both do." Hannah drew back her hand with obvious reluctance.

Her tender touch had been very pleasant indeed, and Gavin was sorry she must stop. Still, he knew it was the right thing for both of them. They would keep their association cordial and professional until the day came when he was free to speak. It would go against his impetuous nature to act with such deliberate restraint. But that would be his tribute to Clarissa…and to Hannah. When the day came that he could make his honorable intentions known, it would be all the sweeter.

A hesitant tap on the sitting room door made them both start as if they had forgotten anyone else in the world existed. Gavin clasped Hannah's hands and gave them a swift, warm squeeze that he hoped would convey his feelings until he was at liberty to tell her in greater detail.

Then he sprang from the sofa and called, "Come in."

The door swung open, admitting Lady Benedict, who held tight to Peter's hand. She cast Hannah an apologetic look, perhaps to beg her pardon for not keep-

ing the child occupied any longer. Gavin was not altogether sorry for the interruption. If he'd spent too many
more minutes staring into Hannah's eyes he was not
certain his honorable intentions could have prevented
him from kissing her.

"The cook here is very nice," announced Peter. "She
made us up a tray and she gave me a biscuit to hold my
stomach."

A maid bustled in behind them with the tray and set
it on the table in front of the sofa.

"Is something wrong, Miss Hannah?" Peter climbed
up beside her. "You look like you've been crying."

For a moment, Hannah seemed as if she meant to
deny the charge, but her eyes and nose were quite red
and she still clutched Gavin's sodden handkerchief. "I
was, but not because anything is wrong. Your father
told me he means to come back to Edgecombe with us
and that made me very happy."

No happier than it made him, Gavin reflected, to
think of making a true home with her and the children.

"Well, that's good." Peter still sounded puzzled by
the strange notion of happy tears.

While they were talking, Lady Benedict began to
heap food on their plates. A smug little smile hovered
on her lips.

Hannah wrapped her arm around Peter's shoulders.
"As soon as you have eaten, we must get you to bed,
young man. It is a wonder you have kept your temper
so well after such a long day."

Much as Gavin wanted to return to Edgecombe, see
the twins and begin the next phase of his life, his son's
well-being mattered more to him. "Since you have come

all this way, we should show you a bit of London before we go home. If you would like to, that is, and if it would not be too great an imposition on Lady Benedict."

"Not in the least." Her ladyship's bright tone conveyed her approval of his suggestion. "It would allow me a longer visit with my dear friend without taking my husband away from his duties."

Gavin sensed their hostess was eager to learn what he and Hannah had discussed in her absence. He did not mind Lady Benedict knowing that she need not exert herself to find her friend a husband.

He and Hannah would take care of that in their own time.

Hannah, Gavin and Peter spent an enjoyable few days in London as guests of Rebecca and Sebastian. They took the child around to see London Bridge, Saint Paul's Cathedral and other sights that might one day provide a basis for his history instruction.

Hannah and Rebecca enjoyed these outings quite as much as the child, having led very quiet lives until recently. What made Hannah even happier was the unspoken sense that she, Gavin and his son were already becoming a family. It still troubled her a little to imagine what Peter's mother would have thought of her place being filled by her son's governess. But she hoped and believed the countess had found peace and love beyond human understanding. Surely she would not begrudge the happiness of those she had left behind.

Rebecca helped to set Hannah's mind at ease on the subject.

"You will be fulfilling the promise you made to her."

She gave Hannah's hand a reassuring squeeze as the Edgecombe party prepared to depart. "Whatever she may have felt toward you and the earl, there can be no doubt she loved her children with pure, unselfish affection. I am certain she would approve any arrangement that promised to be so very good for them."

"You talk excellent sense." Hannah caught her loyal friend in a warm embrace. "I wish I had you near all the time to keep me from fretting about such things."

"We will see one another far more often now." Rebecca glowed with delight at the prospect. "And Marian, as well as the others, I hope. Besides, you have another friend now in whom you can confide."

Her teasing little smile told Hannah exactly whom she meant.

Just then Gavin returned from the kitchen with Peter. They had gone down to thank the Benedicts' cook for a supply of warm gingerbread nuggets she had baked for him to nibble on the journey home.

"I hope poor Cook will be content here once you go," Rebecca fretted, not entirely in jest. "I fear she may leave us for a family with little ones she can spoil."

"Surely she can be patient awhile longer," Hannah replied, "for you and Lord Benedict to oblige her."

From the way Rebecca and Sebastian had responded to Gavin's children, Hannah knew they must be eager to welcome a child of their own. How fortunate she felt that when the time came, she would have a ready-made family.

"Speaking of Sebastian," said Rebecca, "I hope he will get back in time to bid you farewell. That horrid Bonaparte is almost as much trouble in captivity as he was on the loose. I shall be heartily glad when his future is settled."

Hannah cast a covert glance at Gavin as she stooped to wipe a crumb of gingerbread from Peter's chin. The earl's mouth tightened and his dark eyes flashed in response to Rebecca's remark. Though he had decided to put the war behind him and concentrate on his family, she sensed that the situation still mattered a great deal to him. She hoped with all her heart it would not be mismanaged again, leaving Gavin prey to undeserved regrets.

He must have been thinking the same thing. "I quite agree, Lady Benedict. I would be the last person to take your husband away from his duties for the sake of civilities."

No sooner had he spoken those words than Hannah heard voices in the distance, followed by the sound of brisk footsteps approaching. A moment later, Sebastian strode in, looking rather anxious.

"Thank goodness you're still here." The viscount addressed himself to Gavin. "I was afraid I might have missed you."

Gavin started to repeat what he had just told Rebecca, but Sebastian interrupted him.

"This has nothing to do with polite leave-taking. I have been charged by Lord Bathurst to give you this." He thrust a letter into Gavin's hands. "Whatever you said to Buckinghamshire the other night seems to have made an impression. The Board of Control has withdrawn its objections to the use of Saint Helena as a place of exile for Bonaparte."

"What wonderful news!" Rebecca cried.

Hannah swept Peter into a joyful embrace.

"Are you certain?" Gavin tore open the letter and began to read it, his eyes darting back and forth. "This is an end to it, then?"

"An end to what?" Peter demanded. "Why are you all so happy?"

"Because it is an end to many years of war." Hannah strove to explain in a way a child might understand. "And an end to the worry that it might begin again."

She sought to catch Gavin's eye to communicate her delight at this new development and her pride in him for the part he'd played. When she glanced toward him, she did not see the wide smile she expected, but a furrowed brow and an anxious scowl.

Sebastian clearly noticed, too. "What is the matter? What does the letter say?"

"Just a lot of political nonsense." Gavin's lips curled upward then, in the most grotesque parody of a smile Hannah had ever seen.

She suspected it must be for his son's benefit and she was certain of it when he addressed the child. "I say, Peter, would you mind going out with Lady Benedict to check if our carriage is ready?"

An opportunity to do anything involving horses distracted the boy from his father's abrupt change of mood. "I shall be glad to, Papa."

Rebecca quickly grasped what was required of her. She took Peter's hand and headed away with him. "Perhaps we can stop by the kitchen and see if Cook might spare some carrots for your horses."

The minute they were out of earshot, Sebastian asked

the question that clamored in Hannah's mind. "What does Lord Bathurst *truly* say?"

The viscount did not question Hannah's right to be there, for which she was grateful.

Gavin heaved a sigh. "The government has resolved to send Bonaparte to Saint Helena, but they want *me* to go along as his custodian. In recognition of my intense desire to ensure that he should never again pose a threat to peace in Europe."

Hannah lifted a hand to her chest, for her heart felt as if it might plummet into her feet. She should have known a happy future with Gavin and the children was too good to be true. What had she ever done to deserve such happiness?

Another thought rose up to comfort her. It urged her to trust in the infinite generosity of divine love and seek to be a channel of it.

"Dash it all," Sebastian muttered. "I have no doubt you would be an ideal man for the post but…. What will you do?"

Gavin looked from the letter to Hannah and back again, all the while silently shaking his head.

"I will leave you to think on it," said Sebastian as he discreetly withdrew.

When he had gone, Gavin looked up at Hannah again. The painful struggle that waged within him showed on his rugged features and in the stormy depths of his eyes. It was as vicious a battle as he had ever fought, for it was not against an oppressive enemy who must be vanquished at all costs. Instead, it was a severe contest between two greatly desired events, each of which must exclude the other. Such a battle could yield no true victory—only bitter disappointment and regrets.

Or could it? Perhaps in surrender and sacrifice, Hannah could help him find peace. Was that not more important than winning what *she* wanted at the cost of his peace of mind?

"I think you should go." Those were the hardest words she'd ever had to speak—welcoming her worst fear. Yet once they left her lips, she knew they were the right ones.

The look of bewilderment that came over Gavin might have made her laugh under other circumstances, but not now. Instead it compelled her to make him understand. "I know how important this is for so many people and how much it means to you. I also realize what I should have all along—that you are not using this as an excuse to abandon your children. I know you will come home to them…and to me, at your very first opportunity."

The furrows in Gavin's brow smoothed out and the rigid set of his mouth relaxed.

"If you want the children and me to come with you to Saint Helena," she continued, "we will."

Though she meant it with all her heart, Hannah could foresee many difficulties.

When Gavin shook his head, she found herself torn between disappointment and relief. "Alice and Arthur are not yet weaned, and it is a long voyage. The children would be much better off at Edgecombe."

It was not an easy decision for him, she could tell, but one he made out of tender concern for his children's well-being. For the first time, Hannah could truly believe her father might have felt the same way when he'd sent her and Sarah to live with his sister. "Then I will look after them until you return, as governess or mother, whichever you think best."

"You would…marry me…right away? Won't you mind what people might say?"

"A little," she admitted. "But your peace of mind matters more to me than the comments of others. Do what you must and you may rely on my complete support."

A sincere, mellow smile replaced Gavin's earlier look of perplexity. "I know I can rely on you. That was something I sensed even when I did not much care for you otherwise."

With slow, deliberate steps, he approached her. "I want you and the children to be able to rely on me, as well. How can I do that if I am an ocean away, playing nursemaid to General Bonaparte? I do not believe Molesworth would approve of that in the least."

He tossed aside the letter and took her hands in his. "What is more important, it is not what *I* want for our family and our future. I know I said I would not speak of it yet, but just this once, I must. I love you, Hannah, with all my heart and I could not bear to be parted from you for any reason. I want to put the war and all the other troubles of our past behind us. I want us to embrace the future with love and happiness."

His voice rang with confidence and certainty that gladdened Hannah, and yet… "What about General Bonaparte? Who will serve as his custodian if you do not? Is there a chance he might not be sent to Saint Helena if you refuse to go?"

"Are you *trying* to get rid of me now?" Gavin's dark eyes twinkled in a way Hannah hoped she would often see in the years to come.

"You know very well the answer to that." Hannah was not accustomed to the sort of gentle banter she had heard Rebecca and Sebastian exchange, but she found she enjoyed it. "I love you so much that I am afraid of letting you down. I want to be quite sure you will not regret your decision."

"Not for a moment." He raised her hands and pressed a kiss on them. "I am confident that when I exercise my newfound powers of persuasion upon Lord Bathurst and the other gentlemen, they will find someone just as well qualified for the post and far more eager to accept."

"Does that mean we will have to stay in London a while longer?" Much as Hannah enjoyed spending time with Rebecca, she yearned to see the babies with an intensity that was almost painful.

An answering look of longing came over Gavin. He shook his head. "I have had my fill of London. We will go as soon as I can dash off a quick reply to Lord Bathurst. I once thought I would never say these words, but I can hardly wait to get home."

Epilogue

Kent, England
June 1816

In many parts of England, there would be celebrations on this day to mark the anniversary of Waterloo. Gavin doubted many would be as joyful as the one soon to take place at the parish church of Saint Alban's Edgecombe.

That terrible day, when he had staggered into this place of worship with a heart full of guilt and failure, now seemed like a bad dream from which Hannah had wakened him. Indeed, his whole previous life felt that way. Only in the past year had he truly come alive—taking on challenges he once would have shunned, opening his heart to family and friends.

"It will all be worth the wait, you'll see," Sebastian whispered as he and Gavin took their places at the foot of the chancel steps. "It was for Rebecca and me, and it will be for you and Hannah."

Was Sebastian referring to his own somewhat lengthy betrothal? Gavin wondered as he waited for the arrival of *his* bride. Or did he mean the months he and Rebecca had waited and hoped to start a family? The moment the Benedicts arrived for the wedding, Hannah had guessed her friend was with child. She and Gavin were delighted for them.

Gavin turned for a moment, his gaze sweeping over the small congregation with a sense of satisfaction. He had managed to gather almost all of Hannah's school friends for their wedding. The beautiful Lady Steadwell had a glow about her as she sat with her husband and his three daughters. Vivacious Miss Shaw was sitting with Captain and Mrs. Radcliffe to help out with their infant son. Only Evangeline Fairfax had not been able to make the journey down from the Lake District, though she had sent a gift and warm letter of congratulations.

On the other side of the church sat two of Gavin's cousins, a number of his fellow cavalry officers and as many of the Edgecombe servants as could be spared from preparations for the wedding breakfast. Peter was there, of course, with his nursemaid. Gavin tried to catch his son's eye, but the child was too busy staring at the Radcliffe girls and Lord Steadwell's youngest daughter. He seemed delighted to have so many children visiting.

Hannah had insisted Alice and Arthur must attend the ceremony, as well. Gavin's little daughter sat quietly on her nurse's lap, staring around her at the stained-glass windows, which were brilliantly illuminated by the morning sunlight. Young Arthur refused to have any of that. Instead he staggered up and down the side aisle with Mrs. Wilkes clinging tightly to his leading strings to prevent him from taking a tumble.

Just then Hannah appeared at the back of the church.

She looked quietly radiant in a modest dress, her bonnet trimmed with flowers from the Edgecombe gardens. In her hands she held a matching nosegay. Even from a distance, Gavin could not mistake the love that glowed from her whole countenance. Love for him, for the children and for Edgecombe itself.

He had spent the past several months proving to her and to himself that he could be the kind of husband she needed and deserved. Today at last, he could pledge her his love and loyalty for all the years to come. When they made their wedding vows to each other, he and Hannah would have the confidence of knowing the lengths to which they would both go to honor such promises.

"I promised our host I would keep my toast short," Sebastian announced with a wry chuckle as the guests paused in their appreciative consumption of the wedding breakfast.

Hannah ducked her head and blushed, for she knew the viscount was about to pay tribute to her. She had never been comfortable accepting praise.

But no amount of unease on that account could temper her joy. Today was the happiest in her life, not only because she had wed such a fine man and become the mother of three children she adored. Her pleasure was compounded by the presence of so many of her dear friends. Like Rebecca, the years had not changed them in essentials. Grace was still as kind and understanding as ever, Leah still as irrepressible and Marian still had the brave heart of a true champion.

As well as Hannah and her friends got along after all their years apart, their husbands had also taken to one another like old comrades. Even Lord Steadwell and Sebastian had overcome the awkwardness of mistaken impressions formed before they became better acquainted.

The children were having a wonderful time together, too. Lord Steadwell's eldest daughter, Charlotte, doted on the babies while the middle daughter, Phoebe, had bonded with Peter over their shared love of horses. The youngest of Lord Steadwell's daughters, Sophie, had become great friends with the Radcliffe girls. Peter was delighted to have three high-spirited playmates of his own age. Looking ahead, Hannah foresaw many pleasant visits between their families.

"When Rebecca first told me about her school friends," Sebastian continued, "I must confess I thought they sounded too good to be true—particularly the incomparable Hannah Fletcher. But having become acquainted with the lady, I can now assure you my dear wife did not exaggerate. Gavin is a fortunate man to have secured such a fine wife, as are all the gentlemen who have wed her friends."

"Hear, hear!" cried Gavin, Lord Steadwell and Captain Radcliffe with touching enthusiasm.

Sebastian laughed along with the rest of the company. Then he raised his glass. "Ladies and gentlemen, pray join me in drinking to the health and felicity of the new Countess of Hawkehurst!"

It gave Hannah an odd feeling to hear herself called that. To her, Gavin's first wife would always be the countess. Being Mrs. Gavin Romney was as precious a title as she could ever wish for.

Once the company had drunk to her health and Sebastian resumed his seat, Gavin rose. "I have one announcement to make, after which I promise you there will be no more speeches."

"Hear, hear!" Leah quipped to everyone's amusement, including Gavin.

"Perhaps you will think differently after you hear me out, Miss Shaw, for it concerns you and your friends."

The others all cast Hannah questioning looks, but she could only reply with a mystified shrug. She had not the least idea what Gavin intended to announce.

"Lord Benedict, Lord Steadwell, Captain Radcliffe and I have been talking," Gavin continued, "and we have decided the best way to honor our dear wives is to endow a new school to replace that horrid Pendergast place—a school that will be run on truly Christian principles."

He was interrupted by cries of delight from Hannah and the others. What a comfort it would be to think that another generation of girls need not suffer what they had and worse. Already Hannah's mind was churning with ideas for how to make the new school an example of what such institutions could and should be.

"We will need the very best people to run it." Gavin's words echoed Hannah's thoughts. "We hope Miss Shaw and Miss Fairfax might be persuaded to take on the task."

Hannah, Rebecca, Marian and Grace hailed the announcement with delight and called for Leah to accept.

"If anyone could make our school a happy place, it is you, Leah," cried Hannah. "Please say you will!"

But Leah shook her head, her hazel eyes twinkling. "I wish I could oblige you, but this sounds like an ideal project for Evangeline. You know what a born leader she is. I am too much a rebel—we would come to blows in no time."

Though her friend's answer disappointed Hannah, she could not deny the truth of it. Evangeline was much better suited to the challenge of establishing and running a new school. Besides, Leah hated being tied down in one place for too long. She moved from position to position with an eagerness that a homebody like Hannah could never understand.

Gavin concluded his speech to a flurry of applause.

When he sat down, Hannah reached for his hand under the table and gave it a squeeze. "The school was *your* idea, wasn't it?"

Her husband replied with a nod and a rather shamefaced grin. "I hope you approve."

"You know I do." She gazed deeply into his eyes, basking in the warmth of love that glowed in them. "It is the most thoughtful, generous gift, from the kindest husband a wife could ask for."

Love like theirs was the best gift of all, Hannah reflected as she cast decorum aside to offer her husband a tender embrace. Steadfast and abiding, without conditions or standards, it would enrich their lives and their children's with an abundance of happiness in the years ahead.

* * * * *

Dear Reader,

Unlike my earlier Glass Slipper Brides stories, this one took more effort and changes. Perhaps that's appropriate for a story about dealing with failure. Failure is a scary thing that can shatter our self-confidence and burden us with guilt. Fear of failure can make us reluctant to take on challenges.

Burdened by a sense of failure, Colonel Gavin Romney feels he must atone by keeping a battlefield vow. His ideas about God were influenced by his judgmental father. Hannah Fletcher pushes herself hard to win the regard of others. She has lost too many people she cared for to believe *anyone* can love her unconditionally.

When circumstances force the wounded warrior and the capable governess together, they discover that forgiving themselves and risking their hearts will require something more than hard work and courage. It will take a leap of faith.

Deborah Hale

Questions for Discussion

1. When Gavin arrives at his wife's funeral, Hannah assumes his unsteady gait and rough appearance mean he's been drinking. What makes Hannah so quick to believe the worst of Gavin? Have you ever let past events color your judgment of someone?

2. Gavin quickly becomes fixated on bringing Napoleon Bonaparte to justice. Why do you think he lets that idea consume him to the degree it does? Have you ever focused on something external as a way to avoid unpleasant feelings or problems within yourself?

3. As Gavin and Hannah become better acquainted, they realize they have more in common than they once believed. What sorts of things do Gavin and Hannah have in common? In what ways to they differ? In what ways do their similarities and differences draw them together?

4. When Hannah prays, she reflects that she does not often pester God by asking things for herself. Why do you think she feels her prayers might "pester" God? Do you ever feel some things are too trivial to pray for? What do you think Jesus might have said about that?

5. How do you think Gavin's view of God is influenced by his relationship with his father? Are

there any ways your early relationships might have shaped your beliefs?

6. Gavin feels the failure of his marriage to Clarissa was entirely his fault. Do you agree? What factors do you think contributed to the problems in their marriage?

7. Gavin believes people should only do those things they have a natural talent for. Hannah believes it is possible to do anything with enough hard work. Which do you think is more important—natural ability or determined effort?

8. Hannah advises Gavin that the Bible "may not be as current as the *Times* or the *Morning Chronicle,* but it contains words of wisdom that could well apply to the present situation." Can you think of a time when you found words of wisdom in the scriptures that helped you deal with challenges of modern life?

9. Hannah wonders if there is "part of her...still held captive by her past, which needed saving?" Have you ever felt that way? Was someone able to help you or did you find a way to free yourself from destructive influences of the past?

10. Through the course of the story, Gavin learns some important lessons about handling failure. What do you think he learns? Can you think of any scripture passages that might help someone deal more constructively with failure?

REQUEST YOUR FREE BOOKS!

2 FREE INSPIRATIONAL NOVELS
PLUS 2
FREE
MYSTERY GIFTS

Love Inspired.

HISTORICAL

INSPIRATIONAL HISTORICAL ROMANCE

YES! Please send me 2 FREE Love Inspired® Historical novels and my 2 FREE mystery gifts (gifts are worth about $10). After receiving them, if I don't wish to receive any more books, I can return the shipping statement marked "cancel." If I don't cancel, I will receive 4 brand-new novels every month and be billed just $4.74 per book in the U.S. or $5.24 per book in Canada. That's a saving of at least 21% off the cover price. It's quite a bargain! Shipping and handling is just 50¢ per book in the U.S. and 75¢ per book in Canada.* I understand that accepting the 2 free books and gifts places me under no obligation to buy anything. I can always return a shipment and cancel at any time. Even if I never buy another book, the two free books and gifts are mine to keep forever.

102/302 IDN F5CN

Name _____ (PLEASE PRINT) _____

Address _____ Apt. # _____

City _____ State/Prov. _____ Zip/Postal Code _____

Signature (if under 18, a parent or guardian must sign)

Mail to the Harlequin® Reader Service:
IN U.S.A.: P.O. Box 1867, Buffalo, NY 14240-1867
IN CANADA: P.O. Box 609, Fort Erie, Ontario L2A 5X3

Want to try two free books from another series?
Call 1-800-873-8635 or visit www.ReaderService.com.

* Terms and prices subject to change without notice. Prices do not include applicable taxes. Sales tax applicable in N.Y. Canadian residents will be charged applicable taxes. Offer not valid in Quebec. This offer is limited to one order per household. Not valid for current subscribers to Love Inspired Historical books. All orders subject to credit approval. Credit or debit balances in a customer's account(s) may be offset by any other outstanding balance owed by or to the customer. Please allow 4 to 6 weeks for delivery. Offer available while quantities last.

Your Privacy—The Harlequin® Reader Service is committed to protecting your privacy. Our Privacy Policy is available online at www.ReaderService.com or upon request from the Harlequin Reader Service.

We make a portion of our mailing list available to reputable third parties that offer products we believe may interest you. If you prefer that we not exchange your name with third parties, or if you wish to clarify or modify your communication preferences, please visit us at www.ReaderService.com/consumerchoice or write to us at Harlequin Reader Service Preference Service, P.O. Box 9062, Buffalo, NY 14269. Include your complete name and address.

LIH13R

*Can a gift from a mysterious benefactor save a dying
Kansas town? Read on for a preview of
LOVE IN BLOOM by Arlene James, the first book in the
new HEART OF MAIN STREET miniseries from Love
Inspired. Available July 2013.*

The pavement outside the Kansas City airport radiated heat
even though the sun had already sunk below the horizon.
Tate held his seven-year-old daughter's hand a little tighter
and squinted against the dying sunshine to read the signs
hanging overhead.

"That's it down there," he said, pointing. "Baggage
Claim A."

Lily Farnsworth was the last of six new business owners
to arrive, each selected by the Save Our Street Committee of
the town of Bygones. As a member of the committee, Tate
had been asked to meet her at the airport in Kansas City and
transport her to Bygones. With the grand opening just a week
away, most of the shop owners had been at work preparing
their stores for some time already, but Ms. Farnsworth
had delayed until after her sister's wedding, assuring the
committee that a florist's shop required less preparation than
some retail businesses. Tate hoped she was right.

He still wasn't convinced that this scheme, financed by a
mysterious, anonymous donor, would work, but if something
didn't revive the financial fortunes of Bygones—and soon—
their small town would become just another ghost town on the
north central plains.

Isabella stopped before the automatic doors and waited

for him to catch up. They entered the cool building together. A pair of gleaming luggage carousels occupied the open space, both vacant. A few people milled about. Among them was a tall, pretty woman with long blond hair and round tortoiseshell glasses. She was perched atop a veritable mountain of luggage. She wore black ballet slippers and white knit leggings beneath a gossamery blue dress with fluttery sleeves and hems. Her very long hair was parted in the middle and waved about her face and shoulders. He felt the insane urge to look more closely behind the lenses of her glasses, but of course he would not.

He turned away, the better to resist the urge to stare, and scanned the building for anyone who might be his florist.

One by one, the possibilities faded away. Finally Isabella gave him that look that said, "Dad, you're being a goof again." She slipped her little hand into his, and he sighed inwardly. Turning, he walked the few yards to the luggage mountain and swept off his straw cowboy hat.

"Are you Lily Farnsworth?"

To find out if Bygones can turn itself around,
pick up LOVE IN BLOOM
wherever Love Inspired books are sold.

SADDLE UP AND READ 'EM!

This summer, get your fix of Western reads and pick up a cowboy from the INSPIRATIONAL category in July!

THE OUTLAW'S REDEMPTION
by Renee Ryan
from Love Inspired Historical

MONTANA WRANGLER
by Charlotte Carter
from Love Inspired

*Look for these great Western reads AND MORE,
available wherever books are sold or visit*
www.Harlequin.com/Westerns